The Passage

The Passage

by Finnegan Joshua Middleton Tailor

as told to Bill Simpson

The Passage

A Novel by

Thomas William Simpson

Published by

Simpson Books

THE PASSAGE

A Simpson Book/August 2014

All rights reserved.

©2014 by Thomas William Simpson

No part of this book may be reproduced or transmitted in any form without permission in writing from the publisher.

Contact simpson-books@icloud.com

Thomas William Simpson

is the author of *The Ferryman, Annie's War, This Way Madness Lies,*
and many other entertaining and stimulating novels
on a wide range of subjects.

Go to www.simpson-books.com
for a complete summary of the Author's Work
and Life.

For my curious, adventurous, & silver-tongued son,
William Charles Simpson
May his Passage through Life be filled with
Intrigue and many Narrow Escapes.

passage, n. [ME., OFr., from passer, to pass]

1. the act of moving from one place to another; migration.
2. change from one process or condition to another; transition.
3. a road; a path; an opening.
4. happenings between people; an interchange of blows or vows.
5. an occurrence, event, or incident.
6. a passing away; decay; death.
7. a portion of something spoken or written.
8. an old game played by two persons with three dice.
9. in medicine or everyday life, a bowel movement.
10. an event, act, or ceremony marking a person's evolution from one stage of life to another; for example, from boyhood to manhood; a boy's rite of passage.

I sat on the train waiting for it to leave the station on the day the world stopped. Like everyone else, I just wanted to get home. Only nobody got home. Not that day, and not the next. We all had to make do the best we could.

I had a bag of dried fruit, some almonds, half a bottle of water, a dead cell phone, and two novels I'd already read more than once. I was desperate for something to read, something to occupy my troubled mind.

I looked across the aisle and spotted a stack of manuscript pages in a cardboard box. No one occupied the seat so I picked up the box and turned to the title page.

The story right away caught my attention. It was about a teenage kid, a boy, who sets off on a journey across America with his estranged father.

I read maybe ten minutes before a young man came down the aisle and took the seat earlier occupied by the manuscript. He looked at me, saw me reading.

I pointed to the box of pages. "Sorry, this yours?"

He nodded.

"You write it?"

"I did."

"Mind if I keep going?"

He was a good looking kid, late teens, maybe twenty, mop of unkempt hair, scruffy beard, thin and loose limbed. "Knock yourself out," he said. "But hey, we're both just sitting here, nowhere to go, nothing to do. Why don't I tell you that tale instead of you reading it?"

So that's what he did. Young Josh Tailor told me his story, while we waited…and waited…and waited some more for that train to leave Union Station.

The Boot

I think I'll start with the boot.

Halfway home from my best buddy Retro's house I had a little run-in with Mom's boyfriend. Mr. Homer Otis.

The big nasty SOB came out of nowhere.

Homer rode up alongside me in his bright yellow Hummer H2—the official car of guys with little peckers and big egos—over on a quiet stretch of Church Street.

"Hey, Josh," he called out the window, "where you going?"

My instincts told me to bolt but I decided that'd be cowardly. "Home."

"Want a lift?"

"Nope."

"Come on," encouraged Homer, a big smile on his phony face, "hop in."

"I don't think so."

"I want to talk to you."

"About what?"

Homer halted the Hummer. It looked like a gigantic yellow refrigerator lying on its side. "I hear you're going to make a little trip with your old man."

"Could be."

"He in town?"

"He will be."

"So where you two headed?"

The Passage

"What's it to you?"

"How long you going for?"

"Hard to say."

Homer smiled and stepped out of the Hummer.

My legs twitched but I stayed put.

Even though Homer was a big guy, an inch or so over six feet, he could've used a stepladder to climb out of that SUV. For some reason Homer had on a denim shirt, tight blue jeans, and a pair of fancy cowboy boots.

I'd never seen Homer wearing cowboy boots or cowboy duds before. We lived in Jersey. Not many cowboys in Jersey.

"What's up with the outfit, Homer? You been to the Garden State rodeo?"

I should've kept my trap shut. Nipped my sarcasm in the bud. But like my old man, I'm a talker.

Homer took two quick steps and put a leg in motion. He kicked me square between the legs, dead on the gonads. The blow sucked all the oxygen out of my lungs. I doubled over in agony, saw black stars before my eyes. My testes felt like they'd been rocketed up into his chest. I stayed on my feet for a second or two, then collapsed onto my knees.

Homer said, "That's for cracking up the convertible, you little shit."

Oh yeah, the convertible. Mom's brand spanking new Mellow Yellow VW Beetle convertible. A recent gift from Homer O.

I tried to lift my head but couldn't. Off to the side I could see Homer's fancy cowboy boots. They looked like real rattlesnake hide.

A split second later one of those boots started to move. And before I could roll out of the way, the toe of that boot kicked me flush in the butt. Smack on the right cheek. A hard, solid shot that sent me spiraling flat out and facedown on the sidewalk.

"And that's for being a wise-ass, Josh. For that crack about the rodeo."

Against all reason I moved my mouth. "Hey, tough guy, why don't you eat me raw with a flavored straw."

Homer didn't kick me again. Instead he worked up a foul goober and blew it out of his mouth onto the back of my neck. The warm gooey spittle slipped under my tee shirt and slid down my back.

Homer laughed, and soon thereafter he climbed up into his refrigerator and drove off.

I didn't move for quite some time. I just lay there and writhed in all that pain and humiliation. And reflected on the nature of revenge.

Big Jack

Now just so we're clear, every word of this story's true. Even the stuff about the Indian. Especially the stuff about the old Indian.

My full and legal name's Finnegan Joshua Middleton Tailor, but I prefer Josh. My friends call me Josh. My mom and grandmother call me Joshua. Only my father calls me Finnegan. And then only when he wants to rile me up. Get under my skin.

The family name used to be Tatum not Tailor, back before I was born. But Big Jack—that's my old man—tossed Tatum when he pulled out of Jersey City as a young man. Hard to say why. A man's motives are as mysterious as the moons of Jupiter. Ask Big Jack why he changed his name and he'll tell you a thousand different tales. Big Jack lived like a wild wolf roaming the tundra—by instinct and impulse. Intellect brought up the rear.

And forget the Truth. Big Jack didn't bide the Truth anytime at all.

Big Jack abandoned Mom and me when I was still just a kid and for that I hated him and was pissed off for a very long time.

He used to visit on occasion but he never stayed long, sometimes less than a day, less than an hour.

"Things to do, kid," he'd say, slapping me on the back as though emotion had no place in the world at all, "places to go, people to see."

But he came back that summer.

And when he left he took me and Retro and Bones with him.

The Trailer

A couple days after school let out the three of us—me and Retro and Bones—piled into Big Jack's Chrysler Town & Country and hit the road.

Of course, it wasn't that simple. Like countless westbound pioneers from days gone by, we had things to do and people to placate before pulling up stakes. I had to argue with my mom about what to bring and how to act, about how often I'd call home and how long I'd be gone. I had to hug Gram and reassure her a million times I'd be polite and careful. I had to listen to Pop lecture me about the absolute necessity of visiting Mt. Rushmore in the Black Hills of Dakota. Seems my grandfather had seen Rushmore as a boy and had been made a better American for the visit.

On the day we left I was up in my bedroom with my girlfriend Amy who shoved a calling card in my hand and kept telling me to call her morning, noon, and night.

I knew that wouldn't happen but assured her I'd do my best. I stuck the card in my otherwise empty wallet save for a picture of Mom and the hundred bucks Pop had slipped me the night before.

I heard a horn toot and when I looked out the window I saw Big Jack roll in the driveway. Time to go.

Before I could get downstairs and out the front door Mom had started yelling at Dad, telling him she'd have him killed if anything happened to me. Then she threatened to call the state police and the FBI if he didn't have me home safe and sound within two weeks.

My mother and father, you'll soon enough come to see, didn't exactly get on like peas in a pod. Mom hated Dad, though of course she still loved him too.

Big Jack stepped out of that van and blocked out the late morning sun. Tall and rangy, he wore faded jeans, no socks, moose hide moccasins, and a gray tee shirt. He listened to Mom's rant, leaned against the minivan, and smiled.

The minivan, let me tell you, was quite a shock, but I didn't say a word. I figured the old boy had good reason for driving the soccer mom's limo. So I made a beeline across the lawn, opened up the wide-mouth rear hatch, and tossed in my gear. More than anything I just wanted to roll. After all the recent trouble I needed some space between me and Bridgeton, between me and Mom, me and Homer O, me and law enforcement.

"Take it easy, woman," Big Jack said to Mom. "You'll hurt yourself. Josh'll be back tight to your bosom soon enough."

"Don't tell me to take it easy, Jack Tailor. I won't rest easy until he's back here where he belongs, away from your noxious influence. I never should've agreed to this trip, and if I could stop it now I most definitely would."

Big Jack just laughed, but I'd heard enough. Their bickering was embarrassing. I jogged back across the lawn to where Mom stood at the foot of the front porch with Gram and Amy. I gave her a hug and a kiss and told her I'd call in a couple days. Gram and Amy got hugs and kisses too.

And then, finally, me and Dad climbed into the Town & Country, backed out of the driveway, and made our getaway. But not before I looked through the windshield at Mom and Gram and Amy—three generations of women waving and looking solemn—and felt this weird sensation rumbling in my gut. I'd never felt anything like it before. It was like I'd been shot through the heart by a soft bullet moving in slow motion. It didn't really hurt all that much, not like when Homer had kicked me in the testes, but I can tell you off and on for days it sure did ache.

We drove over to Retro's house on High Street. Big Jack had a conversation with Retro's mom while me and Retro tossed Retro's gear in the back of the Chrysler.

"What's with the minivan?" Retro wanted to know.

I could only separate myself from it with a shrug.

Retro kissed his mom, said so long, and then we headed over to get Bones.

Bones had a real name: Peter Edward Zeller. The Zeller's had a few bucks and lived in a big new colonial just outside town. Bones' parents, a couple of scientific types with like eight PhDs each, had already talked the trip over with my dad both on the phone and in person. It was Big Jack's sales prowess and great charm that won Bones his freedom. But when we pulled in to pick him up, Maw and Paw Zeller needed an additional bit of stroking before we could load and bolt.

The sight of that Chrysler minivan gave them confidence. What, after all, could be more reassuring, more American, than a minivan? Big Jack was a sharp guy. He could see what the Zellers needed. And he enjoyed giving it to them. Right from the get-go he had the Zellers buffaloed. He had them convinced he was a good, moral, upstanding, hard-working father sacrificing much to take his son and his son's two chums on this cross-country sojourn. He assured the Zellers—small, bespectacled folks—that Bones would be touring national parks, historical battlefields, important geological sites. Big Jack threw around names like Lewis and Clark, Thomas Jefferson, George Washington, Yellowstone, Glacier, Grand Teton. It all had the proper effect on the Zellers. Stroking their intellectual chins, they nodded their approval.

Little did they know Big Jack was a car salesman extraordinaire and a scam-meister supreme. He could sell wings to a whale.

And finally it was proclaimed we could depart, begin our journey, venture off into the western wilderness. And so we did. We threw Bones' gear in back, climbed into the minivan (from here on out I'll just call it the van), and took off for points west.

But we didn't get far before we ground to a halt. We drove through Bridgeton and over the bridge into Pennsylvania. But instead of continuing west, we turned south on the river road for six or eight miles. Finally we slowed. We made a right turn and drove half a mile or so down a tree-lined gravel lane before coming to an old stone house with its mortar crumbling and half its windows busted out. Behind the house was a big old wooden barn with a sagging roof.

Big Jack pulled up in front of the barn. A second or two later a tall wooden door slid open on a rusty and creaky hinge. A short squat guy, a bodybuilder gone to seed, stood in the doorway. He wore a Philadelphia Phillies baseball cap and stroked a long gray beard.

"You boys wait here," Big Jack ordered as he turned off the motor and stepped out onto the weedy lawn. "Best right now if you don't get out of the van."

That threw some mystery on the dash. Had Big Jack said something like, "They got a mastiff on the property who'll rip your leg off," or "The ground's contaminated with PCPs," I might've sat tight and kept quiet. But knowing my old man and his wild ways, I right off got curious and wondered what was up. The bearded guy looked creepy. No way did I want him trekking west with us. Once when me and Jake were kids and Mom and Dad still lived together, we left on this vacation to the Jersey shore. About halfway there Dad stopped to pick up these two grungy pals who then spent the whole week with us at a rented house in Wildwood drinking and smoking and eating every morsel of food Mom bought. They smelled bad and cursed hard and stayed up all night plucking out-of-tune guitars and singing Eric Clapton tunes in raspy off-key voices.

Big Jack disappeared inside that old barn. Too dark for us to see what was going on in there, but finally both him and the bearded dude stepped out into the daylight. Big Jack climbed into the van, turned it around, and backed most of the way into the barn.

"What's the deal?" I asked him.

He left the van idling and stepped out again. "Not right now, kid."

The deal was this: a black and silver box trailer about five feet wide and maybe eight or ten feet long. It wasn't a horse trailer or anything fancy. Just a simple box on wheels with no windows and a large swinging door on the back. A sturdy steel bar and a heavy-duty padlock kept the back door secure from prying eyes.

While Big Jack and the bearded guy hitched the trailer to the van, me and Retro and Bones watched through the windows. We'd been told to stay put. No way that early in the trip were we about to buck a direct order.

The hitching-up process took about ten minutes, after which Big Jack powwowed briefly with the bearded guy in hushed voices. Then they shook hands, Big Jack climbed back into the van, and we pulled out of the barn and down that gravel lane. At the river we turned south.

"So," I asked, "what's in the trailer?"

Big Jack didn't answer. Not right away.

I thought about asking him again, but didn't.

Finally he said, "The trailer, right. You know, kid, stuff. For the trip. Sleeping bags, propane stove. A tent. Things we'll need out west."

That all sounded a little squirrelly. I mean, don't you usually buy that stuff at a sporting goods store? You don't get it out of some old barn. But what did I know? I didn't know squat. I was just a kid. Knotted in the middle of his troubled teenage years. So I sat back in my wide comfy seat and waited to see what might happen next.

I kept an eye on the digital compass/thermometer on the overhead console. The temp hovered between 79 and 82, but the direction remained steady: S, for south.

I said to Big Jack "So, where we headed?"

"West, kid. We're headed west. Go west, young man."

"The compass says south."

He took a look. "So it does."

"South's not west."

He glanced over at me. "What's the story here, Finnegan Tailor? Don't tell me you've matured into a large pain in the ass."

Retro and Bones laughed.

My father said, "You never used to be a pain in the ass."

I squirmed in my seat.

"You used to be a pretty cool and easy cat."

"Things change," I muttered.

"Maybe so," my old man fired back, "but we don't need you turning into your mother at the onset of this life-altering adventure."

I did some more squirming. Retro and Bones stayed quiet. They knew the sound of a family wrangle when they heard it.

Big Jack said, "Listen, boys, before we steer west we have a little history trip to make. It won't take but a couple days, then we'll be off."

None of us much liked the sound of that. It hummed of school, a prison we'd just days ago escaped.

And so despite my reprimand it fell to me as team leader to raise a hand. "History trip, huh. Where to?"

Big Jack took a long look at me, then he studied Retro and Bones in the rear-view mirror. "So, you boys are the curious types, huh? Curious minds, inquisitive, all that jack-shit. You gotta know where and when and how come? No going with the flow with these triplets. Okay, I can roll with that. Just please swear to me you're not gonna bust my balls. I get all worked up when someone busts my balls."

Not exactly the kind of chatter we heard from the tight-lipped, well-groomed, politically-correct pappies back in our hometown of Bridgeton, NJ. It left me and Retro and Bones speechless.

But not Big Jack. Big Jack was rarely at a loss for words. He drove another mile or so, then he looked us over again and boomed, "Here's what I suggest, boys! I suggest you sit back and soak up the stim-u-lie! Let your eyes and ears WANDER! Let 'em turn into great big oversized sponges! Because what you got before you over the next days and weeks is OPPORTUNITY! Do you hear me, you little deaf-mute cretins of suburbia? OP-POOR-TUNE-A-TEE! To EXPAND! To EXPLORE! To use your eyes and ears and CONTEMPLATE THE GODDAMN USA!"

Big Jack stuck his fingers between his teeth and whistled loud enough to call back a sheep dog clear over in the next county. Then he blew the horn of that Chrysler Town & Country. He blew it long and loud at nothing and no one. He just blew it to blow it, to make some noise.

"I'll tell you this much," he told us. "First stop: Washington, D.C.! The District 'o Columbia! The Capitol city, boys looking to be men, of this rich and fickle nation, the greatest and greediest country on earth."

Then he gave us a wink and made some popping noises with his mouth before settling his eyes back on the road ahead.

Now I should tell you, I hadn't spent much time with my old man for a number of years. Just about no time at all if you added it all up. But all that was about to change. I was about to spend days and weeks with him in very close proximity. And there I sat, watching him out of the corner of my eye while wondering if I'd entered the world of a madman.

The General

I'd been to Washington before. On a class trip. But I'd never been there with Big Jack. Big Jack, let me tell you, handled things a little differently than my teachers and the parents who'd come along to chaperone.

We got caught in a traffic jam somewhere between Baltimore and Washington. For like an hour we sat without moving. Big Jack, never the dean of patience, stayed reasonably cool. A few times he muttered under his breath that the northeast had too damn many people and too damn many cars and he couldn't wait to reach the wide open spaces of the west.

It got dark and grew late. We had burgers at Friendly's, except for Dad who had a piece of apple pie and a cup of black coffee. After dinner we checked into a motel hard by the highway. They had only one room left. It had two double beds—me and Dad in one, Retro and Bones in the other. Bones said he had to call his parents.

Big Jack said, "Easy, boy. You only left home a few hours ago."

Which meant no way could I call Mom, despite my desire.

Dad said, "You dudes go to sleep. We're risin' early."

So we went to sleep while Big Jack read by the lamp beside the bed.

I woke up sometime later with bladder bursting from way too much Coke. Dad was still working on his book. The digital clock next to my side of the bed read: 1:49. I peed then slipped back between the sheets. The old boy gave my arm a squeeze and asked me friendly if I needed anything. I said no and noticed for the first time the title of his book: The Terrorist Next Door: The Militia Movement and the Radical Right.

"How's the book?" I asked.

"Not too shabby."

"What's it about?"

"It's about these whack jobs who want to overthrow the government."

I nodded and fell back to sleep. Before I knew what hit me Big Jack shook me wide awake. "Burnin' daylight, Finnegan. We're gone in thirty minutes. Sleep, shower, shave, watch TV, pull your pud, whatever you desire. But we're in the van in half an hour. Pass the order."

And with that Big Jack rose and headed for the bathroom. It was 5:31.

Less than an hour later we pulled up to the Washington Monument. The whole area was deserted except for a couple cops who eyed us suspiciously. Big Jack told us to hop out and take a look. I remember the sun hung low in the early morning sky. It lit up the east side of the tall white obelisk. A long shadow reached out toward the Capitol at the far end of the Mall. It was cool being there that early with the quiet and just a few birds chattering in the bushes.

We pulled out of D.C. soon thereafter and ate breakfast at some no-name diner. Me and Retro and Bones ate eggs and pancakes and home fries. Big Jack drank some OJ. I remembered him being more of an eater and said so. He said, "Food's overrated, kid. Eat to live, don't live to eat." When he paid the tab he pulled a thick wad of bills out of his pocket, thicker than my wrist. The bill on top was a hundred, had a picture of old Ben Franklin on the front.

After breakfast we took a tour of Mount Vernon, the Virginia plantation of George and Martha Washington. The front gate was still locked when we walked up to pay. Dad told us to relax, things would open up in a few minutes. "Once we get inside," he said, "you're on your own.

Just keep the horseplay to a minimum."

The gates opened, Big Jack paid, and in we went. He went his way and we went ours. For the next couple hours we toured the plantation, a swell spread that in George Washington's day had encompassed eight thousand acres and supported nearly four hundred folks, over three hundred and fifty of them African slaves.

The mansion was a big place made of wood that looked like stone. It had plenty of rooms and lots of windows. The front windows looked east across a wide swathe of lush grass and down a high embankment to the Potomac River. The Potomac must've been a mile across in front of George's spread. Sailboats and speedboats cruised by.

Retro elbowed me in the gut and pointed. Out there on the far edge of the lawn stood Big Jack, yakking into a cell phone. We couldn't hear him but we sure could see him moving his mouth at rapid speed and gesticulating wildly with his hands.

We saw George's study with his books and his writing desk and his globe of the world circa 1795. There wasn't much of the United States to see on that globe west of the Mississippi. Just about nothing at all but open space.

Upstairs we saw George and Martha's bedroom with George's custom bed to fit his 6 foot 4 inch frame. The general towered over his fellow countrymen, which some say was why they made him general and then President.

Our gray-haired tour guide, none too happy to have three ornery young males on her first tour of the day, informed us General Washington (she always referred to George as General Washington, never President Washington or just plain George) had died in that bed.

"Died of what?" Bones, ever curious, wanted to know.

"An infection," came the answer.

"Infection of what?"

"The throat, actually."

"The throat? Really?" said Retro. "I had an infection in my throat last winter. I got some pills and in a couple days felt spiffy again."

The old girl smiled, almost. "That's because your doctor probably prescribed you antibiotics. If there'd been antibiotics during General Washington's time he would have survived his infection and lived many more years."

Our little quartet warmed up some after that and the gray-haired girl patiently answered our six million questions. Like when I asked if the pictures on the wall were pictures of George and Martha's kids. She told us George and Martha hadn't had any children of their own. The kids were Martha's from an earlier marriage. Martha's first husband had died of one of those blasted infections. Seems back in those days there were lots of broken and blended families because people died young of infections and viruses and the like. Today we got an equal number of broken and blended families, only now it's caused not by disease but by divorce. Though I guess if you think about it divorce is a kind of disease.

A while later we found Big Jack still out on the front lawn overlooking the wide and mighty Potomac. All my life I'd thought the Delaware was cool, but man oh man, the Potomac was awesome. It made our river back home in Bridgeton look like a trickle.

Not too much later we got back to the parking lot where we found two police cars and four cops surrounding the van. Big Jack ordered me and Retro and Bones to stand back and stay cool. He moved forward while we watched from the edge of the lot.

Words we couldn't hear were exchanged between Big Jack and the cops. Big Jack pulled out his wallet and produced his driver's license. The cops took turns looking it over. Next Big Jack pointed to us. The cops glanced our way. We squirmed. Big Jack opened the van and dug through the glove box. He located the registration and the insurance card and handed them over. It all took time.

My curiosity killing me, I took a few steps forward. Retro and Bones followed close behind.

We got close enough to hear one of the cops say, "We'd like to search the van and the trailer, Mr. Jacobs. Any problem with that?"

Me and Retro and Bones exchanged looks. Who the heck was Mr. Jacobs?

"No problem at all," answered Big Jack. "But might I ask a couple questions?"

"Go ahead."

"First off I'd like to know if you have a warrant? And second, I wouldn't mind knowing exactly what you're looking for."

"I'll tell you, Mr. Jacobs," said one of the cops, a big bruiser who must've been in charge, "I could get a search warrant if you don't mind waiting. And as for what we're looking for, well, I got a suspicion you might already know the answer to that."

Again, me and Retro and Bones exchanged looks.

Big Jack shrugged and said, "Actually, officer, I don't have a clue what you're looking for, but go right ahead. Search away. Knock yourselves out."

The search lasted maybe ten minutes. The four cops took a long look through the van. They even opened our duffel bags and rifled through our underwear. Then Big Jack opened the trailer and two of the cops climbed inside.

The boys and I maneuvered into position so we could watch the search. We, too, were plenty curious about the contents of that trailer.

But there was nothing in there but sleeping bags and a tent, a propane stove and some other assorted camping gear. Not really much at all.

The cops climbed out and Big Jack locked up. The head cop had another brief chat with Dad. Dad nodded a few times but didn't say much and what he did say we couldn't hear. At the end of the chat he got back his driver's license, his registration, and his insurance card. Soon after that he signalled us to get in the van.

A minute or so later we pulled out of the parking lot and flew the coop.

"What was all that about?" I asked.

Big Jack shrugged, easy as can be. "Appeared to be a case of mistaken identity. They were looking for some guy named Jacobs."

We pushed for more info but Big Jack put some music that sounded sort of like rock and roll into the CD player and ordered us to pipe down till further notice.

The Shenandoah

We led a wild chase over the next couple days. Big Jack tore south through the Virginia countryside delivering us to Thomas Jefferson's Monticello just hours after Washington's Mount Vernon. He didn't take the tour with us but instead hung back and worked on whatever deals he had cooking. I liked Washington's house better than Jefferson's but probably because I'm a river guy and Mount Vernon sprawled easily along the Potomac whereas Monticello sat isolated on a mountaintop looking regal but I thought lonely.

We spent the night at a motel outside Charlottesville, then got up at dawn and started north along Skyline Drive. The sun just rising we saw dewy vistas across the Shenandoah Valley and eagles soaring against a blue sky and whitetail deer scurrying through the woods with their newborn spotted fawns. At one pull-out Bones took a photo of me and Dad standing on a stonewall with the Shenandoah as a backdrop. I keep a copy of that photo in my wallet. Big Jack's got his arm around me and his best broad smile working big-time.

All morning long Big Jack had the Blues bleeding loud and unruly through the speakers. I asked him about it.

He said, "The Blues is the daddy of jazz and the granddaddy of rock 'n roll."

There was this cool guitar pickin'. I asked, "Who's that playing?"

"That's Mississippi John Hurt. *Make Me A Pallet On Your Floor.*"

We all took a listen while Mississippi John sang:

> *Don't let my good girl catch you here,*
> *She might shoot you, might cut and stab you too;*

*There just ain't no tellin what she might do.
So make me down, oh make me down,
Oh make me a pallet on your floor.*

I tried to get all that straight in my head but couldn't.

Late in the morning we drove down off Skyline Drive to eat. But we didn't stop at some generic fast food joint. Big Jack pulled into a small gravel parking lot beside this fast moving, rock-strewn stream. Against the back of the parking lot was this hole-in-the-wall dive called Leonard's with a tin roof and peeling paint. Leonard's was owned and operated by Mr. Leonard White. Leonard was also cook, waiter, busboy, and maître d'. He was a big broad beefy black guy, must've stood six and a half feet tall and I'd guess upwards of three hundred pounds. He greeted Big Jack like a long-lost brother.

"Damn, Earl!" he shouted soon as we rolled through the rickety front door. "I say where you been, boy? I've been expecting you near a week now! Your goods are growin' heavy!" Even when Leonard spoke softly it rumbled loud out of his mouth.

He gave Big Jack a bear hug—lifted my dad, a six foot one hundred and seventy-five pounder, right up off the ground. I got the same treatment the second Leonard White heard I was Big Jack's son. Only Leonard didn't call Big Jack Big Jack; he called him Earl. Earl What? Earl Jacobs? I never knew.

Leonard sat us down at a big round table back near the kitchen. He served up succulent spareribs, mashed potatoes with gravy, black-eyed peas, corn on the cob. It was a feast to behold. Even Big Jack ate. In great quantity. He drank beer with his meal. Me and Retro and Bones drank sarsaparilla.

For dessert Leonard offered up Shoo Fly pie that I didn't think I'd like but did and piled in two slices. After the pie Dad told us to scram.

"Take a hike along the river," he suggested. "But no swimming. Come back wet and I'll tan your hides."

I knew the history of that and so didn't argue.

Me and Retro and Bones left the dim light of Leonard's and went out into the bright afternoon sunshine. We walked down to the river's edge. But with full and bloated bellies we didn't feel like hiking. Instead we found a soft shady spot along the riverbank and one by one nodded off.

Big Jack rousted us sometime later. A couple hours later from my reading of the sun. It had rolled out west of the Shenandoah.

"Rise and shine, boys."

We got up, stretched, and followed Big Jack away from the river and back to the van. I started to climb into the passenger seat but something wasn't right.

"Hey," I said, "wait a second. Get a load of that trailer. That's not our trailer."

Dad, Retro, and Bones all stopped and took a look.

"Our trailer was black and silver. This one's black and white."

Big Jack said, "No one'll ever put one over on you, Finnegan Tailor. Maybe we'll call you Sherlock. You're right, that's not our trailer. I had to switch trailers. Had a little problem with the axle on the old one. It was making an awful racket."

I hadn't noticed any racket, but then, I hadn't been listening.

The Romance

Before we head west I want to drag you briefly into my family's past so you'll know how and where The Troubles began. Don't worry, I won't drag you back to ancient times when Middletons first set foot in the New World. I won't put you through the misery of Tatums starving to death in Ireland during the potato famine (though believe me they did). I'll stick to Mom and Dad and how they wound up together and later begat me and later still my little brother Jake.

My mother, Lisa Anne Middleton Tailor, is the only child of Edna and Thomas Middleton. I think Gram and Pop might've lost one, or maybe even two, in the womb, but on these matters I've never been fully apprised.

Lisa grew up in the big Victorian on Cherry Street in Bridgeton. Like me, she went to Bridgeton Elementary and South Hunterdon High. In high school she swam on the swim team and ran on the track team. She didn't apply herself much to her studies. I've seen some of her old report cards. She got Bs and Cs in the easy stuff like history and English and Cs and Ds in the tougher subjects like chemistry and geometry.

Mom was a looker. She had blue eyes and blond hair and pearly white teeth behind lips that curled up into the prettiest smile you ever saw. She had a smile that mostly got her what she wanted, and sometimes what she deserved. She had long lean legs that to this day knock men's socks off.

As a senior Mom got voted Best Looking. That same summer, after graduation, she was voted Miss Hunterdon County at the annual Flemington Fair. That meant she got to compete in the Miss New Jersey beauty pageant against twenty or so other county beauties. And you know what? Mom came in second place. Something to this day she's still proud to tell people.

If Mom came from what you'd call a solid, middle class family, my old man definitely didn't. John (Jack) Matthew Tatum (Tailor) grew up on the river also, but not the Delaware. Dad grew up a stone's throw from the Hudson, up in Jersey City, across from the Big Apple. Dad lived in a high-rise apartment, really a tenement, a few blocks from the river. He was one of five kids. He shared a bedroom with his two brothers—my Uncles Ray and Frankie—who I've met but only a handful of times.

Their dad, my other grandfather, I've never met and only seen once in a family photo (he's laughing with a baby in one arm and a bottle of Jamison's Irish whiskey in the other). He fought fires for the Jersey City Fire Department. But he lost that job when he turned up once too often soused and punched his captain in the choppers. A hard drinkin' hard livin' Irishman, Kenneth Tatum was a good-natured drinker till he poured one too many. Then he turned into a drunk who liked to clobber things, especially his wife and kids. When his boys got a little older and started to fight back, Ken headed for the hills leaving nothing behind but a bunch of dirty shirts, unpaid bills, and black eyes.

The family, though plenty poor, was overjoyed to see Ken go.

My dad went to Jersey City public schools. He was a pretty fair athlete, but he never played organized sports like me, not even Little League baseball or Pop Warner football. He played stickball in the streets and basketball on the asphalt playgrounds with bent rims and no nets. Instead of running on the track team like Mom, Dad ran from the Jersey City cops after swiping candy or cigarettes from the corner store. He also ran with a gang of Irish toughs who frequently brawled with the Italians or the Puerto Ricans—the inner city version of the suburban Saturday afternoon football game.

At 16 Dad quit school to work at a car dealer out on Kennedy Boulevard near St. Peter's College. His dad long gone, the family needed money. At first Jack cleaned and waxed the new cars. I think they were Buicks but they might've been Pontiacs. Dad loved the work, all that shiny new sheet metal. When not cleaning cars he was studying them, learning the specs on all the models. Pretty soon he knew more about the line than the salesmen. They'd call him over if a customer had a more in-depth question about, say, engine torque or interior cargo space or gross vehicle weight.

When he turned eighteen the sales manager gave him a shot on the floor. That same day Dad sold his first car, made himself a hundred bucks along the way. "Easiest dough I ever made," he once told me. "Spic family. Came in looking to buy used but I showed 'em the beauty of financing new. The wife, this hot little dark-skinned dish, took one look inside that vehicle, all spiffy and smelling good, and her old man knew there'd be no more nooky till she got that car. They spoke only a little broken English and they didn't really get the whole haggling process, so I had no problem getting sticker."

The sales manager knew he had a star in the making. By the time Dad turned twenty he was the dealership's top salesman. He moved more units for more profit than anybody else, including Nick Maglione, Dad's car-selling mentor. Nick, a silver-haired slickster who always had an unlit stogie in his mouth, drummed one simple message into young Jack when foot traffic was slow. "You're a car salesman, kid, not a social worker or a Good Samaritan. You apply whatever pressure necessary to close the deal. And never, ever, let 'em outta the showroom till they give you some green."

People trusted Jack. They shouldn't have, but they did. He was a smooth-talking, easy-going, good-looking Irishman with a mile-wide smile and no conscience at all. The truth or a lie—it didn't matter so long as he sealed the deal. Big Jack (who'd taken on the moniker to separate him from Little Jack who worked in service) could sell a Ferrari to a blind man with no legs.

"Let me tell you," he used to tell me and Jake when we were kids, "hawking those crappy American cars back in the seventies was no picnic. Those cars were pieces of junk. You'd go for a test drive and the windows wouldn't go down or the wipers wouldn't wipe or the radio wouldn't play. You had to be quick on your feet. Detroit was pumping out some of the ugliest, worst performing vehicles in automotive history and handing 'em off to guys like me to sell to the American public. It was like being on the frontlines during a war. The customers were armed and suspicious. You had to have guts and skin thicker than moose hide to go to work in the morning."

Around the age of twenty-three Dad got sick of living in the city and decided to head for the country. That's when he made the move from Hudson County to Hunterdon County, from the Hudson River to the Delaware. I've heard rumors maybe he made this move not exactly voluntarily, that a young girl in a motherly way might've been involved in his decision to relocate.

He moved into a house in Frenchtown with a couple other guys. The house was kind of a beat-up ramshackle place but it overlooked the river and had a big deck off the back where you could sit and watch the sunset over the Delaware. That's where the guys would bring their girls for a romantic evening before trying to coax them back into the house for a tussle between the sheets.

When not pursuing women Jack continued to sell cars. When he first moved to western Jersey he worked at Chrysler/Plymouth/Dodge on Route 202 in Flemington. But it soon became clear to management that this kid Jack Tailor was far too valuable an asset to waste on common domestic stock. Within a year they moved him across the highway to the high-priced shop where they sold BMWs and Porsches. It was there in the BMW/Porsche showroom where Dad met Mom.

They met totally by chance one afternoon when Lisa and a couple pals went shopping in Flemington. After buying jeans and bras and racy underwear they went to check out the new cars. Had Lisa and Jack missed each other that day there's a good chance they might never have met. Which means this story never would've happened. I never would've happened. So, did fate pull them together? Destiny? I don't know. I don't think so. I don't buy into those lotteries. I'd call their meeting plain dumb luck. And really everything that happened afterwards the flip of a coin.

Big Jack, thirty, had mastered the slick look for expensive foreign car sales. He was fit and slim and tan. He had dark eyes and wavy dark hair and almost olive skin. He looked Italian even though he had mostly Irish blood pumping through his heart.

The day Mom sauntered into that BMW/Porsche showroom with her two pals she was just nineteen years old. Still a few months shy of twenty. But more than a decade and a whole host of experience separated Lisa and Jack. Those years were just one small ledge of the abyss that loomed beneath them.

It was August. Dog days. Hot and muggy. The sun, filtered through a thin layer of clouds, blistered everything in its path. The sheet metal of the cars in the lot could've fried an egg. Inside the cool, quiet showroom the salesmen languished. They sat at their desks reading the sports section of the Ledger or checking out photos of the new BMWs due in the fall. Business was dead slow. Barely a customer had turned up all day. It was too hot. Everyone was at the beach or up in the mountains.

The girls, all three of them young and thin and oh so pretty, one of them a beauty queen, stepped out of a low-slung Camaro. They wore nothing but flip-flops, halter-tops, and hot pants. Back in the showroom one of the salesmen spotted the sexy trio through the large front window and right away alerted his fellow scalpers to the visual treat. They all knew there wasn't one chance in a million those girls had the dough to buy a Buick, let alone a BMW or a Porsche. But hey, it was a slow day, a dull day, so Jack Tailor, always on the lookout for babes, waited for the trio to enter the showroom, then he slid out from behind his desk and slipped over for a closer look. Even with both the temp and the humidity in the 90s, Jack looked cool and collected in his summer-weight suit and polished cordovan loafers. He said hey and the girls said hey and he asked if they were in the market for a hot new car and Lisa's pals, shy in the presence of this hunk with the slicked-back hair, shrugged and dropped their eyes. But Mom, practiced in the art of poise, held his gaze and said, yeah, a fire-engine red one with a convertible top.

The story of Lisa Anne Middleton and Jack Tailor goes on from there, on and on, I tell you, year after troubled year. I ought to know. I might've missed the launch, the damn prologue, but before long I had a front row seat.

Probably someone should've foreseen all the pain and torment and nipped the whole business in the bud before it had a chance to root and bloom. But hey, it doesn't work that way. Dad didn't say, "I gotta go to the head, girls. My buddy Al here will help you with that red convertible." Mom didn't say, "Would you mind if a saleswoman helped us? I don't trust that predator-like look in your eyes, buster."

No, those words did not pass between them. Instead Lisa and Jack locked onto one another, momentarily blocked out the universe, and exchanged both chemical and biological signals that sent their brains and libidos into hyperactive sexual overdrive. The fix, as they say, was in.

So despite the fact he knew his sales manager would have a conniption, Jack brought around a red-hot 911 Cabriolet and offered the stunning young beauty the driver's seat. Lisa grinned at her pals and slipped into the leather bucket. Jack climbed into the passenger seat. He went over the controls and the features of the $68,000 German sports car and then asked, "So, would you like to go for a little test ride?"

Lisa thought that sounded like a swell idea. "Oh yeah," she cooed, "I do."

Off they went. But none too smoothly. Mom had never handled a clutch before. She stalled that high-tech engine over and over. And when finally she got the sports car moving it hopped across the parking lot like a drunken rabbit. A few minutes of this and Jack suggested maybe he should drive. They switched seats and set off on a long cruise through the rolling countryside of Hunterdon County. Jack knew all the back roads where he could let that Porsche roll. He was an awesome driver. He shifted with precision and swept the 911 through the turns with the greatest of ease. He was a man in control. Lisa knew she was in the hands of a real man, not some idiot boy. She'd been waiting for a real man to take her for a ride.

They were gone at least an hour, maybe more. A mighty long test drive. They put over fifty miles on that Cabriolet. They even parked for a while at a farm stand piled high with just-picked Silver Queen and the season's first local peaches. They almost had their first kiss at that farm stand, but Lisa, who'd only ever kissed boys, grew nervous and shied away. Or maybe she was just playing hard to get. On the way back Jack wondered aloud about dinner and a movie on Saturday night. Lisa said she'd have to think about it but then thought about it and said okay, why not, it might be fun.

By the time they got back to the dealership the sales manager had gone on the warpath. The second Jack pulled into the parking lot the sales manager, who secretly hated Jack because Jack sold the most cars and picked up the most chicks, tore out of the showroom wild-eyed and sizzling mad. He demanded to know what the hell Jack was doing disappearing with a brand new 911 for half the afternoon. Jack, cooler than a white linen suit, just shrugged. Which drove the sales manager's blood pressure even higher, turning him redder than a cooked beet. Right on the spot he fired Jack, ordered him to gather his gear and get off the lot. ASAP.

Jack, so goes the family legend, didn't flinch. He just smiled and said, "Alrightee then, if that's the way you want it, Bob, that's the way it'll be." Easy as pie he brushed past the sales manager, went into the showroom, and cleaned out his desk.

On his way out Jack winked at Lisa. "See you Saturday night, good lookin'. I'll pick you up at seven." Then he turned, flipped the sales manager the bird, and vanished into the shimmering August heat.

See, Big Jack's like an island. Isolated and alone. The man has never done well with authority. He does as he pleases, and so long as you leave him alone, don't hassle him, he moves pretty easy through the world. But Jack Tailor (Tatum), the wild Irish kid from Jersey City, has another side, a devilish side, a manic side, a side that can slip out of control when the roads get slick. When this side surfaces, brother, you learn to watch out! Stay clear! Find a place to hide!

The Three Rivers

After leaving Leonard's with our new trailer, we drove north and west. The sun went down. We kept driving. I asked Big Jack if we were going to stop for the night. He didn't answer. It grew dark. By and by I guess I fell asleep.

And when I woke up the van was parked and empty except for me. It was still plenty dark out. I checked my Timex Explorer: 4:21 am. I'd been asleep for hours. But where had everyone gone?

I figured we'd pulled into an all-night service station and everyone had gone to pee. But I didn't see any cars or gas pumps or buildings. All I saw was darkness and some faint lights flickering in the distance. But then, in the shadows, I spotted something sprinting toward the van. I had myself a quick little panic attack. But then that something turned into someone—my old buddy Retro.

I opened the door and stepped out. "Hey," I said, cool and casual like I hadn't been all wigged out just a couple seconds earlier.

"Hey," he said, "you awake?"

"Oh yeah, I'm awake. What's up?"

"Big Jack sent me to get you so you could see the river."

"What river?"

"Three rivers, actually. Come on, let's check it out."

I took a step forward but over my shoulder saw the trailer gone. Again.

"Big Jack," explained Retro, without me asking, "pulled into this giant truck stop along the Pennsylvania Turnpike maybe an hour ago. He unhitched the trailer and a few minutes later this big Ford F-350 diesel came along. The driver hopped out, exchanged some chatter with Big Jack, and then they hooked up the trailer to the Ford. The pickup took off and a couple seconds later we did too."

I couldn't believe I'd slept through all that action. I smacked myself on the side of the head. "The guy just drove away with the trailer?"

Retro nodded. "Yup, it all happened in a flash."

I felt like an idiot and vowed to sleep no more. "What did Big Jack say?"

"He didn't exactly do much explaining, Josh. And me and Bones, we didn't much feel like asking."

I thought it over and nodded. "Alright, let's check out these rivers."

Retro turned and took off. I followed him into the shadows.

Retro, I should tell you, was my best bud in the world. Still is. And has been since like the third grade when me and Mom moved to Bridgeton. We'd been living over in our riverside bungalow in Upper Black Eddy, PA. But with Big Jack having ditched us and the unpaid bills mounting, Gram and Pop stepped in and soon thereafter me and Mom moved into the big old Victorian on Cherry Street. Within a few weeks of that move me and Retro, who lived just a few blocks away, wrestled in the mud after a ferocious thunderstorm, bloodied each other's lips, and instantly became best buds.

Retro's real name is Carl Shipley, Jr. His dad was Carl Shipley, Sr. Carl Sr., if I haven't mentioned it, was dead. He died in a plane crash when me and Retro were like nine or ten. Carl Sr. owned his own plane. A small Cessna he used to fly up to Canada where he loved to hunt and fish. Flying home late one Sunday afternoon he got caught in a storm up near Syracuse, New York. No one ever saw Carl Sr. alive again.

Carl Sr. was the coolest father in Bridgeton. Carl Jr., as you can imagine, took his dad's death pretty hard. It was tough on me when my dad flew the coop, but at least I knew in the back of my head Big Jack was still alive. The possibility I'd see him again lived strong in my brain. Retro didn't live with that luxury.

After Carl Sr. died I learned to put my arm around Carl Jr., give him a hug, and tell him everything would be okay. I especially had to do this when Carl Jr. would start balling and telling me how he wanted to die so he could see his dad in heaven.

Anyway, I followed Retro through the shadows, but the shadows soon gave way to another kind of glow—a watery glow that looked plenty familiar after all my years living along the Delaware. I knew water lay dead ahead.

Then I heard Big Jack say, "Good of you to join us, Finnegan. Have a pleasant nap?"

I didn't like the old boy's tone, way too sarcastic and condescending, like I was some kind of pansy for sleeping while they charged ahead into the next adventure. Or maybe I was reading too much into a couple simple sentences. Either way, I knew father and son had a long way to go before all the hatchets were buried and axes ground.

"Where are we?" I asked.

"We're not in Bridgeton anymore, kid."

Bones and Retro laughed.

I got paranoid and wondered if they'd been talking about me. Amazing what can happen when you nod off for an hour. Your whole stupid life can change. I felt like my status in the unit had been compromised, like I'd sunk to low man on the totem pole.

"Forget it," I grumbled. "I'll just have a look around for myself."

Which only made them laugh harder.

While I sulked Big Jack provided some info. "Three Rivers State

Park, Pittsburgh, PA. Confluence of the Allegheny and Monongahela Rivers. That would be the Allegheny pouring down from the north and the Monongahela driving up from the south. They meet here and form the mighty Ohio directly in front of us. Right here, gentlemen, is where the Ohio begins its journey west toward the muddy Mississip."

I stood there and took in the sites. A little bit of dawn brought those rivers into focus. The power of all that water easily drove away my paranoia and inferiority. We occupied a spit of land practically surrounded by water, by those three roiling rivers. In the silence of the early morning you could literally hear the Allegheny crashing into the Monongahela. All this crashing churned up great cascades of white water. Me and Retro and Bones looked upon it in awe. The mild-mannered Delaware never offered up anything like this. Not even during spring thaw when some years huge chunks of ice swept past our town on their way to the Atlantic.

"Gateway to the west!" Big Jack cheered. "Before railroads and dirt roads, before byways and highways, American adventurers traveled by river, especially these three rivers. Meriwether Lewis stood on this spot before floating down the Ohio to St. Louis where he rendezvoused with William Clark and off they went on their incredible journey across the Plains and over the Rockies to the Pacific Ocean. You boys've been itching to head west since you climbed into the van back in Bridgeton. Well here it is!"

The speech got us revved up. I could hear my pump and the pumps of Retro and Bones thumping louder than usual. We stood there and took it all in while time and the last dregs of night slipped away.

But then, silent as a specter, a cop crept out of the shadows and scared us, at least me and Retro and Bones, half to death.

"Well, folks," said that Pittsburgh policeman after we'd all calmed down and he could see we weren't murderers or marauders, "the park's closed from ten p.m. till eight a.m. There were signs out in the parking lot, but I guess you didn't see them."

"Actually, officer," began Big Jack, his storytelling prowess kicking instantly into high gear, "I've taught my fine son here," and he put his arm around my shoulder and squeezed my neck, "to never tell a lie. So I'd be a hypocrite if I told you one now. I did see that sign, sir, but I pulled in anyway. See, these boys and I, we're on a cross-country swing this summer. We're out to see, touch, and smell America. We're goin' from Jersey clear out to the Rocky Mountains. We've already been to the nation's capital and to Mr. Washington's home in Mount Vernon and to Mr. Jefferson's home at Monticello and to the great battlefield at Gettysburg where I lost an ancestor and I'll bet you did too."

Gettysburg? And what ancestor, I wondered, was that?

But the cop, upon receiving this news, a jet-black revolver strapped to his bulging midriff, nodded and looked reflective. He must've been remembering stories of his great granddaddy beating back the Rebs at Little Round Top or the Bloody Angle.

Jack Tailor, a man who knew how to read his audience, poured it on. "I wanted my boys to see the great city of Pittsburgh. I wanted them to hear the merging of these three great rivers because, in my humble opinion, this, right here, is the front door to the American west. This is where the great westward expansion began and so no matter the hour, we couldn't push on without first taking a gander at this incredible sight."

Oh yeah, Big Jack, my dad, make no mistake, could really empty the tank when he felt so inclined. A natural salesman with a powerful gift of gab, he could've been, had he led a cleaner life, President of these United States.

Eventually we all walked back to the parking lot together, fast friends. And then that officer, who never bothered to ask for license, registration, or insurance card, shook hands all around before giving Dad directions out of town.

Back on the road, steering west, Big Jack was still in a mood to chatter. Up until then he'd been fairly docile verbally, but that was about to change. Me and the boys just sat back and listened.

"Now cops," he pontificated, "are an interesting phenomenon. They like to hassle you. It's their job to hassle you. I believe they enjoy it. So, when you encounter a cop, it behooves you to gain the upper hand. Never," Big Jack advised, "be belligerent to a cop. Belligerence will only bring down the iron hammer, the iron heel. But at the same time you can't be submissive. Oh no, you need to walk a fine line. You have to let them think they're in charge while at the same time exuding confidence. This doesn't take much use of the brain matter since cops tend to think linear. Throw a cop a curve and he gets all cross-eyed and confused. Like a young lass when you first tell her you love her."

We kind of got the analogy and so nodded.

"And remember," Big Jack warned, "all kinds of cops roaming the streets. A lot more than just the few in uniform. Here in America we're top heavy with cops. Just about everyone these days in a position of authority—parents, teachers, coaches, crossing guards, judges, shrinks, sportscasters, even cartoon characters for chrissakes—is a potential cop. And all these cops have one thing in common—they wanna tell you what you can and can't do, where you can and can't go, how you should and shouldn't live your life. They wanna tell you how to think and behave. They wanna get in your face, squelch your freedom. You gotta be crafty to stay ahead of them. You gotta be quick on your feet, keep a clear head. You absolutely need to have strong, tasty verbal skills. The right words more than anything else can keep the cops at bay, keep your own personal liberties in tact. Trust me on these points, boys, if few others, for I know of what I speak."

We digested this fodder, some of which I recalled from my youth back before Dad deserted the family. There didn't seem much for me or Retro or Bones to add to Jack's dialogue, so for a few minutes we drove along in silence. During that pause I heard my buds breathing slow and deep in the back seat. Exhausted from the long night they'd finally crashed with the coming of dawn.

I said to Big Jack, "So where's the trailer?"

Big Jack thought it over. "The trailer, right… Had a couple bad bearings."

"First the axle. Now the bearings. All kinds of problems. I wonder what next?"

Big Jack gave me a look, a wink, and a smile. "Hard to say, kid. Always new problems on the horizon. But don't worry, we'll get her back down the road a piece."

"I'll bet we will."

Big Jack—parent, teacher, cartoon character—gave me a long, leisurely stare. He looked amused. "Kid, you're a piece of work. But you're my kid so I guess I'd expect no less. Now let me tell you something of interest. That trailer is something bringing up the rear, something I keep tabs on when I glance in the mirrors. You have no reason to worry about that trailer, son. Best if you stay focused on what lies ahead. On the future."

"You think so, huh?"

"Oh yeah, I do."

I checked to make sure my buds were asleep, then said, "Well I think you're up to no good with these trailers and fake names and—"

"You think so, huh?" he asked, mimicking me.

I ignored him. "I'm not saying you're on the illegal side of the law or anything, but with those cops back in Mount Vernon searching high and low through the van and the trailer, well, I have to wonder."

The Passage

That was a mouthful and Big Jack said so. Then he said, "If I didn't know better, Finnegan Tailor, I'd think you were a cop."

"I'm no cop."

"You say that," Big Jack said, "because you don't know what a cop is. A cop is someone who minds someone else's business. But okay, I suppose you have the right to some small amount of information, so I'll level with you. This little westward sojourn has a few complexities beyond the stated purpose of a father/son adventure. I can't at this early juncture go into all the various details and demarcations, but there's one mighty interesting piece of the puzzle we might right now slip into place."

"Oh yeah?" I replied, fully expecting some more Big Jack double talk. "And what piece of the puzzle would that be?"

"One unseemly piece of shit named Homer Otis."

That got my attention like a punch in the head. "Homer Otis? What about him?"

Big Jack glanced in the rear-view mirror. "Those boys asleep?"

I checked. "Seems so."

Big Jack, who rarely spoke below a boom, made his announcement in a voice I could barely hear. "I know," he whispered, "about Homer."

My voice right off went low too. "You know what about Homer?"

Big Jack shifted his gaze to mine. "I know it all, kid. I know he's one sadistic and abusive son of a bitch. I know about every pinch, every poke, every punch, every smack, every backhand, every bruise, every black eye, every insult, every abuse... every kick in the balls."

I pressed my legs together remembering what Homer had done to my balls just a couple weeks earlier.

"But how?" I asked. "How do you know all that?"

"I'm your father, boy," Big Jack answered in that formidable whisper. "It's my job to know. And know too that in the days ahead you and me will be deciding exactly what punishments will be meted out to that bastard for his crimes against my wife and son."

Wife? I thought as we drove through that Pennsylvania dawn. Didn't he mean ex wife? I didn't ask.

Big Jack said, "We've been communicating, Finnegan, but I'd say not with any great commitment."

I didn't jump on that, so Big Jack added, "I guess we've got time."

"Guess so," I said.

"Anything you want to tell me?"

There was no end of stuff I wanted to tell my old man, but I shook my head and answered quick, "Nope."

"You're full of shit, boy. Probably you wanna tell me I'm a rotten son of a bitch and you hate my guts for running out on you and Mom. And I don't blame you. Not for a second. So go ahead, get it off your chest."

"You're a rotten son of a bitch and I hate your guts for running out on me and Mom."

"Feel better?"

"Not really."

Big Jack made eye contact with me. I looked away fast.

"Tell me about the VW, Josh. About the crash. And after that tell me about this lumber you boys supposedly stole from that construction site. Give me the facts. Give me your side of the story. I've heard Mom's side. Now I wanna hear your side."

So with the boys sawing lumber in back and us finally headed west, I got my mouth moving. I told my old man a story. Of course, I didn't tell him the whole story. No way. You never tell the whole story. You just tell those parts you think that particular audience wants to hear.

The Crash

We had quite a crew at the big old Victorian that night. With Mom out with Homer and the grandparents down in the City of Brotherly Love, the back door might as well have been a turnstile at Grand Central. I was there. And Retro. And Bones. And Young and Johnson and Eddie the Owl and Stinky Cogan and the new kid Laramie who smelled to me like trouble. Plus a whole bunch of other lowlifes and hangers-on I'd mostly not invited. Plus a few girls too. But not Amy. She stayed clear of that crowd.

We hung out in the family room watching MTV and listening to Nine Inch Nails and the Grateful Dead and playing Ping Pong and throwing darts, and when all that got boring the guys started pushing me, taunting me, egging me on.

They wanted me to fire up Mom's brand new convertible VW Beetle—Mellow Yellow with a black top—and go for a little joy ride.

My chums, however, did not consider the many problems plaguing their desires. 1) I wasn't even supposed to have anyone in the house that night. 2) It was absolutely verboten for me to drive that or any other car. 3) I still had quite a while to go before I possessed a valid NJ driver's license. And 4) Mellow Yellow might've been Mom's new ride, but Homer O., who'd bought the Beetle, had his name on the registration.

Obviously, none of these problems struck the dozen or so birds hanging out on my home turf that Saturday night as particularly relevant. They wanted to cruise.

I believe Retro, my all-time best bud, said, "Come on, Josh, your grandparents won't be back for hours. And your Mom, hell, she probably won't be back till morning."

That got me thinking. And plenty ticked off too. As no doubt Retro knew it would. See, Mom was out with Homer. Mr. Homer Otis. Josh Tailor Enemy Number One. He'd swung by a couple hours earlier in his hot to trot BMW Z8, swooped up Mom, and then buzzed off into the night. I hated Homer. And I hated Mom too for going off with him.

So what did I do? I went up to my room on the third floor of that big old Victorian and dug out the box under my bed. I kept various items of import locked up tight inside that box. For instance, I had two hundred and eleven dollars in there, just in case I ever got the desire to hit the road and search for Big Jack. I had an antique gold pocket watch Pop had given me on my twelfth birthday. I had a couple condoms in the event Amy and I decided to, well, you know. And I had my very own illicitly obtained key to the brand new Mellow Yellow VW convertible.

Here's how I came by that key:

The previous weekend I'd been out in the garage with Pop fixing the lawnmower. We needed a part to finish the job. Pop told me to hustle inside and grab the key off the hook to his Mercury Grand Marquis. So I went in through the back door and grabbed Pop's keys. But instead of rushing back out to the garage, I paused. I paused because hanging there on the next hook was the key to Mom's new convertible. And Mom was off for the weekend with, who else, you got it, Mr. Homer Otis. Dining and dancing in the Big Apple. So I, clean as can be, dropped that VW key into my pocket.

Homer'd out of the blue given the new Beetle to Mom as a present. It wasn't even her birthday or Christmas or anything. Homer, you see, was a rich guy. Maybe the richest guy in our little riverside settlement. But money didn't prevent him from being a mean, spiteful, sadistic son of a bitch.

Until recently me and Pop would've driven over to McPherson's

Hardware on Center Street to buy the needed bolt. But the giant Home Depot in Flemington had forced old man McPherson to close up shop after nearly forty years in business. "A shame," Pop called it. "A damn shame."

So while Pop searched high and low in that gigantic Home Depot for one little crummy bolt, I slipped away, located the key-making department, and handed over the VW key to a smiling fat man in an orange apron. "My mom," I lied, "wants me to have an extra one of these made."

The guy in the orange apron made me an extra key, no questions asked, unlike old man McPherson who would've been all over Pop making sure the new key was legit.

I slipped both the old key and the new key into my pocket and went off to find Pop. And later, not wanting Pop to know I had the spare key, I walked right out of Home Depot without paying for it. Yup, I stole it. Not exactly the right or Christian thing to do, but that's what I did.

Anyway, that's how I'd come by my own key.

And for my troubles I had my buds hounding me.

"Come on, Josh, let's roll."

"Yeah, this is Dullsville."

"Let's cruise over to PA and get some burgers at Dell's."

Oh yeah, the peer pressure was on. Wound up tight.

I could see the new Beetle sitting out in the driveway between Mom's old Civic and Gram's Mercury Mountaineer. The convertible was so new it still had the temporary license plate taped to the rear window. The car beckoned to me. It was a temptation so tasty you knew the Devil loitered nearby.

It must've been about nine o'clock when the six of us piled into the VW. It was late May. A crescent moon hung over the Delaware. I remember thinking this was a bad idea, cruising in Mom's new car owned by Homer O., but we climbed in anyway and I stuck the key in the ignition and fired up the engine, a spunky little turbo-charged number with plenty of pep even with an automatic trans.

The passengers demanded the roof be lowered. I said no way, we'd be way too visible to the neighbors and to Bridgeton's boys in blue. But I was outnumbered five to one. Down went the roof.

With Retro riding shotgun and with Bones, Young, Johnson and the new kid Laramie stuffed into the back seat, I put the bug in motion. I backed down the drive and steered cautiously along Cherry Street away from the main part of town. Thank God the good citizens of Bridgeton had retired to their love seats and recliners to watch TV and enjoy a snack before bed. Had any friends or neighbors been out for a stroll or sitting on their front porches they would've spotted us in a heartbeat. Which actually might've been a good thing. Because maybe they would've called Police Chief Walters and he would've intercepted us before the actions of stupid teenage boys spiraled out of control.

We turned off Cherry onto Water Street. Water Street took us down under the old railroad trestle to the river. In the woods just beyond the trestle was an abandoned shack we used as a hangout. I parked the bug in front of the shack. We all piled out. Under the shack we kept our stash. That night the stash contained three warm cans of Budweiser and enough grass to roll one thin joint. We rolled and smoked and passed around one of the Buds. The combination of the beer and the grass pretty soon got us to giggling like idiots and shoving each other around. Bones went into the shack and got the boom box so we could listen to some Weezer , but the batteries went dead so we took a walk down to the river. I said something about the reflection of the moon glistening on the surface of the easy flowing Delaware.

Retro said, "Watch out, boys! Tailor's about to launch into song."

To the new kid Laramie he said, "Josh here is our resident poet. He's got all kinds of lofty ballads rolling around in his head. Since he's part Irish he thinks he's the next Bono."

I told Retro where he could stick it and then we piled back into the Beetle with our two remaining cans of Bud. We took River Road north out of Bridgeton. Within a couple minutes we reached some wide-open country. We cracked a can of Bud and passed it around. I definitely had a pretty good buzz going. More buzz than I should've had behind the wheel with my minimal driving experience.

Being a serious athlete and hopefully college-bound on scholarship, I didn't drink much and I almost never smoked dope, so in my system a little went a long way. But I can tell you, the buzz gave me courage. The buzz made me double stupid. Where at first I'd been driving well below the speed limit, slow and easy, now I started to rip around corners and let loose on the straightaways.

The boys urged me on. Retro cranked up the radio. The rapper 50 Cent blasted from the speakers. He wanted us to kill cops and have sex with our mothers. Retro said, "Screw this jerk-off!" and tuned in some classic rock. The Stones, I think. Street Fighting Man. Everyone moved to the music. Retro tapped on the dash. Bones drummed on the top of my head. A whole lot of singing and shouting rolled through Mellow Yellow.

Retro kept pointing and telling me to turn, to go this way and that way. I spun the wheel and made the turns. Pretty soon I didn't know where we were. Didn't really care either. We were just cruising. Yucking it up. Staying cool.

I think I might've been looking at the moon when the bug drifted off the road, spun wildly in some loose gravel, slammed into a drainage ditch, and got airborne in a very big hurry.

Hard to say about the moon. I've always loved the moon. I've always been kind of a dreamer. Add to that the open roof, the booze, the grass, and some excessive speed, and, well, you have a recipe for automotive disaster. Definitely we all could've been casualties of the teenage wars. SIX LOCAL TEENS DEAD the headline could've read. The bodies of six local boys were found dead in a drainage ditch last night after their car overturned along Hamilton Road on the south side of Delaware Township.

But it didn't work out that way. The Devil might've tempted us, but God had his eye on us. That is, if you believe in God and the Devil and all that stuff.

I can tell you this: all six of us flew out of that bug like confetti tossed at the circus. I like to think the combination of the booze and the weed saved our lives. We were all too fucked up to stress out. We just let it happen. We flew through the air with the greatest of ease. Fricking acrobats. High wire men.

We floated, then splattered in a field of timothy. The long, flowing grass (destined for cutting the very next day) cushioned our fall and made our return to earth relatively painless. It was like a parachute jump behind enemy lines. A minute or so passed before we reconnoitered and surveyed the damage. Plenty of it, but none of it life-threatening or even in immediate need of medical attention.

The brand new Mellow Yellow had not been so lucky. The Beetle lay on its side looking scraped and dented and dead. I remember the front wheels still had life. They kept spinning, running free.

One by one the six of us gathered around the battered bug. Some small effort was made to get the wheels back on the ground so we could make our getaway. To where and to what end we had no idea, but it seemed senseless to just stand there. So we put our shoulders to work and started the old heave-ho.

The sound of a siren halted our efforts. We paused and listened. The siren grew louder. We looked at each other in the dim light, then turned and bolted across that field of timothy and into the nearby woods.

From the relative safety of the trees we watched as first one police cruiser arrived on the scene followed soon thereafter by a second police cruiser. Police Chief Walters of the Bridgeton P.D., and Pop's best friend, stepped out of that second cruiser. He'd been the police chief for like a hundred years. He was a good guy, fair and friendly, so long as you didn't mess up.

I'd just messed up. Big-time.

Police Chief Walters and the other cop shined their flashlights on the bug. They checked the interior of the VW for dead and or mangled bodies. Finding none, they cast their beams along the road and out across the field. We instinctively backed up a few paces, secreted ourselves behind those trees.

"I don't see anyone," said Police Chief Walters.

"Me neither," said the other cop.

"Whoever was in the car," said Chief Walters, "must be okay. They must have started walking. Maybe to get help."

"Maybe."

"I'll tell you something though," added Chief Walters.

"What's that, Chief?"

"I can't say for certain, but that looks like the new convertible Tom Middleton's daughter Lisa got a couple weeks ago."

Chief Walters took another look around with his flashlight. We didn't draw a breath or move a muscle.

"Look there," said Chief Walters, and his light fell upon our escape route. "The grass is all trampled down."

"Maybe whoever was in the car went that way."

"Must have. Strange though. Why would they head for those woods?"

The other cop shrugged. "I don't know."

"Maybe someone's hurts," said Police Chief Walters. "We better have a look."

The two cops started into the field. We couldn't see their faces but we could see their flashlight beams dancing across the timothy. Old hands at avoiding trouble and authority even at our tender ages, we silently continued our retreat.

Boys, I can tell you, move more swiftly and with greater purpose than men. We had no hassles at all avoiding capture. Slipped into the night and stole away. Too bad I had a mass of other problems. Like how to explain the condition of Mellow Yellow to Mom and Pop and Gram. And Homer. Homer'd be plenty hot when he found out. He'd raise all kinds of hell. Kick me clear into the middle of next week if I gave him half a chance. (Which, as we've already witnessed, he did and then some.)

While I ran through the woods and open fields I pondered my options. I could return to the big old Victorian, stretch out in front of the tube, and go to sleep. When folks started arriving home and quizzing me about the absence of the convertible, well, I'd just shrug my shoulders and tell them I didn't have a clue. It might sound suspicious, but hey, they had no proof I'd been out joyriding. No proof at all. Maybe someone had stolen the car out of the driveway, driven it into the hills, and smashed it up.

Or maybe not.

I ran and ran. And as I ran I realized one thing: I was screwed.

We halted our retreat behind the Pratt's barn out on Old Dutch Road. It must've been midnight by that time. We went over our casualty list. All of us had scratches and abrasions, bumps and bruises. I had a finger that was definitely busted. Bones had a sprained wrist. Retro's knee was bruised and swollen. Young and Johnson complained of various aches and pains. The new kid Laramie had a nasty egg on his forehead.

We went into the barn and up the ladder to the hayloft. For an hour or more we talked it over, all the details. Finally, exhausted, I told everyone to get some sleep and we'd decide what to do in the morning. Like I was the boss or something. There was some grousing and finger pointing, mostly in my direction, but one by one we all settled down to get some zzzs on that musty hay.

Or so I thought.

I closed my eyes. And immediately drifted off.

A second later I heard crows squawking and roosters screaming. Dawn already?

I opened my eyes. At first I couldn't figure out where I was. Life was a blur. The fourth finger on my left hand throbbed like a beating heart. Then I remembered. It all came back to me in a flash. The whole mess. That's when I glanced around the hayloft and realized my cohorts had checked out of the game. In the middle of the night those cowards had made some decisions without me.

Not that I really blamed them. They hadn't stolen their mother's new car. They hadn't been stoned behind the wheel and drinking Bud. They hadn't run into that stupid drainage ditch. They'd just been along for the ride. Riders caught in a storm. Had I been in their shoes, I probably would've blown free in the middle of the night also. Hell, why should five guys lose their heads just because one guy's heading for the guillotine?

So what did I do? I made a run for it. I figured I'd get in touch with Big Jack. I'd track him down. He'd take me in. We'd hang out together, be a team. A boy and his father. Hey, it beat facing the Inquisition of Mom and Pop and Gram and Homer.

For a couple hours I bushwhacked through the woods so I wouldn't have to show my face on any local roads. By midmorning I'd worked my way over to Flemington where I started hitching north on U.S. 202. I'd hitched some over the years, but not much. Mom had drummed into me the world was full of murderers and pedophiles. Getting in the car with a stranger could spell disaster. But when we were kids Dad used to tell me and Jake stories of him hitching all the way to Florida in winter and out west in summer. So I figured if he could do it, I could too.

It being a Sunday morning it was pretty quiet out there. But after a while a car stopped. A dark blue Pontiac Bonneville. Not too new and not in great shape. A noisy muffler and lots of rust. I didn't care. I ran for it before the driver changed his mind. As soon as I pulled open the back door I saw two black guys—one driving and one riding. I was right away scared shitless. I'd been pretty well programmed to fear black men. I don't know why. I'd never had any problems with black men. All my troubles, if I thought about it, had been with white men. My own father, for one. And of course the world's nastiest SOB, Mr. Homer Otis.

"Where you going, kid?"

"Down the road," I answered, after a pause long enough to slaughter a hog.

"Down the road where?" It was the driver asking the questions.

His buddy worked on a Marlboro, blew smoke rings the size of a basketball hoop.

"Down the road a piece," I said, I think because I'd heard James Dean or Marlon Brando say it once in an old movie.

The black guys looked at each other and laughed. They were cool. They didn't rob me or kill me. In fact, they bought me breakfast. At the Circle Diner up in Somerville. While we ate our eggs and pancakes they gave me some advice. "You got to watch your ass hitchhiking, kid. These be bad times we live in. There be some bad dudes out there won't be buying you breakfast. No sirree, they'll be eating you for breakfast."

I told them they sounded like my mother. They laughed and stuffed eggs over easy and heavily buttered white toast into their mouths.

After breakfast they dropped me where Interstates 287 and 78 converge. My plan was to head west, that's where I figured Big Jack would be. (Big Jack had a good laugh when I plugged in that detail.) I thanked the two black guys for the food and the ride and headed down the I-78 entrance ramp.

Half an hour later an eighteen-wheeler pulled onto the shoulder at least half a mile up the interstate. That truck was so far in the distance I thought it had nothing to do with me. But then I heard its horn give a couple of short blasts. I made a run for it. It took some time. I climbed up, pulled open the passenger door, and swung myself up into the seat. The driver was huge, easily in excess of three hundred pounds.

Before he could ask I told him I was headed for Pennsylvania.

"Is that so?" he said.

"That's so," I told him.

He studied me hard while he slowly shifted that big rig through its five thousand gears. I tried not to look at the thick folds of fat on his arms and neck and face. He had a big-time fetish with Reese's peanut butter cups. During our half hour together he must've put away a hundred of the bite-sized morsels. He just kept shoveling them in, one right after another, as fast as he could pull free the tin foil wrappers.

The fat man turned out to be a squealer. Though I guess you could look upon him as a Good Samaritan. Out in Bloomsbury he exited the interstate, telling me he needed fuel. But when we got to the service area there were two New Jersey state police cars sitting in the parking lot. Seems the fat man had heard an APB on his shortwave just a minute or so before spotting me standing on the shoulder of the highway with my thumb out. He'd radioed the state police before I climbed into his cab.

Two muscular state troopers approached the truck.

I turned to the driver. "You're a rat, fat man. I hope your brakes fail and you slide off a bridge into the river."

He just popped another Reese's and smiled. Probably the fat man was doing me a favor, protecting me from my own idiocy, but I didn't see it that way.

The state troopers wanted to know if I was Joshua Tailor of Bridgeton. I scowled and nodded. They put me in the back of one of the squad cars and hauled me off to the state police barracks a few miles down the road. No one said much. They put me in a room by myself and locked the door. I sat on a folding metal chair and watched the clock on the wall. The second hand swept around and around. So did the minute hand, only more slowly. Time passed. My life ticked away. I wondered if I'd go to prison.

Forty-seven minutes and twenty-three seconds after I sat down in that metal chair the door opened. In walked Mom and Pop and Gram. Oddly, they were all happy to see me. Overjoyed you might even say. Mom and Gram had tears in their eyes. I got great big hugs. Wet kisses planted upon my cheeks and forehead.

"Thank God you're all right, Joshua."

"Longest night of my life."

"You had us worried sick."

"You should have called. Always call, Joshua. No matter what happens, no matter how bad you think it is, always call."

"We're your family. We're the ones you turn to when things go wrong."

Not exactly what I'd been anticipating, but I lapped it up as I knew it couldn't last.

Mom and the grandparents powwowed with the state police. A bunch of papers were signed. No formal charges were filed. But I would have to appear before the local juvenile board. The board would decide my punishment, typically several months of community service. In the meantime, I was free to go.

On the ride home the great outpouring of love and relief gave way to a more somber tone. Pop gave me the lecture of a lifetime. Words like selfish and stupid and irresponsible spilled from his lips. He reminded me several times that I could have been killed.

I sat in the back of the Mercury Marquis next to Mom. She held my hand and shook her head a lot.

And how did I feel? What did I have on my mind?

Less than you might think. I felt bad about wrecking the bug and putting my buds in harm's way. I didn't want to wreck that car. I loved that car. I loved all cars. Old and new. Fast and slow. Domestics and Imports. Hardtops and convertibles. After all, my daddy, Big Jack, was a car salesman. He'd instilled in me from an early age the muscle, magic, and splendor of the automobile. Big Jack used to say a boy becomes a man when he first climbs up behind the wheel, turns the key, engages the transmission, and mashes the accelerator. Well, I guess I'd proved Big Jack's theory dead wrong when I plowed into that drainage ditch. I definitely was no man. Not yet.

I knew I'd screwed up. But in my mind my screw-up hadn't been easing the bug out of the driveway for a little joyride. Or taking a couple tokes off that reefer. Or a few swigs of Bud. No, my screw-up had been taking my eyes off the road. My screw-up had been looking at the moon.

My screw-up had been getting caught.

The Wad

As soon as I finished telling him about The Crash, Big Jack wanted to hear about the lumber we'd allegedly swiped from the bridge construction job just south of Bridgeton.

But I felt like I'd divulged enough, so I insisted he give me a few more details on the Homer Otis front. See, Big Jack's brief and whispered reference to the evil bastard had put a whole new optimistic spin on my little world: Me and Big Jack—aligned against Homer O! What could beat that? But though I pushed the old boy to say more about his plans, he blew me off and slipped some old Blues into the CD player.

The Blues right away woke up Retro and Bones putting the quietus on our little father/son chitchat. For a time that morning we rode along the eastern bank of the Ohio River north and west through western PA listening and tapping our feet and drumming our fingers to the loose and lazy rhythms. The river ran so close I could've spat in her had I been on the left side of the van.

Up near Beaver where the river swung west, we stopped at a diner and got Taylor ham and egg sandwiches on hard rolls with ketchup, salt and pepper. The yolks broke when I bit into mine and happy was I for having Big Jack on my side against Otis, and for the warm, salty pig taste that filled my mouth. Big Jack took his coffee black and spent most of the meal yakkin' into the black and chrome pay phone over near the door to the men's room. Too bad I couldn't hear him over the din of noisy diners masticating their food and smacking their lips while talking politics and weather.

Back in the van we turned due north and hooked up with the PA Turnpike. That shoved us west to the border. "New state, boys!" shouted Big Jack. "New state! Ohio state line! See it now or miss it forever!"

Tough to miss the huge white billboard: WELCOME TO OHIO! THE BUCKEYE STATE!

"What's a buckeye?" I asked my father.

"A buckeye? It's a... well... it's a type of horse. The buckeye horse. Like a big plow horse. Settlers used the buckeye back in the old days to tame the land."

I bought the buckeye story, lock, stock, and barrel, but found out later Big Jack had lied like a rug. The man didn't have a clue what a buckeye was. But that didn't stop him from making something up. He had to have an answer, couldn't stand not knowing, and so lied as easy as breathing.

A buckeye's actually a tree not a horse. Ohio nicknamed itself the Buckeye State because when Ohioans joined the Union in 1803 Buckeye trees covered the place from Lake Erie all the way south to the Kentucky line.

We pushed a mile or so into Ohio. Big Jack proclaimed, "We've done Jersey, boys. We've done Delaware, Maryland, Virginia, West Virginia, Pennsylvania, and now Ohio. Seven states under our belts already with plenty more to come. And don't you boys worry, I won't cross a single state line anytime day or night without spreading the word loud and clear, like Paul Revere proclaiming the approach of the British into Boston harbor."

Another few miles and Big Jack broke back into song. He announced that "for a period of time" he'd been a long haul trucker. "I drove a big rig, an eighteen wheeler, back and forth across this fine but tormented country."

This was news to me. I thought my father had only ever been a car salesman. But I didn't let my ignorance out of the bag since no way did I want Retro and Bones to see, feel, or hear the distance between me and Big Jack.

Big Jack said, "I did most of my driving at night. Quieter then. More peaceful. Just me and the headlights and my thoughts drifting off into the deep dark."

I glanced over at my father sitting there behind the wheel waxing poetic and I wanted to ask him what he thought about while driving his big rig. I wanted to know if he thought about me and Mom and Jake, God rest the little man's soul, but before I could get my mouth open Retro asked him what kind of stuff he hauled.

"Anything needed hauling, Carl. I drove a Kenworth Supreme for J. Vanderpoel Trucking of Kearney, New Jersey. Vanderpoel hauled anything for anybody so long as that anybody had the coin."

"But like what kind of stuff?" Retro persisted.

"Well, for instance, I might haul steel reinforcing rods from Newark, NJ out to Spokane, Washington. Then I might pick up a load of pine flooring in Boise, Idaho and haul it down to Jacksonville, Florida. Then run empty up to Macon, Georgia for a load of car batteries bound for Detroit, Michigan. In Michigan I might pick up, say, a thousand storm doors for delivery back to a Home Depot warehouse in Delaware. I've zigzagged across this country a thousand times. Been to every state now except for Alaska and Hawaii. But move over! I'm on my way. I'll get everywhere, and you boys should too. It's a big old world out there and this is the only lifetime you got to see it. Forget about Heaven and Hell or coming back as an eagle or an Eagle Scout. This right now is your chance to shine. So don't be hiding out letting the days slide by without a fight."

Now this was more like it. More like what I'd imagined when I lay in bed back in Bridgeton with my hands behind my head pondering the trip—the four of us out on the open road, Big Jack Speechifying and

Postulating on the ways of the world. I was certain we had nothing but good times and wide-open spaces ahead.

Bones wanted to know if Big Jack had ever been to California. Dad said sure a thousand times, and started in telling us about when he'd gone to San Diego to haul out a load of antique pick-up trucks. "Folks up in the northeast," he explained, "like those old pickups. Forty-nine Dodges and fifty-two Fords. Only the ones in that neck of the woods rot from rust so they pull the old farm trucks out of Arizona and southern California where there's no snow and no salt on the roads. You ever get salt in an open wound? It stings like a mother, makes you yelp like a dog. Well, you get salt up underneath the paint of an automobile or a pickup and you can hear that sheet metal screaming in pain. Anyway I was hauling these pickups from San Diego out across the Mojave Desert when—" Jack cut himself short when his cell phone began to chirp. He pulled the phone from his shirt pocket, glanced at the display, gave me a wink, popped the cover, and said, "Yeah?"

After a couple seconds listening he said, "You got that right." Then after another glance my way he reached forward and switched on the radio. Turned it up plenty loud too. Some weatherman informed us the Ohio Valley would have a hot and humid day with some clouds and maybe a thunderstorm late in the afternoon.

Big Jack half turned to the window and spoke out of the left side of his mouth. I did my best to eavesdrop but about all I got were a few random tidbits. "Yeah." "I'm on top of it." "No problem." "That'll work." "I'll be there."

He hung up and slipped the cell phone back into his pocket. Figuring he needed to say something he said, "My broker. Guy's always on me to buy some crazy stock."

Oh yeah, and I'd be batting cleanup for the Yanks come spring training.

A couple hours later, still flying down I-80 west of Toledo, Big Jack yawned. "I need some shuteye, boys, before I run this van into the back of a semi."

We pulled off the interstate and parked in the hinterlands of an enormous service area. There must've been a square mile of asphalt, plus a gas station and a slew of fast food joints—burgers, pizza, donuts, ice cream, coffee.

Big Jack pushed back his seat, closed his eyes, and said, "You boys lay low for a while. Get yourselves a Whopper or a Tastee-Freeze. Take a walk. Smell the roses. Do whatever you want. Just stay outta trouble. Be back in an hour and I'll be ready to roll."

Me and Retro and Bones slipped through the doors and steered toward the smell of frying meat and hot coffee. To get there we had to maneuver around tractor-trailers, monster RVs, and caravans of Fords, Nissans and BMWs. It was summertime. America was on the move.

Retro said, "I gotta tell you, Josh, your old man's one weird dude."

I right away narrowed my eyes. "Yeah?"

"He's like some guy you'd see in the movies. Maybe an old western. Riding his horse across the desert."

"What are you babbling about?"

"I'm just saying."

"Look," I said, "I don't need you complaining about him. I've barely seen the guy for like the past six years. He's as strange to me as he is to you."

Retro gave me a shove. "Ease off, big boy. Don't get yourself in a dither. I'm not complaining. And hey, at least you got a father."

I right away felt bad.

We walked on.

We peed, bought cans of Dr. Pepper, and headed over to a bank of video games we plied with quarters as fast as we could pull them out of our pockets. When mine ran out I slipped away to make a couple phone calls with my calling card. First I called Mom, but no one answered, not even Gram, so I left like a ten second message. Then I almost called Amy, you know, just to say hi, but halfway through dialing I decided it was uncool to call so I hung up. Which was good because right then Retro and Bones showed up and no way did I want them to see me calling my girl.

We got chicken-on-a-stick, fries in a paper cup, and more Dr. Peppers, then sat outside on the curb to eat. Americans of all colors, shapes, sizes, and ages drinking and eating a wide variety of foods and beverages similar to our own came and went. We just sat and ate and watched them come and go.

After a while we headed back to the van. We came out from behind an RV the size of a bowling alley and there stood the Town & Country. Only the Town & Country no longer looked the way it had earlier. It now had a trailer attached to its hindquarter again. Only it wasn't the black and white trailer we'd picked up back at Leonard's Rib Shack in Virginia. This trailer was black and silver and looked to be the same trailer we'd hauled out of that old hay barn back in Pennsylvania.

Big Jack stood beside the trailer yakkin' with this dude who stood taller than an NBA forward but wasn't any bigger around than a lamppost. He wore a ragged beard, a green John Deere cap, cowboy boots, dungarees, and an Allman Brothers tee shirt.

Jack and the tall skinny guy kept talking.

Retro and Bones pushed forward but I held out my arm. "Hang on."

The tall guy must've been chewing tobacco because every few

seconds he would pucker his lips and spit some brown goo out of his mouth onto the hot asphalt. This went on for a few minutes, then the tall guy reached into the pocket of his faded dungarees. A second later he pulled out a wad of cash. A thick wad. I'm talking several inches thicker than the fat wad Big Jack had been hauling around. The tall guy handed the wad over to Big Jack. Who didn't even look at it—just quick as a cat shoved it into his pocket.

Then the tall guy climbed into a dark green Dodge Durango and raced off with little or no concern for fuel economy. Big Jack didn't bother to wave.

We hung back for another minute or two then started forward. No way did we let on like we'd seen that wad of cash exchange hands. Big Jack said hey and we said hey and then we got back on the road—I-80 due west.

While we sped over flat Ohio terrain I fought a pretty fair battle with myself about whether or not to mention the wad of cash. Call it a battle between my curiosity and my cool. In the end my curiosity, and I guess too my attitude, won out.

I turned to Big Jack and said, "I saw that guy give you money. I saw the wad."

He glanced over at me. "Oh yeah? What guy? What wad?"

"The guy back at the service area. The tall skinny dude."

"You saw some tall skinny dude give me money?"

"I sure did."

Big Jack smiled. "What's the deal, kid? You spying on me now? You a secret agent man?"

"I don't think so. I just know what I saw."

Big Jack's smile grew broader. He had a hell of a smile. Big bright blue eyes and white teeth and dimples the size of the Hawaiian Islands. For years he drove Mom crazy with that smile. Even after he smacked her and cheated on her and abandoned her she still couldn't get enough of that smile.

"Sorry, kid," he told me, "but your eyes must've been playing tricks on you. It was me giving him money. For fixing the trailer. You did take note of the trailer attached to the back of the van, Sherlock? Good, because it cost me some hard-earned dough to get that trailer fixed and hauled out here so we could use it on the long push west. If you get my drift."

I got his drift all right. Big Jack could talk a blue streak when he had a mind to. He could talk till you lost all track of what train you'd come to catch. Mom would say, "When your father starts talking plug up your ears or run for your life."

Still, I didn't feel like taking his jive. So I turned to get some help from Retro and Bones. Retro had himself sprawled across the third row seat. Bones sat reading a book about the infinite size of the universe in the seat directly behind Dad. The book, which Bones had been reading aloud to us off and on, had as its central theme the idea that earth was a miniscule zit on an organism vastly larger than anything humans could comprehend. It also theorized that humans were little more than bacterial blobs living large off the juices of said zit.

When I turned around Retro and Bones pretended like they hadn't even been listening to me and Big Jack hash it out. They acted like Switzerland.

"Come on," I pushed them, "'fess up. You were there. You saw what happened. You saw the skinny dude pass over the wad."

Retro played stupid. Clearly he wanted to stay on Big Jack's good side. And who could blame him? Not only was Big Jack our commanding officer, but he had control of our transportation needs and was also footing the bill.

I nevertheless called him a weasel and turned my efforts to Bones.

Who right away showed his favorite color was yellow. "I didn't see anything. I was busy eating my chicken-on-a-stick."

Which caused me to freak out and hurl some curse words around the van.

Which caused Big Jack to break into a hearty laugh. "Looks like you're rowing this boat alone, secret agent man."

"I saw what I saw."

"Maybe you saw what you shouldn't've saw."

"Huh?"

"Or maybe you just saw what you wanted to see."

"What?"

"Forget it, kid," said Big Jack as he reached under his seat and pulled out a road atlas. He tossed that atlas on my lap. "Finnegan, my man, you have way too much time on your hands. It's time you had something useful to do. From here on out you're going to give up the vocation of minding other people's business and take on a new trade. I'm designating you the official navigator for the remainder of the trip. You'll keep track of where we are. Plot the day's route. Find an alternate route if and when the primary route gets bogged down. Do you understand your assignment?"

Sure I did, but I didn't much like being drafted. I prefer volunteer work, and not much of it. But I loved maps and so kept quiet.

"Alrightee then," said Big Jack, "here's your first job. In about an hour we'll reach Gary, Indiana, followed soon thereafter by Chicago, Illinois. This'll be by far the largest metro area we'll pass on our way to the Rockies. The roads can be a mess. Study the map and find the best way to the other side. I'll want a report in thirty minutes."

Maybe the old boy figured I couldn't handle the rigors of being the navigator, but he had it figured wrong. I knew how to read a map. He didn't know it because he'd run out on us, but I'd been handling the road maps and navigating for Mom for years. After all, I was the man of the house after Dad did his disappearing act.

But no matter how long I studied those maps, I kept coming back to the same basic problem. And the only thing I could do to solve that problem, to my great irritation, was turn to Big Jack.

"I know where we are and where we've been," I told him. "But I don't know where we're going? I can't plan the route without a destination."

"Good point, kid. We're steering for the Rockies. Northern Montana. But we have a few stops along the way. First one's in Illinois. Little town called Port Byron."

I looked up Port Byron in the index. Found it in the northwest corner of the state. Right smack on the Mississippi a few miles north of Moline. The Mississippi River! Just the squiggly blue line on the page made my heart drum a little faster.

I could see we had a couple choices. We could either stay on I-80 and keep pressing west or we could veer off to the north once we got south of Chicago and then head west on I-88. I mentioned all this to Big Jack.

He said, "You pick."

That sounded like a lot of pressure, so I tried to pry some more info out of him.

He said, "It's your call, my man. You pick the route. After all, you're the navigator. I'm just the pilot."

So I pondered the situation a while longer, weighed the pros and cons of both routes, and finally made my decision. "We'll stick to I-80. 88 would probably be okay, but moving any closer to downtown Chicago seems like a risk not worth taking."

"Good call, Josh. Especially with the afternoon rush gearing up."

And that was it. That was all Big Jack said. He didn't question me or demand to see the map or cast doubt on my decision. He gave me the responsibility, then he stuck by me. Stuck by me even after we got caught in some brutal stop and go traffic where 80 and 294 intersect. He didn't mutter a word, just plugged in some Blues and drummed his fingers on the steering wheel.

All this navigating business might seem like a lot of nonsense about very little, but if you think that, well, I have a hunch you don't know fathers and sons. Boys need their father's approval, even on stuff as trivial as reading a map. My relationship with Big Jack was complicated and plenty convoluted, but the man was nevertheless my father. I needed him to think good of me. I needed him sing my praises.

It took some time but we finally broke free of that traffic snarl and pushed our speed back up 75 mph. But less than an hour later, out of the blue, out near La Salle, with the sun still high in the summer sky, Big Jack announced, "Calling it quits for the time being, boys. I'm sick of driving."

This shook me since I'd been thinking we'd probably keep driving night and day till we reached the Rockies. But Big Jack had a different plan. I had to remind myself he was mostly unpredictable.

We exited at the next exchange. It was Retro's turn to fill the gas tank. I checked the oil and inspected the tires. Bones cleaned the dead bugs off the windshield. It was all part of the routine we performed every time we pulled off the highway.

Afterwards we drove down the street and checked into what looked like a brand new Hampton Inn. On the big neon sign out front it read: POOL. BAR. HBO. FITNESS CENTER. Everything a weary traveler could want.

We got two rooms. One for Dad and one for the rest of us.

Big Jack said, "I got some phone calls. You boys behave

yourselves. Absolutely no going in the water unless there's a lifeguard." He locked onto my eyes. "Got me?"

I nodded. I knew about staying out of the water. I'd learned my lesson early.

"Good," he said, then added, "If you want dinner go to the restaurant. Charge it to the room. And remember every step of the way to act like men, not boys."

We didn't see Big Jack again till morning.

Me and Retro and Bones lounged around in our room for a while. I'd lost track of the days but it must've been a weekend because sports filled the TV—baseball mostly but also tennis and car racing and some X Games on ESPN 2. We flipped through the channels, each of us taking a pull on the remote. When that got tiresome we went out and hung by the pool but didn't go in as per Big Jack's orders. When we grew hungry we headed for the restaurant next to the front lobby. We ordered spaghetti and garlic bread and salads we didn't eat.

After dinner we went back to the room and watched movies on HBO, including one with a pretty wild sex scene—lots of flesh, plenty of moaning and groaning. Retro farted. And then I farted. And then Bones farted. We farted and belched and bludgeoned each other with pillows and generally worked ourselves into a frenzy till the guy next door (not Big Jack, he was across the hall) pounded on the wall and ordered us to pipe down. Which we did after some guffawing and a few more farts each.

At the crack of dawn Big Jack burst into our room. "Rise and shine, girls! Up and at 'em! Let's go go go! Shorts! Tee shirts! Sneakers and socks! You girls look soft! You girls need some ex-a-size!"

Five minutes later Big Jack the drill sergeant had us in the Hampton Inn parking lot doing squats and jumping jacks. "Up, down! Up, down!! Look alive, Zeller! This ain't a camp for couch potatoes!"

Ten minutes of jacks, then off we set on a five-mile run. The terrain was flat and the pace moderate, but nevertheless, by the time we got back the only one still running was Big Jack. Me and Retro, we'd slowed to a lazy jog. And poor Bones, he'd just about gone down on all fours.

From there we went straight to the fitness center where I got to see my old man's physique for the first time in a long time. He was in his late forties but had the body of a guy twenty years younger—trim and fit and sturdy as steel with six-pack abs and a V-shaped back. His arms, chest, and neck swelled as he pumped the free weights.

Bones, still trying to catch his breath, still skinny as a stick, sat on the sidelines and stared at Big Jack. Me and Retro played it a little cooler. We did some bicep curls while we snuck glances at Big Jack out of the corners of our eyes…

Now you've been with me on this trip since we left Jersey. You've seen Big Jack in action. You know he's a man in motion, never a dull moment. So wouldn't you think after the long overnight, after the workout, the showers and breakfast, Big Jack would've had us back on the road? Back in the van and making haste for points west?

Well, it didn't happen. After a long and leisurely breakfast, wherein Big Jack ate some bacon and eggs, he informed us we'd be hanging at the Hampton Inn for a few hours. He told us to pull on our swimsuits and kick back till further notice.

So that's what we did. It was another hot day with a high blue sky. We hung by the pool, worked on our tans, went swimming, read some mags, laid low. Big Jack kept disappearing into his bedroom, I guess to make phone calls. But most of the time he hung out at the pool with us. He told us stories about growing up in Jersey City, about the time he sold a 911 Cabriolet to Jack Nicholson, about the tornado that blew his tractor-trailer clean off the highway outside Abilene, Kansas. Irish through and through, my old man knew how to tell a story. I can tell a story too, but not like Jack. I got my storytelling prowess diluted with all that stodgy English Middleton blood.

And still our train sat idle in the station. Rumors flowed from car to car. An explosion on the track. A rolling blackout across the northeast. Terrorists at the gate.

I had no idea what to believe.

Sometime in the early evening, dusk just beginning to settle, the conductor came to our car and made an announcement. He claimed there were problems with the tracks farther up the line. I asked him what kinds of problems. He wouldn't say.

I asked when we could expect the train to leave the station. He would not even venture a guess.

It would have been nice to call home but I had a dead cell phone and no interest in leaving the train. A massive and unhappy crowd jammed the platform. No way did I want to give up my seat and get swept into that throng.

And so I encouraged Josh to continue with his cross country adventure...

The Nuptials

While we steer west for the Mississippi and Port Byron, I'd like to take another quick trip back to check up on my parents during their younger, wilder days. It won't take long. I feel like we left them hanging in the hot August breeze back there on the eve of their first date.

Jack and Lisa had a stormy ride in the days and weeks and months following their chance meeting at Flemington Porsche/BMW. They took that test drive and never turned back. They went to dinner that Saturday night, the sparks flew, and so began an era of lust and love and loss.

When Mom and Dad first started dating Lisa lived at home and went to junior college in Trenton. Up till then she'd dated mostly bright-eyed boys in blue jeans. Pop had no problem intimidating these smiling idiots. But right off he knew he had his hands full with Jack Tailor. Not only was Jack a decade older than Lisa, but he was a fast-talker wearing fancy French loafers and driving a hot German sports car. And to boot he often showed up at the house smelling of beer and whiskey and smoking a cig. Sometimes he wouldn't even bother to get out of the car and come to the door—he'd just lean on the horn and wait for his sweetie to come a-runnin'. Which she always did. Usually with her scowling father standing in the doorway forbidding her to go. But forbidding, I can tell you, doesn't always make it so. Forbidden fruit and all that jive.

Big Jack and Lisa Anne listened to no one. They had a lustful relationship, one that could not be reined in by parents, friends, or rational reasoning. Like a lot of folks, Jack and Lisa mistook this vigorous physical lust for love. Real love. Tender, sweet and everlasting. And so despite warnings from far and wide, from friends and family, Lisa moved out of the big Victorian on Cherry Street and into Jack's bachelor pad. This move followed directly on the heels of Lisa having a knock-down drag-out battle with her folks after arriving home in the wee hours sans pantyhose, skirt askew, and half the buttons on her shirt gone forever. Her parents had waited up all night. By the time Lisa rolled through the front door Pop was tired and ticked off and eager for a fight.

Gram, the calmest of the calm even during major emotional hurricanes, did her best to keep her husband and daughter from ripping each other apart. She did fine, only she couldn't keep Pop's trap shut. In the heat of battle he called his daughter a number of unsavory names, names that typically tumble out during times when people might be better off in different states, forget about standing in the same living room.

So Mom, headstrong and oh so spoiled, got her hackles up, hurled a few choice words of her own, and bolted for the door. While she stormed down the front walk, Pop stepped out onto the porch. As dawn unfurled, in a voice heard by early-rising Bridgeton residents half a dozen blocks away, he informed his daughter that if she left now she'd never set foot in his house again. To which Mom turned and shouted an expression best left up to your imagination. She then spun on her pumps and with her shirt flapping in the breeze marched off at a spirited clip to begin Life With Jack.

For over a year Mom lived in Dad's bachelor pad in Frenchtown. I think Dad's pad was pretty much a dump with a lot of ne'er-do-wells coming and going and crashing on the floor or out on the dilapidated back porch that hung precariously over the river. A one-endless-party kind of pad. Not exactly Lisa Anne Middleton's cup of tea, but she put up with it because she loved her man, or thought she did, and because no way was she about to crawl home with her tail between her legs.

Lisa worked at the River Café in Frenchtown serving soup and sandwiches to locals and transients passing through town. One day Mom returned home from work early due to a fever and an upset stomach. She found Dad in bed—in a compromised position. Some screaming and shouting and throwing of objects ensued. Mom threw a shoe at the woman. The heel of this shoe clipped the chippie on the chin and brought forth a gush of blood. The bleeding hussy grabbed her gear and made a run for it.

Big Jack needed a couple weeks to soothe the situation over. He kissed Mom's feet, bought her endless flowers, begged forgiveness, and promised to never ever again succumb to temptation. Mom, young and naïve and some might say stupid as a stick, gave an inch here and another inch there and pretty soon allowed Dad, car salesman extraordinaire, back into her bed. Undoubtedly she should've run for her life, gotten a BA in English or Education, taught 2nd grade for a year or two, then married a respectable doctor, settled down in one of Bridgeton's better neighborhoods, and pumped out a few kids. But nope, she stuck to the notion that Jack was her man.

Lisa had only one demand before resuming normal relations. She insisted they evacuate Dad's pad on the River Styx and move into a house for rent up in Milford. Big Jack, full of false guilt and remorse, agreed to the move and promptly started packing.

And for a while their lives in the small house in Milford went along smooth and easy. No real problems at all. Then, several months after they moved to Milford, a guy walked into the River Café. He ordered a tomato and mozzarella sandwich, then stood there staring at the girl behind the counter. Now Mom, like good looking women the world over, get men staring at them all the time. It goes with the territory. Men can't help but stare at pretty girls. It's in the genes. But this guy stared so long Mom grew antsy and finally asked him if he was okay or should she maybe call a doctor.

Well, long story short, the guy recognized Mom as an ex Miss New Jersey. He told her his name was Stan Morrow and he owned a talent agency in New York. Then he told her she was beautiful and should be a star. But truth be told—not every beautiful woman gets to be a star. Some just grow orchids or teach music or go mad or make sandwiches at the River Café. But Stan the Man told Mom he wanted her to come to New York and do an audition. He said they needed a fresh young face for an upcoming TV commercial. Stan thought Mom would be perfect for the job.

So that night, all excited, Lisa went home and told her man about the big TV offer. Well, Big Jack, so goes the story, was not exactly thrilled with the prospect of his woman doing TV ads. First he dismissed Stan as nothing but some smoothie on the make, probably not even a talent agent at all. Then when that attitude ran low on steam he started ranting and raving about Madison Avenue being nothing but a meat market and a den of thieves and the bottom of the American capitalist barrel.

Big Jack Tailor, Mr. Cool, was feeling threatened.

But despite Dad's bad attitude, Mom slipped in to see Stan on the sly. And it turned out Stan had a legitimate office on Madison Avenue. He had secretaries and assistants and phones ringing and no end of hustle and bustle. But he made time for Mom. He took her into his studio and shot a five-minute video of her. Mom didn't do much—just stood there and smiled into the camera. At first she was nervous but Stan told a joke about a rabbi and a priest. Mom relaxed. She began to ham it up. She tossed her long blond locks around and kicked up her heels. Stan told her she was a natural and assured her he'd call in a few days.

Stan called and invited Mom back to audition for the commercial. Mom wanted to tell Dad, but, well, didn't. And so into the Big Apple she slipped on the sly again. The instant the actual director of the commercial saw Mom through the camera lens the deal was sealed. She was told to report back the following week for three days of shooting.

Back home the time came to tell Jack the good news. Only Lisa was afraid to tell him. She didn't want him getting all riled up. Despite his massive cool Big Jack had a short fuse and a hot temper. So she lied. She told him she was taking a few days off from work and going to the beach with a couple friends.

And right here the story gets a little fuzzy. Lisa went to New York to shoot a commercial. No doubt about that. I've seen the commercial, on video, and I can tell you Mom looks good. She looks hot. They dressed her in this scanty little outfit, basically a bikini with some fringe hanging off her hips. She stood on a tall glass pedestal in the middle of a mock showroom crowded with shiny new Toyotas while a high-energy salesman rushed around shouting about Camrys and Corollas. Mom held up a large sign: TOYOTA SELL-A-THON GOING ON NOW!

So Lisa spent three days in the Big Apple shooting the commercial. Big Jack thought she was down in Avalon with a couple friends. On Friday Lisa arrived home. Jack asked her if she'd had a good time. Lisa said yeah, sure. Jack wanted to know what she did. Lisa said not much, just hung out on the beach. Jack looked her over and said she didn't get much of a tan. Lisa said there'd been a lot of clouds. Jack said the skies had been clear as a bell over the Delaware. Lisa shrugged.

All that blew over, but a couple weeks later Dad was sitting in the living room drinking a Bud and watching the Yanks on the tube. Mom was in the kitchen yakking on the phone. Suddenly she heard Dad shout, "Lisa, Jesus! Get in here!" Mom went, but none too quick. By the time she reached the living room the baseball game was back on but Dad was on his feet looking hot under the collar. He said he swore he'd just seen her on TV. On a commercial! A car commercial!

Lisa, knowing Jack watched a lot of sports, had figured this would happen. Well now it had, but she wasn't prepared to face the music. "No," she said, "it must've been someone who looked like me." And back she went to her phone call.

Big Jack let her go without further fanfare, but he definitely smelled a rat. He returned to the tube with an increased intensity. Not only did he watch the Yanks on PIX, but he flipped through the channels in hot pursuit of that Toyota Sell-a-thon ad. He didn't have to pursue for long. Toyota had their new ad all over the dial. Dad spotted the Sell-A-Thon on ABC, CBS, and NBC. And every time he saw it there stood his hot young blond blue-eyed bombshell girlfriend waving her stupid Sell-A-Thon banner with bellybutton on full display for horny sports hungry American males from sea to shining sea. Big Jack roared and freaked.

Oh yeah, that fight lasted all day and well into the night. At first the combatants battled over the fact that Mom had lied about doing the commercial. But within a couple hours that particular facet of the fight had been pushed to the rear, all but forgotten. You see, Big Jack, a guy who couldn't be trusted and so had a tough time trusting anyone else, got it in his craw that Mom had been messing around behind his back. No doubt he figured if he could give in to temptation, so too could she.

He demanded to know where Mom had slept during her three-day absence. Mom insisted she'd slept at a cheap motel in Hoboken. Dad didn't buy that for a second. He knew with absolute certainty she'd been shacking up with this dude Stan the Man the talent agent. Mom told him he was ridiculous, Stan was married with two young sons and a daughter. Dad told her to quit lying, married men cheated all the time. Mom said she wasn't lying. Dad said she was. Mom said she wasn't. Around and around they went, cursing and shouting and kicking chairs.

I personally do not know where Mom slept those nights. Hoboken. The Ritz-Carlton. Stan's skank pad. I don't have a clue. Maybe she had a fling, maybe not. The truth's a shady and slippery business.

I do know this: sometime after midnight, six or eight hours into the battle, Dad's jealous nature, Irish temper, and relentless consumption of the King of Beers finally reared its ugly head.

Mom shouted, "I've had it! Enough's enough! I'm going to bed." She turned and headed for the bedroom.

Dad didn't much like seeing Mom's backside at that moment. He took a couple quick hostile steps forward, grabbed Mom's shoulder, and spun her around. And right here's where things still could've gone either way. But as they often do in the heat of battle, things swung the wrong way.

Dad clocked Mom on the left cheek with a right jab. Down went Mom.

Yup, you heard me right: Big Jack whacked Lisa Anne. Whacked her pretty good right in the puss. No turning back from that action. No way. No how.

Big Jack had bloodied Lisa's cheek and blackened her eye. Which, as you might imagine, brought about an immediate ceasefire. Dad turned instantly docile. He fell upon Lisa with affection and contrition. He told her as he gently held ice to her puffy cheek and stroked her hair that he'd flipped out, lost his head, lost his cool. Never, not in a million years, he promised, would he ever touch her in a violent way again. She could count on that. Take that pledge to the bank. Absolutely. As good as gold.

For a solid hour Big Jack voiced his disgust and dismay with himself, his life, his attitude, his personality. Mom listened like a priest in the confessional as Dad poured out his heart. Only, of course, it wasn't Dad's heart pouring out, just his fear Mom might tell him to take a hike, might call the cops, might call her father.

After he finally ran out of gas and even shed a few tears, Mom, bludgeoned but not beaten, scowled at her man, thumped him hard on the chest, and demanded, "You promise me, right here, right now, you'll never hit me again! Ever! No matter what."

Between blubbers Big Jack sobbed, "I promise. Of course I promise. My God I'd kill myself before I'd hit you again. I love you, baby. I love you so much."

Lisa immediately softened. Her pink tee shirt all wet from tears and the melted ice, she whispered in a subdued but dire voice, "Okay, baby, it's okay. I know you didn't mean to hit me. I know you love me. I'm sorry I lied to you. I shouldn't have lied. I'll never lie to you again. Ever. I love you too. I love you more than anything in the world."

And believe it or not, that's how easily Lisa Anne let Big Jack off the hook.

They did some teary-eyed loving and the next day Jack rolled off to work. He arrived home that evening toting fifty blood red roses. That's right—fifty! He pressed the enormous mass of fragrant blooms into Mom's arms. Mom swooned. But Dad was just getting warmed up. He sat Mom down on the sofa, knelt in front of her on one knee, took her hand, and pulled a huge diamond ring out of his pocket. "You're the most beautiful girl in the world," he told her. "The most beautiful girl who ever lived. I adore you and worship you and love you more than my own life. Marry me, baby. Be my wife and I'll make you happy forever."

Mom, her eye all black and blue and her cheek all puffy and bruised, immediately broke into tears. And I'm not talking tears of rage here—I'm talking tears of joy. Tears of overwhelming happiness. Lisa Anne threw her arms around Big Jack, drew him close, kissed him on the mouth, and exclaimed, "Yes! Yes! Yes! Of course I'll marry you. Of course I'll be your wife!"

Jack slipped the ring on her finger. Fates sealed.

So there you are, there you go, that's my mom and dad. That's their early story and I'm sticking with it. Big Jack cheats on her—Lisa takes him back. He beats her—she takes him back. He proposes—she accepts. What are you gonna do?

They got hitched a month later at the Episcopal Church in Bridgeton with a few close family members and friends attending. Pop walked Mom down the aisle, but I've seen photos and can tell you—my grandfather did not look pleased with the duty.

The happy couple went to Bermuda on their honeymoon. And they must've made me because nine months later I made my first appearance at the Hunterdon Medical Center over in Flemington. 9 lbs. 6 ozs. of fuss and bother. Finnegan Joshua Middleton Tailor.

The Cargo

It might've been moving toward evening but it looked more like high noon with that early summer sun still high in the sky. At six o'clock it was 70 degrees inside the van, 88 degrees outside. And unbelievably bright out there. You had to wear shades or you would've gone blind. I had on some very cool Wayfarers Big Jack had given me.

I-80 stretched out long and straight. The land did not undulate. Illinois—all the way to the Mississippi River—ran as flat as the wooden floor in our gym over at South Hunterdon High. Farms, green and abundant, stretched all the way to the horizon. I could identify corn growing in the fields, but the rest of the crops drew a blank. Big Jack pointed out wheat and soybeans and rye, but I had my doubts.

There weren't many trees. The only ones I saw were tall shade trees—maples, beeches, and sycamores—standing guard over the farmhouses and barns. Beneath those shade trees I could see tire swings and swimming pools and trampolines.

I'd never been too far west of the Delaware, so this flat country spreading out mile after mile had my eyes burning.

"This is it, boys," Big Jack announced. "Right outside your window, live and in color—Middle America. The Heartland. The Breadbasket. Some of the most fertile soil on the planet lies out there for as far as you can see and for the next six or eight hundred miles down the road."

I spent most of my time staring through the glass but occasionally I glanced at the map. I didn't want to lose focus and blow my assignment—

Port Byron. Which was why, a couple miles before the exit, I said to Dad, "Coming up on I-74. Head north."

"Got it." Big Jack took the exit with complete confidence in his son.

We drove up I-74. I said, loud enough for Retro and Bones to hear, "We'll be coming up on the river soon. We exit just before the river and head north on Illinois Route 84."

I did my best to sound cool, but my heart had itself worked up in anticipation of my first glimpse of the Mississippi River. Retro and Bones too. After all, we were a trio of river rats. And the Mississippi, well, there wasn't anything like the Mississippi when it came to rivers. The Big Muddy. The Mighty Mississip. Mark Twain. Tom Sawyer. Huck Finn for crying out loud.

My dad, Big Jack, only ever read me one book when I was a kid. That book was The Adventures of Huckleberry Finn.

After a mile or so on 84 we came into Port Byron. Right off we saw the river. I got to tell you, much as I hate to say it—I wasn't all that impressed. Now I'll admit, I had the Mississippi so built up in my brain nothing short of a mile-wide river of pure liquid gold could've played out my expectations. So I suppose some amount of disappointment was a foregone conclusion.

The river stretched farther from bank to bank than the Delaware did at Bridgeton, but not by much. I easily could've swum across and back. But maybe I'm just whining to whine. That old river did have a certain beauty, a calmness. All kinds of boats plied her waters—sailboats, cargo boats, flatboats, fishing boats. I didn't see a paddleboat but my brain had no problem conjuring one up. I even saw old Sam Clemens with his big white moustache standing at the wheel smoking a fat cigar.

Big Jack drove north through town, then turned around and drove back south again. It was just a small river town, maybe a stoplight bigger than Bridgeton. I spotted a couple gas stations, a small supermarket, a pharmacy, rows of modest houses, some of them less than a good stone's throw from the river. Between the road and the river ran a railroad track, and between the tracks and the river ran a narrow dirt path, I figured for walking or running or riding your bike.

Big Jack reached the south end of town, then turned around for a third pass. He drove slow and said not a word, but he kept his eyes active, his head moving back and forth like it operated on a swivel.

On the fourth pass, right about in the middle of town, Big Jack pulled off the road into an asphalt parking lot with a nice view of the Mississippi. He swung the van and trailer around, then expertly backed the rig into the far corner of the parking lot under a large willow tree. He switched off the engine and took a couple deep breaths. Big Jack, let me tell you, looked plenty serious. All business. He said, "Let's have a look at that map, Josh."

I handed him the atlas. He studied it for several minutes. Finally he closed it, pushed it under the seat, and said, "Alright, boys, let's go have a look."

We climbed out and strolled over to the Mississippi River. Big Jack threw us a couple bones. He said across the way was the Hawkeye State of Iowa. Then he said we stood just about halfway between where the river began up in Minnesota and where it dumped into the Gulf of Mexico down in Louisiana.

I said, "I expected it to be bigger, you know, wider."

Retro said he thought so too.

Big Jack said, "You know, boys, our brains have the capacity to make mountains out of molehills. She's a nice river, but still just a ditch filled with water."

Didn't seem to be much to say to that, so the four of us just stood quiet watching the river slide by north to south. Over in Iowa a big red, white, and blue locomotive blew its horn followed by the appearance of a long slow-moving freight.

After that train passed Big Jack said, "Come on, let's get a burger."

We turned our backs on the river and walked across the parking lot. At the south end of the lot was a low squat cinderblock building with a small neon sign hanging in the window: Port Byron Bar & Grill. We steered that way.

Just before we reached the door Big Jack said, "Anybody asks where we're from, you tell them back east and no more. Anybody asks where we're going, you tell them to come see me. Got it?"

We all nodded. But I had to ask, "Why all the mystery?"

"No mystery at all," Big Jack told me. "I just want you to play it close to the vest."

I didn't wear a vest but gave the old boy a nod anyway. A couple seconds later we went up the brick steps of the Port Byron Bar and Grill and through the front door decorated with a small porthole.

The Mighty Mississippi might've been outside, not more than a couple hundred feet of air between us and it, but inside the Port Byron Bar and Grill you never would've known. We just as easily could've been on top of the Matterhorn. The Port Byron Bar and Grill had about as many windows as an outhouse. There was the front window with the neon sign, but that one looked out at the road. It was as though the river was such a colossal part of Port Byron life that the locals ventured into the Bar and Grill to forget about it while they drank a few beers and threw a few darts.

It might've still been as bright as an operating room outside, but inside it was dusky at best. We waited for our eyes to adjust to the lack of light, then we took in the customers and the bar's décor. Not many or much of either. Two guys sat hunkered down on stools at the bar. They took frequent gulps from large mugs of beer. Wooden chairs and tables lay scattered around the barroom. Most, in fact I think maybe all, were empty. I heard the sound of pool balls scattering and sure enough saw in another room off the back two more guys in dusty work clothes playing 8-ball.

A heavyset man wearing an apron and a red St. Louis Cardinals cap came out from behind the bar. "Can I help you fellas?" he asked friendlier than I would've thought.

"We could use something to wet our whistles," Big Jack told him.

At which point the bartender took a long look through the dim light at my father. A big smile broke across his face. He slapped Big Jack on the back and said, "Damn, Ben, I didn't recognize the face without the beard."

Ben? I right away wondered. Beard?

"Yeah, well," replied Big Jack, "it's a different game."

They jawboned some but I didn't catch most of it. I was trying to imagine my old man with a beard as well as wondering how he knew the bartender. I'd been under the impression Big Jack had never been to Port Byron before. After all, my navigational skills had gotten us there. Hadn't they?

The bartender led us over to a table. Me and the boys sat down. Big Jack (Ben) went over to the bar and powwowed with the bartender. I say powwowed because they leaned in close and spoke soft, so soft I doubt the CIA could've heard them.

My buds looked to me for explanations but I could only shrug. We opened the sticky plastic menus shoved into the back of the napkin holder and perused the fare. To give some idea, I'd say the bacon cheeseburger with mushrooms probably pushed the chef to his culinary max.

Dad returned to the table with four Cokes. He told us he'd ordered cheeseburgers all around. We drank our drinks. No one said much. I said something about the lack of windows. Big Jack told us serious drinkers preferred to drink in the dark.

The bartender brought the cheeseburgers along with a jumbo basket of fries and onion rings. We dug in and ate with enthusiasm.

Big Jack asked us when we'd be old enough to drink. We told him we had quite a few years yet. He said, "Well, when the time comes, drink with circumspection." But I got to tell you—the man had a faraway look in his eyes. He clearly had some heavy stuff on his mind I didn't know about, stuff pressing fast against his temples.

It all made me curious. So after I finished my burger I looked over at my old man and asked, "How come the bartender called you Ben?"

Maybe he'd been anticipating the question because right off he answered, "No idea, kid. He must've confused me with somebody else."

I didn't think so, but what could I do? Argue? Demand an explanation?

"Never explain and never complain," Big Jack used to tell me and Jake.

Just as we finished the last of the fries and rings the two guys playing pool quit and retired to the bar. Big Jack suggested we take over the table and play a few games. So that's what we did. Dad right away introduced some special rules. Basically, it was us against him. Three against one. We played Stripes and Solids, a.k.a. 8-Ball. First I shot, then Retro, then Bones, then Dad. So we got three shots to his one. It didn't matter. He won every game. Once it was his turn he knocked in all his balls then drilled the 8, no sweat or bother at all.

"My old man was a drunk," he told us while he stalked around the table shooting and chalking his cue. "When our mom would tell him to watch the kids he'd drag us down to MacAfee's Pub on Garfield Avenue in

Jersey City. While he drank Irish whiskey with beer chasers me and my brothers would shoot pool and throw darts. I got proficient at both, but believe you me, they're skills I'd just as soon not have."

That stuff, let me tell you, came right out of left field. Hit me blind. Knocked me for a loop. My old man was a complex guy.

We must've played ten or twelve games. Killin' time. I drank enough Coke to drown a whale. Dad switched from Coke to ice water. I don't think he drank even one beer. He looked plenty nervous, maybe even spooked. He checked his watch like every ten seconds and glanced into the barroom almost as often.

As night came on the bar gathered a pretty good crowd—twenty or thirty tough looking types, men in work clothes and work boots with frayed baseball caps advertising beer or bourbon or farm equipment. Not the crowd you'd see in the trendy riverside bars and restaurants back in Bridgeton. These guys looked rough but real and stayed pretty quiet. They drank their beers and watched baseball on the two overhead TVs.

Right in the middle of the tenth or twelfth game Big Jack leaned his cue stick against the wall and said, "You boys keep playing. Don't give up the table. I have to go talk to a man. Stay right here till I get back."

Big Jack left the back room and beelined for the bar. Me and Retro and Bones directly pressed ourselves into the doorway to watch his every move.

Big Jack stood at the bar with this gaunt-faced, narrow-eyed dude with close-cropped hair and black work boots. He sported several days of dark stubble on his chin and cheeks. I thought he looked like trouble. He and my old man talked things over for a couple minutes. Then the gaunt-faced dude threw back a shot of whiskey and headed for the exit. After waiting a minute or so Big Jack Tailor gave pursuit.

I didn't hesitate. I ordered Retro and Bones to hold the pool table, then I hustled double time over to the exit.

Too bad Big Jack was no idiot. He stood out on the front stoop, laying for me. He grabbed my arm and gave it a pretty fair squeeze. "You need to learn to listen, boy. I told you clear as day to stay put. And I meant what I said. Now get back inside or first thing in the morning I'll put you and your pals on a bus back to Jersey."

Irked, and in some pain, I pulled my arm free and retreated into the bar.

Me and the boys pushed the pool balls around the table while we speculated as to what might be going down outside the Port Byron Bar and Grill. Retro thought drugs, I thought not. I didn't want my old man caught up in that web.

Bones said he had to take a leak and so left to use the head. He couldn't've been gone a minute before he came racing back into the billiard room. "Josh, you gotta check this out! Quick!"

"What's the problem?"

"No problem. Just come with me."

I told Retro to stay put. Bones turned and bolted back into the barroom. I followed on his heels—straight into the men's room. It was dark and dingy in there. There was a urinal, a sink, and a stall with a regular toilet. On the back wall was a small window. The window'd been pushed open to let out the stale air.

Bones urged me over to the window. "Take a look," he ordered.

I crossed the tiled floor, stood on my tiptoes, and peered out the window. Night had fallen, but a couple of overhead lights illuminated the parking lot between the Port Byron Bar and Grill and the Mississippi River. On the far side of the parking lot I could see the van and the trailer. And then I saw what had Bones so lathered up. A big black GMC Sierra pickup was backed up against the trailer. Two men stood in the bed of the pickup.

I squinted into the darkness. Sure enough I saw Big Jack and the gaunt-faced dude. They had themselves in the shadows of that willow tree but not so deep I couldn't see them.

"What are they doing?" I asked Bones, as if he might know.

He stood beside me on a plastic crate. "Looks like they're moving boxes."

And then I saw Big Jack and his newfound buddy bend down and lift something off the bed of the pickup. Something long and, from the way they strained, heavy.

Bones was right—it was some kind of a box.

"Damn," I muttered. "It looks like a coffin."

"Yeah," agreed Bones, "I thought so too. That's why I came to get you."

They moved the coffin from the truck to the trailer. It must've been plenty heavy because both of them groaned and grunted as they shoved and lifted.

The bathroom door swung open. In staggered a drunk with ketchup all over his chin and denim work shirt. But even a drunken fool can spook two kids peering out a window watching coffins getting moved. Me and Bones hightailed it out of the head and back to the billiard room. Where we swiftly passed on the news to Retro.

"So what's the deal?" Retro wanted to know. "Is Big Jack in the drug biz or the dead body biz?"

"I don't know what's going on," I answered, "but the time's come to find out."

The question was: how? And the other question was: when? No way was Big Jack about to let me swing open the door of the trailer and take a look inside.

And then, while the three of us stood there all a-jitters concocting some fool plan to get to the bottom of it all, in waltzed Big Jack wiping sweat off his brow with a paper napkin. "Sorry, boys," he said, easy as can be, "I had to see a man about a horse."

"A horse? What horse?"

Big Jack laughed. "It's just an expression, kid. Means I had some business to take care of. Ready for another game?"

I told him I'd had enough games and enough pool and enough Coke and enough of the whole scene at the Port Byron Bar and Grill.

Big Jack said, "You know who you remind me of, Finnegan Tailor?"

And I said, "I got an idea."

And he said, "Your mother."

And I said, "Yeah?"

And he said, "Yeah."

And I said, "Well, better her than you. Loser." This last came out soft but came out nevertheless.

But Big Jack only laughed since Big Jack didn't give a toot what me or anybody else thought of him. He was his own kind of man. At least this was the way I saw him even if my image of him wasn't entirely accurate.

Still, our little squall might've turned into a full-blown storm had the bartender not suddenly filled the doorway. "Say, Ben," he told Big Jack, "you might want to think about pulling out."

"Why's that? I got another visitor on the way."

The bartender shrugged. "I got a friend in Springfield. He says ATF received a tip. Word is they're on route. Been on the road a couple hours."

Big Jack thought it over. "A couple hours, huh?"

The bartender nodded.

Big Jack asked, "You got an ETA?"

The Passage

I didn't know ATF but I knew ETA. Estimated time of arrival.

The bartender said, "Depending on traffic, I'd said less than an hour."

Big Jack checked his watch. "I only got half an hour till the next load."

"Best roll anyway," advised the bartender. "A partial load's better than no load and a set of cuffs."

Big Jack nodded. "You got that right." And then to us, "We're outta here lickety split, boys. On the hoof."

The bartender asked, "You know where you're going?"

"Oh yeah. First thing I ever learned: always have a way out."

And then we were out. Cool and under control but quick as cats we slipped out of the Port Byron Bar and Grill. Big Jack had the van revved up and ready to roll before we had snapped our seatbelts into place.

We drove north out of Port Byron. Not too fast. Right on the speed limit. In our Chrysler Town and Country family minivan.

Big Jack kept an eye on the rear-view mirror. No doubt about it: the man was on the run.

He had the road atlas under his seat. When I asked for it he said, "Later on that, kid. Right now I don't want the inside lights on."

We drove through Cordova and a couple other small river towns. I could see the Mississippi glistening off to the left. And then, maybe twenty minutes out of Port Byron, we turned west, climbed up onto a steel bridge, and crossed the Big Muddy. A sign on the far side read: WELCOME TO CLINTON, IOWA. POPULATION 27792.

Iowa was the one and only state we entered where Big Jack didn't make his noisy announcement. Maybe he figured he didn't have to. Or maybe he figured we all saw the sign. Or maybe he was preoccupied eluding the ATF. Whoever *they* were.

We drove west on US 30, then north on US 61, then west again on Iowa Route 64. We made a lot of turns. It got hard to follow. Which maybe, I don't know, was the point. Big Jack never asked me to consult the map. He knew the way.

A couple hours after we'd left Port Byron Big Jack announced, "We'll be driving all night, boys. Feel free to lay back and get some shuteye."

I right away figured this was why he'd been resting up back at the Hampton Inn. He knew he'd be making an all-night run.

It took time, but finally around eleven o'clock, Retro and Bones commenced some light snoring. Big Jack must've been waiting for them to crash. Not five minutes passed before he turned to me and said in a low voice, "The lumber, Finnegan. Tell me about the lumber. Tell me about the bridge."

The Bridge

Don't ask me what I was thinking. Obviously I should've known better.

Too bad the brain of a teenage male doesn't exactly run rampant with rational thinking. Just a few days had passed since I'd totaled Mom's convertible so I should've been on my best behavior. But we had plans and those plans had to go forward.

My alarm went off a few minutes after 5 a.m. I wanted to roll over and go back to sleep but I had to get up and get moving. We had a mission that night and we'd decided to rendezvous before school to go over the details one last time.

I crawled out of bed, pulled on some clothes, splashed water on my face, and headed for the kitchen. I ran into Pop standing at the sink eating a bowl of Frosted Flakes and drinking his morning V-8. Pop always eats breakfast standing. He's way too wired up in the a.m. to sit.

"Hey, Josh. What's got you up so early? Or are you," he added, a twinkle in his eye, "just getting home?"

My grandfather put up with me because of his great and deep belief if you give boys enough rope we'll eventually find our way in the world and maybe even amount to something. Plus, of course, I was his only grandson and therefore his only genetic link to the future. He may even have held onto some unspoken desire that I would one day take over the family oil delivery and burner repair biz.

"Coach Kinum called an early morning practice," I fibbed. "He wants us sharp for the big game tomorrow."

Pop nodded, tipped his bowl, and poured the rest of his Frosted

Flakes into his mouth. Pop loved sugar-coated cereal, ate it every morning with milk as thick as syrup. He called skim milk white water and health food a communist conspiracy. He chewed briefly, swallowed, then said, "Well, time to go to work. Can I drop you someplace?"

I shook my head. "One of the coaches is picking me up."

That suited Pop fine. Mornings he kept to a tight schedule. Arriving at the offices of Middleton Oil Supply over on Bridge Street much later than 5:30 a.m. could make him cranky all day. Pop had made his modest fortune delivering heating oil and fixing oil burners in an honest and timely fashion. No way would he jeopardize his bankroll or his reputation by slacking off.

For countless generations the Middletons had been up and at 'em early folks, Puritan types from the Old Country who believed hard work and minimal play made God happy and kept the Devil at bay. Pop was no different. And no, I'm not making fun of him. No way. I love the big fella. You'll never hear me say a rough word about Pop. Not only did he shelter and feed me and Mom, make our lives secure and comfortable after Big Jack hit the road, but he took it upon himself to father me and love me and teach me the ways of the world despite my robust broken-family anger and my generally rebellious nature. A lesser man would've told me to bugger off.

"Alright, Josh," he said heading for the back door, "you have yourself a good day, son. And remember to give trouble a wide berth."

His advice caused my brow to furrow. Did Pop know I had in mind to do some breaking and entering, some felonious pinching, some swiping? Was he two steps ahead of me on this? I decided no way, not a chance.

I relaxed and poured myself a bowl of Flakes. Like Pop I ate over the sink, then made for the exit. First thing I noticed when I hit the drive was the absence of Mom's Civic. Meaning she'd spent the night with Homer up at his swanky hilltop mansion on the edge of town. Which left me tickled pink and jumping for joy. I hated that mansion with its high fences and locked gates. Of course I hated Homer too.

Have I mentioned there was a time early in their relationship when Mom and I actually believed Homer would invite us to live in his mansion, make a family together, and live happily ever after? Well if I haven't we did which I guess just shows the depth of our stupidity. For soon Homer grew ornery, then nasty, then downright violent. The fairy tale scenario quickly gave way to bruised egos and black eyes.

But still Mom went to him. Her taste in men, despite having such a solid guy for a father, has always been suspect.

I intended to do something about the unpleasant situation with Homer Otis. I had plans to put the man down. Big plans. But not right away. First I had to find the guts.

Anyway, the boys and I rendezvoused at the old shack along the Delaware. The same shack where we'd smoked weed and drank Bud in the hours before I wrecked the VW.

I was the last to arrive. Already milling around inside were Retro, Bones, Young, Johnson, the new kid Laramie, Garcia, and Stinky Cogan. We said hey all around and got down to business.

Only there wasn't much business. By that time we'd been mulling the plan over for weeks. Retro blathered on for a few minutes about security at the bridge. Bones went over a few details about getting in and out. I suggested maybe I should stay home, stay clear of the whole mess, since I'd just been busted for the VW disaster. But I got laughed at and smacked around for that cowardly nonsense.

"So you see," I told Big Jack, "I had no choice. I had to participate."

He shook his head and rolled his eyes but held his opinion on the matter. Big Jack was not and never has been, by any stretch, a follower. And so surely he did not abide that trait in his son.

That night—after school, after baseball practice, after dinner, after studying for finals—I slipped out my 3rd floor window, went down the drainpipe, and dropped to the ground. I could've slept right there in the dirt under the rhododendrons so worn out did my brain and body feel. I'd been up since 5 a.m. Now my watch read 10:46 p.m. and I knew it'd be hours before I got back to bed. Still, I had to go. Had no choice at all.

I moved along the same route I'd taken that morning—over to Main, through the graveyard, and along the path to the old shack. I arrived on time—at precisely 11 p.m.

By five after the hour our small army of eight had gathered. Clouds blocked the stars. Darkness had a pretty good hold. We smudged our faces with some charcoal briquettes, then moved off to the south, single file, silent, and serious as old fools.

It took us twenty minutes at a hard charge to reach the bridge. That would be the pedestrian bridge connecting Jersey to Bull's Island out in the Delaware. On the far side of Bull Island's another pedestrian bridge reaches over to Pennsylvania.

The bridge to Bull's was under repair. The site was chock-a-block with stuff we needed—mostly lumber and nails. Construction crews had hauled in a couple hundred 2x10s and 2x4s for scaffolding and concrete forms. We'd decided to slip in under cover of darkness and nab us a few sticks so we could fancy up our shack.

About fifty yards above the bridge we halted. We smudged our faces again, then, quiet as cats, we closed the distance to the bridge. The darkness was pretty thick but we could see the span hovering over the

Delaware. We made our way up the gravel path to the bridge. A padlocked gate blocked us from walking right out onto the steel span. Me, Retro, and the new kid Laramie climbed over the gate no sweat.

We sprinted across the bridge to the island, maybe a hundred and fifty yards. We made sure all was quiet then I took off back across the bridge to tell the others. Bones pulled a flashlight and a slender file out of his camouflage pants pocket. He went to work on the padlock securing the chain around the gate. It took him less than a minute to pick the lock. It was just one of those odd things Bones knew how to do.

I pulled the chain free and swung open the gate. The boys waltzed out onto the bridge like they'd been invited to a dance. But we didn't dally. I replaced the chain, made it look like the lock had never been bothered, then we took off at a run across the bridge and out onto Bull's.

As soon as we reached the island Retro told us the two night watchmen were on the move. One had started west toward the PA bridge and the other was headed our way. We took cover behind some bushes at the edge of a picnic area. A couple minutes later we heard the watchman coming along the trail. Tough not to hear him. He had a wheezy smoker's cough and must've snapped in half every twig in his path. Plus he trailed a powerful flashlight beam and sent up a billow of cig smoke thick enough to choke a camel.

The guard walked right past us out onto the bridge. We sat tight, suppressing all urges to clear our throats, pass gas, or belch. The guard made his way slowly out to the middle of the bridge. There he stopped, pulled out another cig, and lit up. The flash of the match momentarily lit up his face. He was an old guy, probably retired.

For nearly half an hour the watchman stood out there and smoked. God, he loved to smoke. One after another. Used the dying butt to light up the next cig. Finally he grew weary of standing and came back toward us.

The Passage

He walked within just a few feet of me on his way back to the shanty. I could smell his tobacco breath.

We gave him a few minutes to settle down, then we went to work.

In a clearing just north of the bridge the construction crews had set up an area where they kept materials and stored their tools. Their tools were locked inside a pair of steel workboxes the size of small sheds. Between the sheds stood two large piles of lumber. One pile of 8-foot 2x4s stood as high as a house and as wide as a swimming pool. The new kid Laramie climbed up onto the pile and start passing down the lumber. I took the first load, balanced it on my shoulder, and headed for the mainland.

It took about five minutes to carry my load across the bridge and stash it in our hiding spot in the woods. On my way back I passed Young and Johnson and Stinky Cogan toting their loads. Cohorts in crime, we exchanged cool nods of approval.

On my second trip across the bridge I hauled out a pair of 2x10s. Those bears were heavy. And cumbersome. I had to rest halfway across the bridge, and then, again, once I reached Jersey. But I got the load into the woods. While I caught my breath I took a count of the haul. We already had a pretty fair stack. Of course we still had to carry the goods back up river to the shack, but we planned to do that in stages over the next few days. As long as everything went smoothly.

But then out of the blue things started to go not so smoothly.

When I got back to the island I found Retro all lathered up. He'd been keeping an eye on the watchmen. He said they were on the move again. Headed in our direction. But this time in an awful big hurry.

"How far off?" I asked.

"Maybe a minute," Retro answered.

"We gotta bolt. Across the bridge and north along the path."

No one dallied. We dropped our loads and took off for the bridge.

Halfway to the bridge the old-timer with the nasty smoker's cough spotted us. He yelled for us to halt. That only made us turn on the jets. We reached the bridge to Jersey. But almost immediately Retro, leading the way, ordered us to turn back. "Flashlight beams," he explained. "Across the bridge. Headed our way."

"Probably cops," said Stinky Cogan. "I'll bet someone spotted us, ratted us out."

"To the river, boys," rallied Retro.

We turned and raced north across the island.

Retro, who knew the island best, led us through the darkness. We ran along a narrow path overgrown with weeds and finally reached a clearing. At the edge of the clearing the river spread out before us. Behind us we could hear men shouting and whistles blowing, even a couple of dogs barking.

"We're going in the river, boys," announced Retro. "It's our only way out."

With law enforcement hot on our heels no one dithered. We waded in and moved off to the northeast, silent as fish.

We waded till the water rose over our heads. Then we started to swim. It took us half an hour to navigate our way across the Delaware through the cool, black night. We stayed together, our tight little school of escapees.

Finally the water grew shallow again. We could put our feet down on the muddy bottom. One by one we waded ashore, wet and ragged as rats.

For a minute or so we caught our breath and patted one another on the back. But then, plenty of work left to do, we started north at a good clip along the dirt path.

Fearing a run-in with officers of the Bridgeton P.D., who knew about our riverside clubhouse, we skirted the shack and made a beeline for town. It seemed plenty stupid to get caught at the shack wet and bedraggled immediately after the attempted heist.

Big Jack agreed with me on this point.

At 1:55 a.m. we straggled into the graveyard of the Episcopal Church. We closed ranks. In soft voices we talked it over. It was pretty simple. The plan was to deny. Deny. Deny. Deny.

"If even one of us squeals," Retro reminded us, "all our asses are grass."

"Yeah," I added, the guy with the most to lose, "so stay cool and keep your traps shut no matter what happens."

We agreed to rendezvous the next day and discuss our options. Then one by one we slunk off into the night. I was whipped, tired enough to die. But I knew I wouldn't be able to sleep. Not only was I worried about the cops knocking on my door, busting me and dragging my butt off to jail, but the night before a big game I never sleep well. And the next day's playoff game was easily the biggest game of my life. For me it was the Super Bowl and World Series all rolled into one.

The Passage

The Tip

"So that's the way it happened," I confessed. "That's the way it went down."

Big Jack glanced over at me. His face was illuminated by the dashboard lights. He took his time, didn't say anything for most of a minute. I tried not to fidget.

"Excellent story, Finnegan," he said, head nodding. "Nicely told. And, I assume, mostly true. But I have one question."

"What's that?"

"What the hell were you thinking?"

Now I could've asked my daddy what he'd been thinking back at the Port Byron Bar and Grill cavorting with low-lifes and dealing in dead bodies. But no, I chose not to take that route. I chose the high ground.

I said, "It was a judgment call. I made the wrong one. But," I added, "you have to understand. We haven't actually been caught. Not red-handed. We're just what you'd call suspects. They got no hard and fast proof it was us."

"Well," proclaimed Big Jack, "I guess that makes it all right then."

"I didn't say that. I'm just saying we're not busted."

"But you did do it?"

I hesitated, but not for long. After a quick nod I said, "Just the way I told you. Of course, I told you assuming my telling was just between you and me."

"Don't you worry, Finnegan. My lips are a lock box."

I knew sarcasm when I heard it, but I also knew Big Jack had to be careful. He hadn't exactly set himself up as the perfect male role model. Just about any attitude he offered I could throw right back in his face.

"One tip," he said.

"Yeah?"

"Be your own man, kid. Make your own decisions. Find your own trouble. Don't let the pressure of the pack make you stupid."

It was well after midnight. I was plenty tired and sick of talking. What the old boy said made sense. Not that I was in any mood to label him a sage.

I said, "Whatever," and then I closed my eyes and before long drifted off into an edgy sleep.

That night Big Jack hauled us clear across Iowa while me and Retro and Bones snored away. I can't tell you the exact route he took, but I know we stayed clear of any interstates. ATF on our trail, you know.

At dawn he gave us a wake up call. "Missouri River, boys!"

We sprang awake and looked out the windows. The van pulled up onto a steel bridge spanning the Missouri. The river spread out below. But not for long. Not much more than a long fly ball from bank to bank between Iowa and Nebraska. Not even as wide as the Delaware at Bridgeton. Shallow too. In the early morning light I could see ripples of white water and rocks and boulders poking through the surface.

But I didn't have much time to think about the river. The second we swung down off that bridge Big Jack started shouting, "Nebraska! The great state of Nebraska! The Cornhusker State! Straight ahead and for as far as you can see! Nebraska!"

We rubbed the tired out of our eyes and took a look around while Big Jack got his motor running.

"Under different circumstances," he began, "I'd pull off and take a gander at the Missouri. I'd show you boys where the Lewis and Clark expedition camped for a couple days along the banks of the river on their way west in the wet spring of 1804. And where they camped again on the return trip in the late summer of aught-six. But time's on the fly and the wind's rushing and we got expeditions of our own."

Another hour down the highway we pulled into the parking lot of The Homestead Diner, a glass and chrome relic left over from the fifties. Dad opened his wallet, handed me a twenty. "You boys go inside, get yourselves some chow. I had a long night. Think I'll catch a few winks. Grab me a large black joe on your way out."

So the boys and I went into the Homestead and sat in a vinyl booth with our own personal jukebox featuring Hank Williams and Merle Haggard and Tammy Wynette and where we could see Big Jack napping in the van. We pretty much had the Homestead all to ourselves at that early hour. The waitress, middle age and stick-thin with long blood red fingernails and heavy bags under her eyes, slid over to take our orders. She smiled and said, "Morning, you fellows. What's yours?"

"Huh?" we asked.

She smiled again. Her teeth were kind of yellow. "What'll you have to eat?"

Blueberry flapjacks, sausage, and OJ.

She didn't write it down. On the nameplate pinned to her white uniform it said: Willa. She saw me staring and said, "That's Willa for Willa Cather. Ever heard of her?"

I shook my head no.

Bones said, "Sure I heard of her. She wrote books."

"That's right, young man," said Willa. "Stories about Nebraska. Stories about strong, clear-thinking, independent women. My mama loved Willa Cather. So when I came along she named me Willa. I've been happy with the name my whole life."

Being from Jersey we didn't really know why Willa the waitress was telling us her life story but we listened anyway.

"So," asked Willa, "where you boys from and where you headed?"

I told her back east and out west.

She said, "Can't beat that," then turned and steered for the kitchen.

We watched her go. I said to Bones, "I can't believe you heard of Willa Cather."

He shrugged. Retro leaned across the booth and in a hushed voice said, "Forget about that crud. How we gonna get a look in the trailer?"

We all glanced out the window at the trailer hanging off the back of the van. The question posed by Retro had been much on our minds.

I told them I had an idea but that it was still just an idea, meaning nothing solid, but it had to do with somehow luring Big Jack away from the van so one of us could bust off the lock, climb inside, and get a look at those boxes that looked like coffins.

Willa brought breakfast. "So you're headed out west, huh? Where to?"

"Don't exactly know," I told her. "My dad's in charge." I pointed out the window.

"Well," said Willa, after she took a look, "if I was you I'd head for the Black Hills of Dakota. Up amongst those hills sits Mount Rushmore. You know, where they carved the faces of the Presidents into the rock. You need to see that. It's a sight to behold."

We nodded and stuffed more flapjacks into our mouths.

Between bites I said, "My granddad told me the same thing. He said, 'Josh, make sure you visit Mount Rushmore.' He said he'd seen it as a kid and never forgot it."

Willa, who had a sweet smile and teeth that didn't look so yellow anymore and bags under her eyes that had all but disappeared, said, "Your grandfather's a wise man, Josh. And I can see he knows something about America. We're in a deep pool of hot water these days, hot and growing hotter, problems from sea to sea. But this is a good and just country. Maybe not perfect but mighty fine. Go see Rushmore. Stand beneath those Presidents. They'll make you feel like everything will be all right."

We might've been wise guys, tough guys, cool guys, but Willa held us in the palm of her hand. I thought she might've been, I don't know, a spirit or something. She stayed with us till we finished eating, then she smiled and cleared our plates.

I ordered a large black coffee for Jack, paid the bill of $14.23, and left the rest of that twenty as a tip. I'd never left tips much, but I knew that was a sizeable one.

Willa scooped up the money and dropped it in the wide pocket of her apron. She thanked me, then said, "I know one other place you need to visit."

"Where's that?" I asked.

"East of the Black Hills. A place called the Badlands. And let me give you a little tip. Go to the Badlands at dusk, watch the sunset, and be changed forever. That's what Crazy Horse said, and that's what Willa says too."

"Crazy Horse the Indian?"

"That's right, Josh. Crazy Horse the Indian. The Badlands. At dusk. Don't miss it."

Retro and Bones were already over by the door. I said, "We'll try to get there."

Willa winked and smiled and told me to be strong and to always love and protect my mama no matter what.

I felt confused but assured Willa I'd do my best.

We headed back to the van. Big Jack was sound asleep in the

driver's seat.

Retro said, "Let's bust into the trailer now while he's snoozing."

"Yeah," urged Bones, "I'm awful curious about those boxes."

"No way," I told them. "He'll hear us and we'll never get a good look."

We argued but not long. Big Jack woke up and that was that. He stepped out of the van, stretched, and stood there sipping his coffee in the warm dawn. I looked in the window of the Homestead. Willa sat in our booth smoking a cig and reading a book.

After a while we took off. Willa looked up, smiled, and waved. I waved back. The time had come to get across Nebraska.

The Cornhusker State was more flat. And at least for a while more pristine farms with row upon row of corn and soybeans and sorghum. We knew it was sorghum after Bones asked a guy at the Texaco during a fill-up. He told Bones farmers fed sorghum to hogs and cows to fatten them up. In the long, flat, dull hours ahead we'd see our share of hogs and cows.

We passed through Laurel, Osmond, and Plainview—crossroads towns guarded by towering silos and shiny grain elevators. As the morning wore on we floated west on US 20. No interstate highways for this crew.

The temperature started to rise—75, 80, 85 and still pushing.

Big Jack told me to get out the atlas and locate a little town called Rawlins out in central Wyoming.

"Why?" I right away asked, eyes narrowed. "You don't know where it is?"

He read my thoughts straight off and tossed me a little laugh. "I got a rough idea."

There weren't many roads out in that wide-open country, especially paved roads. We saw mostly pickups and farm tractors as big as houses. We turned west onto State Route 95, then south on Route 11. Driving fast and driving hard. Big Jack didn't ask for directions. He knew where he wanted to go.

Somehow the land grew even flatter. And a whole lot drier. The pristine farms gave way to fenced-in ranches. Crops bowed to herds of grazing animals—horses and cattle. They stood around in vast pastures of scorched grass.

"Meat country," Big Jack announced. "Cows and pigs. More pigs than people."

And to prove it, just a few miles later, we came up close and way too personal with a super-sized pig farm. The smell flew up my nostrils, hit my brain, and just about knocked me cold. In the back of the van Retro and Bones began to retch.

"Oh yeah!" proclaimed Big Jack. "Ten thousand swine living on top of each other eating and making waste. How'd you like to live next to that little piece of paradise?"

The pig farm was a massive complex of low-slung bunkers carrying on for half a mile or more. Pigs covered the ground like outdoor carpet. Never in my life had I smelled anything so wretched as those pigs. It stank way beyond disgusting. The stink got up in my brain and started destroying brain cells. I couldn't believe I'd consumed sausage back at the Homestead Diner that very morning. I vowed never to eat pig again. Retro and Bones, writhing around on the floor in the back of the van, made the same vow.

Big Jack just laughed and laughed.

West of Halsey and Seneca the landscape turned brown and barren. Not much grew but scrub and maybe some sparse grass where they pumped in the irrigation. The only thing growing was the wind. It'd been growing and blowing all day, but out there on the high, dry plain it began to howl and whistle through the van. By noon the temp had soared to 95. Hot, dry, and howling—as different from Jersey as night and day.

Of course we had the Blues. The Blues filled the van each and every mile. Big Jack loved the Blues. He loved the rhythm of the Blues, the way the Blues kept his feet tapping and his fingers drumming. He also loved the lyrics—the lowdown humor about the miseries of life and love and loss and lust.

My life has been in misery
But now I hear you're leavin' me
No matter how bad things get
Life will be better when you're not in it.
Just lost my job and now you're gone
Ain't got no money to carry on
But no matter how bad things get
Life will be better when you're not in it.

I wondered if Dad thought about Mom when he heard that tune.

We drove on. Not much changed. It grew hotter and windier. In Whitman we got gas. We stepped out of the van and the wind—intensely hot and dry and flying out of the south—nearly blew us over. The air whistled with sand and grit that got in our eyes and drove us back into the van after a quick dash for sodas and chips and to use the can.

We turned south on State Route 61. That took us down to Ogallala along the South Branch of the Platte River. The Platte meandered between low, shallow banks. It looked to cut a path of least resistance through that dry and sandy land.

I guess Big Jack figured he'd eluded ATF along the blue highways of Nebraska because south of Ogallala we crossed the Platte and got back on I-80 heading due west.

An hour out of Ogallala the land began to rise, subtle, just an easy grade. On the other side of Sydney we finally hit some low hills, "Sand Hills of Nebraska," Big Jack told us, "where they grow the wheat that feeds the nation." We saw evidence of those wheat fields—golden grass spreading all the way to the horizon in a long lazy undulating rhythm that nearly made music up in my head.

And then Big Jack nodded off. Who could blame him? He'd been driving non-stop save for that catnap back at the Homestead since we'd pulled out of Port Byron sixteen or eighteen hours earlier. The man had endurance. But even Big Jack had his limits. So when the van started to lose speed and wander off the road I slugged him on the arm and gave a shout loud enough to wake the dead. "Yooooo!"

He came around quick, thanked me for saving the rig, then first chance he got he pulled over. The old boy looked plenty tired. He yawned, rubbed his eyes, checked his watch, did some calculating, then turned to me. "What do you think, kid?"

"About what?"

"Wanna drive?"

"Me? Drive?"

"That's right."

"I don't know. I—"

"Listen, we need to reach Rawlins and it's still a ways off. I need some shuteye bad but would prefer to keep moving. That leaves you."

Retro and Bones pressed forward from the back seat.

"Why the big push for Rawlins?" I asked.

Big Jack smiled at me. "You sure got a lotta Middleton in you, kid."

"I'm not really a kid anymore, Jack."

"The hell you're not," he snapped quick as a twig under foot. "Let me give you a little tip, boy. Why we're pushing for Rawlins is my business, not yours. You should just enjoy the ride, and the mystery, if you think there is one. You were expecting a nice little family vacation out west—sorry to disappoint. Now you wanna drive? If not I'll ask one of these boneheads in the back," and he pointed to Retro and Bones.

"I'm not legal to drive," I told him.

"That didn't stop you taking a little cruise in the convertible."

I couldn't deny that.

"So here's a chance," he said, "to redeem yourself. Get in a little flight time."

I thought it over. "You really want me to drive? Even after what I did the VW?"

"You were drinking and probably smoking reefer that night. That was stupid and you'll kindly not do it again. Today you'll drive with circumspection."

"With what?"

"Jesus, boy! You'll be careful. Right?"

I could feel myself nervous, but excited. "Right. Yeah. I'll drive careful."

"Alrightee then," said Big Jack, calm and pleasant as can be. "We got some big, wide, friendly highway ahead. Why don't you just slide on over here into the driver's seat and demonstrate your driving skills for us."

So with that challenge hanging in the air I made the move. Retro climbed into the shotgun position. Bones stayed put. Big Jack rolled into the back where he promptly fell asleep. But not before he ordered me to wear my shades and a baseball cap.

Heart pounding away like a jackhammer, I settled in behind the wheel, adjusted the seat, and prepared to pull out into traffic. There wasn't much. Just about none at all, if you want the truth, which I'm sure was why Big Jack let it happen.

Maybe it was his crazy way of trying to make me responsible.

Or maybe he was just out of his mind.

I waited till the road was as deserted as the moon. Then I got moving. I'd only ever driven the Beetle and Mom's Civic. The van was a whole lot bigger. Especially with the trailer, which felt like a big old barn, hanging off the back. Plus the rear-view mirror was useless. I had to use the side views. A dicey endeavor for the novice driver. But with Retro and Bones acting like extra sets of eyes, I got us up to speed.

We climbed into the Sand Hills, me behind the wheel, less nervous with every mile but still watching my speed and studying my mirrors. We'd been on the flats since Illinois, so the change of scenery, and Dad racking, did us good. We yucked it up some, did more talking than we'd done in days.

We passed into Wyoming, the Cowboy State. No river marked the passage. Just more rolling hills and a large billboard with a picture of a cowboy waving his cowboy hat in the air while hanging on for dear life to a bucking bronco.

And then up onto a high windblown plain where off in the distance we could see tall ragged mountains.

In close, not far off the shoulder of the interstate, we saw our first oilrigs. Not big fields of them, just a single rig here and there in the middle of a field or next to an old barn. The rigs pumped away, their wide steel arms slowly pulling the black gold out of the ground.

A sign read: Cheyenne 32 miles. Retro got out the map, did a little navigating. He figured Cheyenne to be a small city, nothing like Philly or New York, but still there'd be plenty more traffic than we'd seen since I took the helm.

"Maybe," he suggested, "we should wake up Big Jack when we get closer."

"It could get hairy," reckoned Bones.

I had mixed feelings. One side of my brain was plenty nervous about driving in a lot of traffic. But the other side wanted my father to know I could handle the situation. So despite my buds pushing me to pull over, I drove straight through Cheyenne. A driving experience, let me tell you, that would serve us well after Big Jack went the way of the wolves up in the Blackfeet Indian Reservation of northern Montana.

West of Cheyenne the hills turned into mountains. We climbed and climbed. The van had to downshift to handle the grade. The big trucks slowed to a crawl. Even most of the cars felt the strain. Not that we saw many vehicles. Five miles west of Cheyenne and the road ran mostly empty. We'd finally hit the wide-open country of the American West.

We reached Snowy Mountain summit at 8200 feet, higher than me or Retro or Bones had ever been. I pulled off. A sign said the Oregon Trail had passed this way in the 1840s. The first transcontinental railroad had come over the pass in 1867. Highway 30 had pushed over the summit in the 1930s. Interstate 80 in the mid 60s.

It all meant me and Retro and Bones were just the latest travelers in a long line of westbound adventurers to stand atop that peak and take in the incredible view.

I can tell you: America looked awful big from that lonesome summit—vast and still plenty wild.

On the way down the other side, the road snaking through dry hills, we came upon a strange and unusual sight—a row of windmills. And I don't mean a windmill like you might see on a small farm. I'm talking huge. Like eighty, a hundred feet high. Big white three-bladed windmills against a royal blue western sky. And not just a couple of windmills either but dozens of them stretching out along a high open ridge for as far as we could see. A hundred monster windmills. Maybe a thousand. Or more.

I pulled over. We climbed out to take a look. Bones took some photos.

Big Jack woke up and demanded to know why we'd stopped.

Windmill country, we told him. He climbed out of the van. "Government project," he told us. "Experiment in producing passive electricity. Not a bad idea with oil so damn expensive. But really just a band-aid on a gaping wound that'll only get bloodier as you boys grow into men. Energy wars on the horizon, boys."

Then he slapped me on the back, thanked me for taking the wheel, and moved back into the driver's seat.

We descended onto some high plains, refueled, then shoved off for the final push to Rawlins. In Sinclair we passed an oil refinery. It sprawled for a mile or more along the interstate. Tall smokestacks spewed black smoke and soot into the evening air. The whole ugly industrial complex set against a backdrop of open range and wild mountains looked plenty surreal.

Big Jack boomed, "Windmills on the mountain, boys, oil refineries in the valley! All part of the schizophrenia of the New West, of Modern Amurica. Damn society doesn't know if it's coming or going, if it's climbing or descending."

Oh yeah, Big Jack was in a mood.

"All part of why you got to make you own hay, boys! Go your own way! Figure out for yourselves if there's a difference between right and wrong! Between good and evil! Between the man in the mirror and the man you set to walking down the street!"

Rawlins, with its interstate stretch of neon motels and fast food joints, came on next in the slow gathering dusk. Brown and dusty and a million miles from appealing, the cow town nevertheless treated us right.

Rawlins gave us—me and Retro and Bones—an opportunity to take a tour of Big Jack's top-secret trailer.

The Family

As you might imagine, no one, other than maybe the bride and groom, thought a marital union between twenty-one year-old Lisa Middleton and thirty-two-year-old Jack Tailor was a good idea. Most thought it was a bad, even a dangerous idea. In their favor the newlyweds had love and lust, passion and desire. But on the down side they had no end of conflict and quarreling along with raging jealousy. Plus Jack's wandering eye and who knows maybe Lisa's too. And finally they had Jack's fiery Irish temper waiting in the wings. All in all a recipe for marital disaster.

But despite all that, their lives, I should say our lives, settled into a pretty smooth running groove.

Just a year and a week and a day after my birth, my little brother Jake rolled out of Mom's belly. Me and Jake—Irish twins, sprouts from like seeds.

With two boys to feed and wash and watch over, Jack and Lisa surprised one and all, maybe even themselves, and got their act together. I guess a pair of fledglings will do that to you. Make you humble. Give you a fresh perspective on life. From all accounts Mom and Dad lavished me and Jake with love and affection.

An added bonus came when a new Honda dealer opened in Clinton a dozen or so miles north and east of where we lived in Milford. The general manager was an old friend of Dad's from their glory days hawking Porsches. He hired Jack, made him sales manager. Those were the days when Hondas Sold Themselves so the money piled up at the door like snow during a blizzard.

All that dough paved the way for easier and more carefree relations between Lisa and Jack. We even moved into a bigger house over in Upper Black Eddy, PA. And we didn't rent. With Pop's help, Jack and Lisa took out a loan and became mortgage-toting middle class homeowners. It was a two-bedroom bungalow right on the river. So close you could make a wish and toss a quarter into the Delaware from the back deck. We lived in that house from when I was three till I was almost eight. It's where everything started out so perfect, you know, but wound up so bad.

Dad made enough money so Mom didn't work. We had a brand new Honda Civic, red, with special kid seats in the back for me and Jake. Mom used to strap us into those seats and off we'd go a-cruising.

The four of us would have breakfast together, then Dad would give us all great big bear hugs before climbing into his Prelude and heading over to Jersey for a day of wheeling and dealing and selling. "It's what America's all about, boys," he'd tell us over a bowl of Cheerios, "wheeling and dealing and selling."

After Dad went to work Mom would get us dressed in matching outfits and across the river to Grandma's house we'd go. From Gram's we'd fan out in various directions to visit friends and family, to shop and eat and stroll along the river on sunny days.

Late in the afternoon we'd stop at the market in Riegelsville or Frenchtown, then head home to make dinner. Mom would feed and bathe me and Jake and put us to bed with snuggles and a story before Dad got home from a long day of wheeling and dealing and selling. Guys who sell cars for a living work long hours, so plenty of days we saw Dad at breakfast, then didn't see him again till breakfast the next day. But we heard him. He'd come home and commence talking to Mom and being a big-time talker he'd talk for a couple hours about everything that had happened up at the shop that day. He'd tell her about the folks he'd met and the cars he'd sold and the deals he'd made. I can tell you it was comforting to lie in bed beside my brother and listen to our father talk to our mother in a revved up and excited voice. Mom never said much, mostly she just listened and served Dad his dinner, poured him a beer, and dished him up a slice of Boston cream pie. Boston cream was his favorite and so in those days it was my favorite too.

Sundays and Wednesdays Dad had off so the daily routine changed some. On Sundays and Wednesdays instead of riding around with Mom, me and Jake rode around in the Prelude with Dad. Instead of going to see Gram in Bridgeton we'd go over to Bull's Island where Dad would do some fishing and beer drinking with his buddies. Sometimes we'd float down the river in a canoe.

One time the canoe tipped over in some rapids and even though me and Jake had on our orange life preservers Dad had to save us from getting dragged clear down to Philadelphia, out into Delaware Bay, and finally into the vast and lonely Atlantic. All the rest of that day and right up till we pulled into the driveway Dad kept telling me and Jake not to tell Mom about us tipping the canoe and falling into the river. "It'll be our little secret," he told us in a low and conspiratorial voice, "now and forever. No one else has to know. Especially your mother."

That was how I first learned about secrets and how they can pull you close to some folks while simultaneously dragging you away from others.

And so there you go—the good news. But of course the good news couldn't last. Not with Jack Tailor and Lisa Anne Middleton Tailor in the starring roles. The sweet and easy bubble in which we all floated had to burst.

One afternoon Mom decided we'd drive up to the Honda dealer and surprise Dad with a bag lunch. We'd done it before and Dad had enjoyed the surprise, so why not do it again? Only this time when we arrived Dad wasn't around. After some hemming and hawing one of the salesmen told us he'd gone on a test drive. That didn't seem like a big deal so Mom decided we'd wait. Fifteen minutes later Dad still hadn't returned. And no sign of him fifteen minutes after that either.

In those days I knew nada about the famous test-drive Jack and Lisa had been on back during his days at the BMW/Porsche dealer. But for sure Mom knew, so it's not tough to imagine her imagination firing on all cylinders while she sat in Dad's office watching me and Jake rummage through Dad's desk drawers. Every so often the sales crew at Clinton Honda would peer in at us, which no doubt added to Mom's anxiety.

After maybe forty-five minutes one of the salesmen stuck his head in the door and said, "Sorry about the wait, Mrs. Tailor. Did Jack… did your husband expect you?"

"No," answered Mom in a voice I immediately recognized as hostile.

"He left a while ago on that test drive," said the salesman, eyes darting, hands fiddling with his bad tie, "but I think he had to stop at our other shop to do a swap."

"Please," Mom offered in response, "don't patronize me."

I had no notion about this patronize business, but I could tell from Mom's tone that it wasn't anything good.

And then, not ten seconds after that salesman beat his retreat, Jake, four years old at the time, most of his little body buried in Dad's bottom drawer, emerged with some foreign object in tow. He held it high for Mom to see.

"What's this, Mommy?"

Me and Mom turned and had a look at Jake's treasure.

Now no way did I have a clue what was in the slim plastic pouch

Jake held aloft, but definitely Mom did. A condom, lubed with a ribbed tip. Not that I learned these facts till years later.

Mom's face turned crimson. She ripped the rubber out of Jake's hand. Me and Jake right away thought she was going to yell at him for some infraction. But instead, her breathing strained, her eyes furious, she brought herself under control. "That's nothing, Jacob. It's something to… to wipe your hands. You know, when they're sticky."

"Oh!" shouted Jake. "Like the Wet Wipes you keep in the car for when me and Josh get sticky stuff on our faces and on the seats."

Mom shoved that plastic pouch into her purse. And then, as if on cue, an Accord pulled into the parking lot and out from behind the wheel stepped Big Jack Tailor looking suave in his dark suit and polished shoes. A finger snap later a perky brunette with legs up to her neck emerged from the passenger seat.

I think I had the same thought as Mom: On a test drive doesn't the customer do the driving? Or maybe this was a question Mom put in my head during the long tough battles that lay ahead.

Let the Marital Troubles begin.

And begin they did.

The Marital Troubles began right there at the Honda dealer when Mom marched us across the showroom and through the double glass doors and out across the parking lot. Only me and Jake didn't know we were supposed to snarl at Dad the way Mom did. I think had she been just a hair less of a lady she might've spat on him.

Needless to say, I didn't get to lie in bed that night and listen to Dad tell Mom about his day wheeling and dealing and selling. Oh no, other, louder issues dominated the table-talk that night. I might've been a kid, but kids ain't dumb.

I remember lines like: "For crying out loud, Lisa, women walk in and out of that showroom every single day. It doesn't mean I'm having sex with them."

And: "Don't think you can pull the wool over my eyes, Jack Tailor. I've been on a test drive with you. Remember?"

And: "I really think you're being totally irrational, Lisa."

And the line that baffled me most: "What about the condom, Jack? You don't wear one when we make love."

Oh yeah, the claims and counter claims went on for hours and hours, deep into the night. Accusations and explanations.

Finally I slumbered. But when I woke I heard the same refrains. The fighting and yelling went on all day. Went on all week. All month. The entire house felt as frozen as an ice cube. Me and Jake tiptoed around fearful any wrong move might escalate an already ugly situation. We didn't even know what Mom and Dad were so testy about. We just knew the world as we knew it had changed. I remember one night in bed Jake asked me when it was gonna change back to the way it had been. I told him I didn't know but that hopefully it'd be sooner than later. Definitely we were both plenty scared.

The truth: it never changed back to the way it had been. Those two people, our parents, couldn't figure out how to solve their differences. And so they just kept battling, hoping, I guess, to achieve victory, to win. Dad moved out of the house, then he moved back into the house, then Mom told him to get out, then she begged him to come back, then she ordered him out again, but he wouldn't go, and then he did go, and then he came back, and all the while they fought and hollered, and once in a while you could hear them in the bedroom moaning and groaning, but by morning they'd be at each other's throats again, and Dad, bag in hand, would slam the screen door and peel out the driveway leaving behind nothing but the smell of burning rubber.

Oh yeah, the Tailor clan had quite a time for itself.

And then tragedy struck. I say tragedy since that's what it was—a mind-boggling, life-altering tragedy.

It was summer, hot and steamy. Dad had moved in and out of our little house half a dozen times over the past year or so. On what I call Black Sunday he was living in a crummy apartment in Flemington and seeing me and Jake maybe once a week, usually Sunday. On Black Sunday he came and picked us up. We went for a ride and then got hot dogs at the Can Do Hot Dog Stand in Riegelsville. After the hot dogs with mustard we hit the river to cool off. I pulled off my sneakers and tee shirt and dove right in. Jake took a little more time. He didn't swim so good yet and he still had a healthy fear of the water. Mostly Dad held him up while he paddled his arms and kicked his feet.

Afterwards we sat on the bank and let the sun dry us. I asked Dad when he was coming home, and not just for a week or two but, you know, for good.

He said, "Your mother and I have some things to work out."

I said, "So why don't you work them out? Jake and me want you home."

"Yeah," added Jake, sitting between Dad's legs, "I don't sleep good when you're not in the house."

Dad gave Jake a big bear hug and told us he was doing the best he could. Which didn't make much sense to us, but what were we supposed to say? Do better?

We walked back to the Prelude, spread our towels across the seats to protect them from our wet bathing suits, and steered for home. Dad popped in a cassette. I think it was probably The Beach Boys. Little Deuce Coupe, Shut Down, Barbara Ann. Catch A Wave. 409.

Before he discovered the Blues Big Jack loved the Beach Boys. He especially loved the tunes that had to do with cars and driving and cruising for chicks.

So, okay, hindsight says Dad should've given us hugs, dropped us off, driven away, and saved the day. But instead he followed us into the house. He followed us into the house because he wanted to see Mom because no matter what he said he still loved Mom same as she still loved him even though she could never admit it. But right away, I mean even before you could take a breath, the two of them started arguing. Fighting to beat the bandit. Fighting like a couple prizefighters.

Jake stuffed his fingers in his ears and asked them to please be quiet. And right then is when a pretty big thing happened, one of those things that change your life and the whole rotten world. Mom would later try to blame Dad. And Dad would do his best to blame Mom.

My brain doesn't make much sense of those couple minutes. And anyway I can't see how who said what when matters. I mean, in the end, when you're trying to make your peace with the whole terrible mess, neither Mom nor Dad said or did anything on purpose. It was all an accident—a big ugly tragic accident.

So after Jake asked them to please stop arguing, one of them, either Mom or Dad, told us to go out in the back yard and play for a few minutes. We weren't sure we'd heard right because never in the history of the Tailor family had me and Jake been allowed to venture out into the back yard on our own. Always we'd explored the back yard with one or both of our parents on hand.

There were three reasons for this. Reason one: poison ivy. The scratchy stuff grew everywhere, even right up out of the grass. And experience had shown that both me and Jake were pretty allergic to the noxious weed.

Reason two: the swing set. We had this really awesome swing set

Pop had built for us. But we could only use it under parental supervision. Mom and Dad didn't want us falling off and cracking our heads open.

Reason three, and by far the biggest reason of all: The River. Mom and Dad didn't want us anywhere near that river. It was absolutely verboten.

So there we were, me and Jake, the Tailor boys, out in the back yard and on our own. All by ourselves. No one to tell us what to do. We looked around. The place looked a whole lot bigger and scarier than usual.

"What do you want to do?" I asked Jake.

Jake shrugged. "Maybe we should just sit here on the steps till Dad comes." He was by nature a cautious kid.

"No way am I just sitting here," I said. "Let's at least swing on the swings."

"We're not allowed to swing on the swings, Josh. Not without Mom or Dad there to watch. They'll get mad."

"So what?" I reasoned. "They're always mad anyway."

"Yeah," countered Jake, "but they're not mad at us. They're mad at each other."

I couldn't argue with that, so I said, "Well I'm going. You can sit here and act like a chicken if you want."

I stepped off the back stairs and headed across the yard. A couple seconds later Jake followed. He had to follow. He was, after all, the little brother. No way could he just stay behind.

So we swung on the swings. No big deal. Back and forth. Just like usual. Maybe not even as high as usual because probably we were a little bit afraid and also because there was no one to impress.

But through the open windows we could hear Mom screaming at Dad and Dad shouting at Mom. They sounded ready to tear each other's heads off.

Jake, swinging away, said, "You know how you can flip lights on and off?"

"Sure," I told him, "I know."

"I wish I could turn my ears on and off like that. Hear only what I wanna hear."

I swung a little higher. "I know what you mean. I'm sick of listening to them. Let's go down to the river, take off our sneaks, cool our feet."

Jake looked doubtful. "I don't think we should go near the river, Josh. We're not supposed to go anywhere near the river."

I hopped off the swing. "Fine. You stay but I'm going." And off I marched.

It took Jake some time but he finally followed. I knew he would. He came across the yard slow and wary but he kept coming nevertheless.

I already had my sneakers off. Already stood in ankle-deep water. Already knew what I'd say when Mom stepped onto the back porch and ordered me out of the river. I'd shout at her what she loved to shout at Dad. "Go to hell!" I'd shout, loud enough for the whole world to hear.

Jake took his stand about ten yards back from the water's edge. "You shouldn't be in there, Josh. You know we're not allowed in the river."

"That's the old rule," I said. "Here's the new rule: when those two start screaming at each other, you and me, we do as we please." And to show my little brother how the new rule worked I waded into the river till the water rose up to my waist.

Jake got used to me out there, then he took a few cautious steps forward. He sat in the grass and slowly untied his sneakers.

I told him I was gonna swim to Jersey, clear across to Bridgeton.

"No you're not," he said.

"Yes I am."

"No you're not." And he pulled those sneakers off.

"I could," I told him, "if I wanted to."

"Maybe," Jake said, "I'll just get my feet wet. It's pretty hot."

"Yeah," I said like a man, "damn hot."

"I won't go in or anything," Jake insisted. "Just my feet."

I was the big brother and all, yeah, that's true. And I knew Jake couldn't swim so good, couldn't really swim at all. But hey, we were in the midst of an adventure, cooling off in the shallows on that steamy hot summer day. And of course we were just a couple kids. No more sense than a pair of golden retrievers.

So what did I do? I waded into the river till the water got deep enough for me to float.

Jake stood and stepped into the shallows but not too far. The water barely covered his ankles.

I dove under and picked up some smooth stones off the bottom of the river. I stayed under till my lungs felt like they would burst. When I surfaced, Jake had boldly advanced forward. The water reached almost to his knees.

"How is it?" I asked.

"Good," he answered. "Scary."

"Scary's good," I told him and dove down for some more stones.

This time when I surfaced Jake had waded out into water almost as deep as his waist. His face looked giddy and worried all at once.

Without a doubt that's when I should've told him to back off, head for shore, but I didn't do it. Instead I said, "You wanna try to swim?"

He shook his head. "I'm okay just standing."

I swam in and handed him a pile of stones. Those smooth stones made for good skipping. Jake was a master skipper. He started skipping them across the surface. Two, three, four times those stones skipped across the river. Jake was so happy he howled.

I swam out and dove under for more stones. I wanted to keep my little brother happy. To hell with Mom and Dad, I thought, me and Jake only need each other.

When I surfaced this time Jake had pushed his way out into water as deep as his nipples. He looked plenty worried but said, "Hey, Josh, this is way cool out here."

"Yeah," I told him, "as cool as it gets."

He gave me a big toothy grin.

I handed him some more stones. "Just you and me and the river, Jake. The way it should be."

His grin got even bigger.

I dove down for more stones.

When I popped up this time Jake was gone. That's right—gone! He'd somehow slipped beneath the surface.

Don't ask me how. I don't know how. I'm not him. I wasn't there. I should've been but I wasn't. I was under the water, fetching some more stones so Jake could skip them and smile and forget about Mom and Dad fighting and arguing and not being together. I was off doing a good thing.

Either he slipped and lost his balance or he decided to go under and get some stones on his own. I don't know. I can't say. Not with any certainty. It's one of those thing that'll never be known, that'll cloud my days till the day I die.

But I can tell you this—when I finally caught sight of my little brother twenty or thirty seconds later he'd bobbed to the surface and immediately commenced screaming and flailing. His skinny arms windmilled a million miles an hour. He looked more scared than I'd ever seen anybody look.

I shouted to him to stay calm. But he kept flailing away, panicking, trying to get his feet back on the bottom of the river. The current caught him and for a second or two pulled him under.

He came up choking and struggling and even more panicked.

"You got to stay calm, Jake!" I shouted. "You got to stay cool. If you stay cool it'll be okay! I promise."

Good advice but tough for Jake to take.

The current began to pull him downstream. He'd been just eight or ten feet from me, but suddenly he was twenty feet, twenty-five feet, thirty feet, fifty feet. I went after him, swimming as best I could, but my best was nowhere near good enough. I couldn't catch up. It's not like I was a lifeguard or a fireman or anything. I was just a kid, a stupid piss-ant, five year old kid.

Jake started screaming at the top his lungs, all the while swallowing river water and choking up a storm.

I wallowed there in the river for a minute or so paralyzed with fear and no small amount of uncertainty. I didn't have a clue what to do or how to do it.

Finally I decided to make for shore, to get help. It seemed the best plan.

I scrambled out of the river and started sprinting across the back yard. "Mom!" I shouted as loud as my little voice would go. "Dad! Help! It's Jake! It's Jake! It's Jake!"

But they couldn't hear me—not over their yelling and screaming and nonstop arguing.

I had to climb the back stairs, race through the kitchen, and sprint into the living room before I had their undivided attention.

"It's Jake!" I shouted, out of breath and scared out of my guts. "It's Jake… in the river… under the water!"

Dad heard it and got it. He sprang instantly to action. Up and out of the house and across the lawn. Mom needed an extra second. She looked confused. Then she looked like she might be sick. But she rallied. And soon she too was on the move and down to the river's edge. Me in hot pursuit.

None of it mattered. None of it had anything to do with anything.

All their efforts in and along the river were for naught. They were too late. But you already know that. You already know Jake, my little brother, God rest his soul, was dead, drowned in the Delaware. Just above the Frenchtown Bridge. Washed up in the shallows against some rocks. River water in his lungs. A deep, bloody gash on his head. Bumps and bruises all over his little body. His thin arms busted. His skinny legs too.

The little guy's life was over. Finished. Kaput. Before it even had a chance to start.

Josh grew quiet for a while after that.

I might've known, might've seen it coming, but still it was a shock that brought tears to my eyes.

Sometime later the conductor stepped into the car and announced the train would not roll until further notice. We would be spending the night at the station.

Endless and alarming rumors filtered through the train. Rumors of bombings, explosions, executions.

More people than ever crammed the platform outside the train. Also it had started to rain.

Josh and I agreed stay put. It seemed safer and saner.

After a time my companion continued his tale…

The Cache

So that's the way it happened. That's the way we lost my little brother. That's the way Jake slipped away. With us one second and gone the next. Makes you think. Makes you sad. Makes you ticked off. Makes you wonder if the whole battle's worth fighting.

Do I blame myself? Of course I blame myself. How could I not blame myself? It was my fault.

The Family, already spiraling out of control, swirled down the toilet after Jake drowned...

Anyway, in Rawlins we checked into the Best Western. Usual arrangement—Big Jack in his room, me and Retro and Bones in the room across the hall.

We'd been in our room maybe five minutes when Big Jack entered. He floated a hundred dollar bill onto the dresser. "Got some business across town, boys. Go on and get yourselves some dinner. Real nice steakhouse nearby. Bucky's. Just remember to stay out of trouble. Not a good town for trouble." He saluted and left.

A few minutes later we followed. We crossed the access road and started into the center of Rawlins. There weren't any sidewalks. This wasn't pedestrian country. Folks here didn't walk. They drove—mostly heavy-duty pickups and big-ass SUVs.

Off to the right a considerable railroad yard stretched several blocks. The yard had a sturdy steel fence all the way around. Inside that fence must've been more cows than live in the entire state of New Jersey. Maybe I mean cattle, not cows, but you get the picture. A whole massive herd of them stood in there looking mighty crowded and unhappy. They stood head to rump and belly to belly with no room to maneuver.

I wondered aloud why they didn't bolt through that steel fence and stampede down the streets of Rawlins and out into the freedom hills. Bones said maybe because their dream was to get slaughtered and turned into ground beef so Moms across America could make burgers and tacos and meatloaves.

We had a good laugh, even though it wasn't very funny.

I said, "I'm really looking forward to that steak now."

Retro said, "Before we eat let's find a hardware store."

"A hardware store? How come?"

"Because I need some hardware."

We pushed but Retro would say no more.

At Rawlins Hardware we located the locks. Retro looked them over and decided on a large Master lock operated by a key. We paid with the hundred, then headed for Bucky's.

Despite the slaughter yard, we ordered prime ribs, medium rare. While we waited for our beef, Retro offered up his plan. "Tomorrow morning," he said, "we're getting up early. Around five. While Big Jack's asleep…"

Well, let me tell you, I had trouble sleeping worrying about that plan. Tossed and turned for quite some time. Finally I got to sleep, but what felt like twenty seconds later Retro shook me awake. "Up and at 'em, Tailor. Time to move."

By 4:55 a.m. we were out of our room, tools in hand. Out in the hallway we took a quick look under Big Jack's door. Still plenty dark and quiet under there.

We slipped down the corridor and out the side entrance. A little cool outside, maybe a lot cool, but I had the adrenaline pumping big-time so it could've been below zero and I wouldn't've noticed. Dawn hadn't quite opened over the valley yet, but the sky had started to brighten. Some early trucks rumbled along the interstate.

We found the van and trailer at the back of the parking lot. A secluded place to perform our dirty work. I say dirty work because even though it might've been my dad's rig I still felt like a criminal as we slunk through the shadows. Kind of like how I felt when we went joyriding in Mom's convertible and when we heisted that lumber.

I definitely did not want to get caught. Not only because I had enough trouble back home but because I knew the old boy would be plenty peeved. I didn't think he'd thump us—never in my life had he hit me—but I feared getting banished back to Jersey. I didn't want to go home. No way, not yet. Not till we'd solved the mystery of the boxes, seen the Rocky Mountains, and had ourselves a proper adventure.

So you see I had in mind to call the whole caper off when suddenly we stood at the back of the trailer. Retro had a hammer in one hand and a chisel in the other but he didn't bother with the chisel. He just raised that hammer and leveled a mighty blow against the lock. The blow fell slightly off mark. It stung the door of the trailer and momentarily shattered the predawn silence.

Retro would not be deterred. He swung the hammer again and again, each blow more vicious than the last. But he kept missing. That big Master lock flailed around in the early morning air but held fast.

Paranoid of the noise and the dings splattering the trailer, I ordered Retro to hand over the hammer. But he wouldn't comply. He was in full lather. He practically foamed at the mouth. And then it happened! A direct hit! The shackle exploded.

Retro, sweat and a smile on his face, proclaimed, "Oh ye of little faith."

The Passage

Lock gone I was able to lift off the security rod and swing open the trailer door without any trouble. Nervous a dead body would come sliding out, I opened the door a few inches and peered inside. I couldn't see a thing through the dark.

Retro yanked the door out of my grasp and swung it all the way open. The first morning light filtered into the back of the trailer. Enough so we could see the boxes—the coffins—stacked up three-high on both sides of the trailer. Twelve coffins in all—six on the left, six on the right. And behind the coffins, more boxes, smaller and squarer, close to twenty of them. For a minute or so we just stood there—mouths open, eyes wide, imaginations on the roll.

Then Bones reached up and switched on the overhead light. And we saw that Big Jack had secured the goods to the sides of the trailer with heavy nylon straps.

We climbed in and had a look around. Back in PA Big Jack had told us he had camping equipment in the trailer. We'd seen some of that gear when the cops performed their search outside Mt. Vernon. Now we saw it all—sleeping bags, lanterns, a couple air mattresses, a gas stove, even a brand new tent still in the box.

But the camping gear didn't hold our interest for long. We had coffins on our minds. And we wanted to see inside those coffins. At least we thought we did. But first we had to loosen those nylon straps. No easy chore. They were secured with steel ratchets that needed an engineering degree to figure out. Luckily, we had Bones. He took charge while I watched and Retro guarded the door against intruders.

Once we had the straps removed we turned our attention to the coffins. Each coffin had a lid secured by a dozen screws. Every screw was like half a mile long. We could've been stymied right there, save for Retro's handy Leatherman combo tool. Retro never went anywhere without his

Leatherman. And a good thing since one of the tools was a Philips head screwdriver.

It took a good ten minutes to get those damn screws out. It felt like ten hours. I just about flipped out. I sweated and hyperventilated during the long wait.

It kept growing lighter and lighter outside. Big Jack, a man who needed almost no sleep at all, could be up and around at anytime. "Come on, come on, come on," I kept chanting. "Let's go, let's go, let's go."

Finally we lifted off the lid. I expected to smell death. But I didn't smell death. I smelled something far more familiar.

"Oil," said Retro.

Me and Bones nodded and said, "Yeah, oil."

So okay, there weren't any dead bodies in those coffins. No bodies at all—dead or alive. They weren't coffins after all. They were shipping boxes, storage boxes.

To be honest, despite our vast array of knowledge on a broad range of subjects, me and Retro and Bones could not identify the equipment in those boxes with absolute precision. But we did know, without any question at all, that we were staring at automatic assault weapons. I thought Russian or Chinese made AK-47s. Retro thought Israeli made Uzis. Bones thought Tec-9s.

"The Tec-9's a pistol," said Retro. "These are rifles."

Whatever they were, we stared speechless at them for quite a while.

Retro said what we'd all been thinking, "That's some arsenal Big Jack's got. What do you think he's doing with a cache of weapons like that?"

That was the million-dollar question: What the hell was Big Jack doing with all those assault rifles? Twelve boxes. Twelve to a box. 144 in all. Jesus.

I didn't have a clue what he was doing. What did I know? I was just the son.

We moved to the smaller boxes, boxes too short to contain assault rifles. They opened easier due to large clamps rather than screws holding them closed. I released the clamps and pulled off the top. Inside were these things looked like miniature missiles or maybe giant grenades. They looked plenty lethal.

"What are they?" asked Bones.

"I think they're RPGs," answered Retro.

"RPGs?"

"Rocket Propelled Grenades," said Retro. "Kind of like a modern bazooka. I saw a show once on the History Channel about them. You can blow up a tank or knock down a building with one of those suckers. Even blast a helicopter outta the sky."

Me and Bones whistled softly. Pretty wild stuff. Assault rifles and RPGs. Stuff to start a war.

Then a noise outside the trailer gave me a jolt. I thought for sure it was Big Jack coming to get us. But no, it was just the wind... and my imagination. I ordered Retro and Bones to get the lids back on the boxes, secure all screws and clamps.

It took a while. Longer than I wanted. Long enough to give me time to think.

I thought about my father and I thought about Big Jack and I couldn't separate the two. They were one and the same. It was without a doubt my dad hauling automatic assault rifles and rocket propelled grenades—undoubtedly illegal automatic assault rifles and rocket propelled grenades—across the country with his family minivan. But to where and for what? The man had enough firepower inside that trailer to arm an army. But how come? To what end? And who was the enemy? The government?

Big Jack had always hated the government. Maybe marauders? We hadn't talked about the marauders, about the whole international terrorist situation, but I felt sure he had an opinion. Big Jack had an opinion on everything.

I wondered if maybe I should call the cops. Or Mom. Or someone.

Retro and Bones secured the lids, then started in on the straps.

I worked on my thoughts and was still working when Retro asked, "So what are we gonna do, Josh?"

"Yeah," Bones wanted to know too. "What are we gonna do?"

"I don't know about you two," I heard myself say, "but I'm not gonna do a damn thing. You guys can catch a bus or a train home if you want, but me, I'm staying here with my old man. I wanna see where he's going and what he's got himself into."

Retro thought it over for maybe two seconds. "I'm staying, Josh. No way am I leaving you on your own."

I gave my best bud a high five.

Bones needed a little more time. "I don't like it," he told us, "but I guess I'm sticking too. Seems like I have no choice."

So we put our hands together again and vowed to keep our mouths shut and our eyes open. Then we closed up the trailer, secured the new lock, and hightailed it back to our room. I lay in bed thinking and worrying till Big Jack showed up and ordered us to pull on our shorts and sneakers and jog on down the road.

The Bully

Just like I feared following our fiasco at the bridge, I had trouble sleeping. I got home and up to my 3rd floor digs no problem. But once between the sheets I tossed and turned while the demons whipped my brain into a frenzy. Finally I nodded off but I doubt an hour passed before a hand gripped my shoulder. For a second I felt sure that hand belonged to a big muscle-bound NJ state trooper who'd tracked me down and would soon have me in handcuffs and leg irons for swiping that lumber and wrecking that car and giving Mom so much grief and all my other infractions.

But it wasn't law enforcement shaking my shoulder—it was just my imagination running amuck.

And then, before I had time to pull the sheet up over my head, the stairs began to squeak. I figured it was Mom, you know, rousting me for school. But it was Gram, not Mom. She knocked on my door, then stepped into my bedroom. "Morning, Joshua. I hate to wake you so early but you have a visitor."

I glanced at the clock: 6:07. "Way early, Gram. Who's here at this hour?"

"Police Chief Walters."

A wave of panic pinched my butt closed. "Police Chief Walters?"

Gram nodded. "He'd like to speak with you."

I tried to look innocent. "With me? How come?"

Gram didn't answer. She went to my closet and found a clean dress shirt. "Wash your face and comb your hair before you come down." She draped the shirt over my desk chair. "And remember, be polite... and honest."

And with that Gram left me to ponder my fate. I broke into a sweat but managed to climb out of bed. It seemed unwise to make Chief Walters wait. I followed Gram's directive to a tee. While I tidied up I went over my story. Deny. Deny. Deny.

Police Chief Walters was a big man with a wavy mane of silver hair and a pretty fair potbelly. He sat at the kitchen table sipping coffee and yakking with Pop about an upcoming fishing trip they had planned to Barnegat Bay. Police Chief Walters didn't wear a uniform. He wore khakis and a blue short-sleeve shirt, the sleeves busting against burly biceps. He got up and shook my hand when I entered the kitchen.

"Morning, Josh. How are you, son?"

"Fine, sir," I answered, Sunday polite. "How are you?"

"Reasonably well. Only one of my deputies got me out of bed in the middle of the night and that never makes me happy."

That probably would've been Deputy MacAdoo, the Chief's son-in-law and one-fifth of the entire Bridgeton P.D. I knew them all and they knew me; generally thought well of me, too, despite my occasional mischief.

An idea popped into my head. Call it a diversionary tactic. I took a look around the room, then asked, "Hey, where's Mom?"

No one answered, so I made myself nervous and ratcheted my voice up an octave or two. "Has something happened to Mom?"

Gram raced to the rescue. She put her hand on my shoulder and said, "Oh no, Joshua. Absolutely not. Your mother's fine."

I calmed myself down. "Thank God. So what's going on?"

Chief Walters was an old hand at this. He took his seat again, then invited me to sit between him and Pop. He worked his cup of joe, then, easy, said, "Josh, we've had a little trouble. Nothing real serious, not the end of the world or anything, but we're trying to get a handle on the situation.

You understand?"

I sat and rubbed my eyes. "Sure. What kind of trouble?"

"Well," answered the Chief, holding his eyes steady on me and rubbing his chin with his knuckles, "I was hoping you might shed some light on the situation."

"I can try."

"Good. Any idea what I could be driving at?"

I hesitated, but not long. "No sir, not really."

"Well, it seems some boys raised a ruckus over on Bull's Island last night. Like I said, nothing that'll shatter the earth's rotation or cause the icecaps to melt, but you see, they skedaddled and we're busy trying to find them."

I told myself to stay cool. Then I reminded myself that Chief Walters was a whole lot smarter than me. I said, "Bull's Island, huh? I don't really know anything about that, Chief. Last night, with final exams and all, I stayed up in my room."

The Chief gave me a nod. "Yeah, I got that from your grandparents. But I wasn't worried about you being involved in the ruckus, Josh. Not after your Mom's car and all. I know you want to steer clear of any further trouble."

I tried to keep the sweat from forming on my brow. I said, "Absolutely right about that, Chief."

The Chief looked long at me. Long enough that I knew he knew. He said, "I was more hoping you could, you know, tell me who might've been involved."

That sounded kind of tricky. I gave it some thought, then went with this, "I tell you, Chief, not to be disrespectful, but I'd sure hate to get the reputation for being a snitch. If, of course, I even knew anything."

This brought on another nod. "Understood, Josh. And no

disrespect taken. I just don't want to see this situation blow up out of control. We're a small town, Bridgeton is, and we just like to keep our boys on the straight and narrow."

Oh yeah, Chief Walters knew a whole lot more than he was letting on. Maybe he'd already broken Bones or Young or the new kid Laramie or maybe Stinky Cogan who was famous for not being able to keep a secret. I wondered if it might go easier for me if I confessed and cooperated. You know, turned state's evidence for a promise of immunity. Or had I been watching way too many lawyer and cop shows on TV?

Luckily, before I spilled my guts, Chief Walters pushed back his chair, stood up, rested his big hand on my shoulder, and said, "Josh, listen, thanks for seeing me. You know where to reach me if there's anything you need to say." Then he turned to Gram and said, "Edna, finest coffee in town. Sorry for the early morning disruption."

Gram said, "Anytime, Roy."

Pop stood. He and the Chief walked out the back door and over to the Chief's Crown Vic parked in the driveway where Mom's Civic should've been.

Gram put some scrambled eggs and toast in front of me and told me I was a good boy. I didn't feel much like a good boy, just a kid who'd maybe gotten away with something, maybe not, time would tell. Then Pop came back in, leaned down close to me, locked onto my eyes, and asked, "You aren't involved in this mess, are you, son?"

I hated lying to Pop. He'd been straight with me for so long. "No, sir."

"Tell me the truth, Josh. Don't lie to me."

I just about confessed, but not quite. "I'm not lying, sir."

Pop gave me a long look.

I felt like I should repeat my denial, but didn't.

"I'm late for work," Pop growled. "I'll see you all this afternoon." And back out through the screen door he went full of hot and bother.

Gram gave my shoulder a squeeze and retreated up the back stairs. I sat there and pushed those eggs around the plate. I tried but couldn't decide if I was a good kid or a bad kid, a lying, no-good juvenile delinquent or a hard-working, three-sport, academic superstar. Hard to say. Hard to know.

While mulling it over Mom rolled in the back door. She took one look at me sitting there in my dress shirt and right off got herself all stirred up. "What's the matter, Joshua? Why are you up so early? Why do you have that shirt on?"

I might've told her, might've filled her in, except for one small blemish on the face of the earth. Actually two blemishes, and not on the face of the earth, but one under my mother's left eye and one on Mom's arm just above her right elbow.

I hopped up in a rage. "What the hell is that on your face?"

Mom tried to cover it up with her hand.

"Did that sick bastard hit you again?" I yelled. "He did, didn't he?"

"Joshua, no, he—"

"That violent son of a bitch! I swear to God, Mom, I'll kill—"

"Joshua, calm down."

I moved in for a closer look. "Your cheek's all bruised and swollen. He smacked you in the face and then he squeezed your arm hard enough to leave a black and blue mark. I can't believe this shit. I'm gonna kill him, Mom. I'm gonna—"

"Joshua, stop it! It was nothing. Don't get all carried away."

"Oh, don't worry, Mom, I won't get carried away! Just going up to Otis Hill and execute that sadistic slimeball with my bare hands! I'm going to reach my hand down his throat and pull his lungs out of his chest!"

"Stop it, Joshua!"

"Why did he do it, Mom? Because I busted up that stupid convertible? I wrecked his crappy car so the second he gets back from his stinking golf trip to Pebble Beach he treats you like a punching bag? I swear to God I'm going to kill him! He's a dead man!"

All day long at school I thought about Police Chief Walters and Mom and that free-swinging dirtbag Homer Otis. It irritated me big-time thinking of the Chief wasting valuable man-hours on us kids swiping a few sticks of lumber while sick sadists like Otis roamed the planet beating up defenseless women half their size. All through chemistry and history and English I mulled over ways I might torture and execute him.

It took forever for that school day to end. As soon as the final bell rang, me and the other guys on the team rendezvoused in the locker room. We sat through a long-winded pep talk from Coach Kinum. Finally he wound down and told us to suit up.

I took off my street clothes and started putting on my uniform. The coach came over, pulled up a chair. "You look like hell, Tailor. You okay?"

"Seasonal allergies, Coach," I lied. "I feel great."

"You got bags under your eyes the size of cantaloupes, kid. Can I count on you to hustle out there today? Get the job done?"

"Absolutely, Coach. One hundred and ten percent. Just like always."

Coach Kinum slapped me on the back. "That's what I want to hear."

I laced up my spikes, taped my busted finger from the car wreck to the pinkie of my left hand, and hit the field.

It was the last game of the regular season. A win for the South

Hunterdon Owls and we'd be in the playoffs.

And we did win, 5-3, but no thanks to me. I went 0-4, including a strikeout with the bases loaded in the bottom of the 5th. And oh yeah, I also let a ball get by me in right field late in the game. It rolled all the way to the wall. In my defense, I was the youngest kid on the team, the only frosh. I'd been pushed into a starting roll after our regular right fielder, Hansi Kunz, went down with a sprained ankle and our second string right fielder, Mark Post, flunked physics and got kicked off the team.

Mom climbed into the bleachers in the top of the 3rd. She gave me a little wave but didn't get one in return. All she got was a hard look. Which, of course, was petty of me, but what can you do?

Despite it being sunny and eighty degrees Mom wore a long-sleeve silk shirt to cover the bruise on her arm plus a huge pair of sunglasses and a South Hunterdon Owls baseball cap, the brim pulled low, to hide her swollen and discolored eye.

I wanted to make an announcement over the public address system that Homer Otis had punched my mother in the face and I'd pay two hundred and eleven dollars—all the dough I had in the world—to anyone who would bludgeon Homer with a baseball bat.

Too bad such an announcement wouldn't have gone over very well since Homer O. was considered a fine and upstanding citizen who had, in fact, donated most of the money that had built our baseball field.

And then, to my sheer amazement, my old chum, Mr. Homer Otis, arrived in the bottom of the sixth. I couldn't believe he had the balls to show with Mom looking the way she did. But there he was, strutting around like a breeding bull. I almost barfed.

Homer's real name was Samuel Mathias Otis—Sam Otis. Supposedly he'd been one heck of a power hitter during his high school and college days. He'd played baseball for some university down in Florida. His senior year he'd crushed the school record for home runs. He'd taken on the nickname Homer, and for the last two and a half decades he'd used it, I guess, as a way to stay in touch with his glory days. Personally, I wouldn't want to be an adult walking around with the nickname Homer.

So Homer'd been a star athlete and a handsome, well-built dude, and he also came from piles of money. I figure you've ridden in an elevator, and if you have it was probably an Otis elevator. Homer's great or great great grandfather had like invented the elevator a hundred or so years ago. And the family was still living large off the invention. Now all this—star athlete, good looks, buckets of dough—should've made Homer a swell guy. Decent and secure and fun. Too bad it hadn't. Homer was an awful human being—violent, devious, mean-spirited, and worst of all in my book, a bully. A first class dyed-in-the-wool bully.

Look, I don't know why Homer turned out lousy despite his advantages. I'm no head shrinker. Maybe his old man bullied him or beat him up. Maybe poor Homer had severe chemical imbalances. Maybe the proper meds would've put him on an even keel, made him pleasant. Maybe his mother didn't love him enough, hug him enough, spoil him enough. Or maybe she loved him too much, spoiled him more than she should've. Like I said, I don't know. And frankly, I don't give a damn. I just wish the bastard had never come into our lives, especially Mom's. He was never any good for her. But she couldn't see that. All she ever saw was his fancy house and his expensive cars and his country club memberships. And sure, okay, even into his mid forties Homer was still fit and handsome. And yeah, he could be a charmer, when it suited him. He could show up with the flowers and chocolate hearts and say all the right things. But it was all smoke and mirrors. Hocus pocus. A lot of hokum.

The jerkoff rolled into the game in his canary yellow Hummer. Came out of that high cabin in his cool khakis and Polo golf shirt, no doubt fresh from a round of golf. The baseball game might not have stopped for Homer's arrival, but his appearance definitely slowed the show. Everyone in Bridgeton knew Homer, and so long as you didn't know him too well he seemed like a good guy, and generous with his dough, too. Homer had big bucks and a mansion on the hill and a fleet of pricey cars and the hot girlfriend. But people didn't know Homer bullied that girlfriend, slapped her around, marked her up. No, they didn't know he belittled and kicked and spit on her teenage son who might've been a pain in the ass but wasn't really all that bad a kid. They didn't know because Homer was a closet sadist. He did his dirty work on the sly, behind the high brick walls of his hilltop estate. People didn't know because I was too much the weak-kneed, lily-livered chicken-shit to tell them.

So there went Homer up into the stands, the masses parting so he could climb without hindrance. He sat beside Mom and oh so gallantly kissed her hand—the perfect gentleman. No one but me and Mom and Homer knew I'd once seen Homer get so mad at Mom he'd actually bit her on that same hand. Bit her hard enough to draw blood. I kid you not.

I was out in right field thinking about the black eye Homer'd given Mom the night before when all of a sudden I heard the crack of the bat. A split second later the ball rushed over the head of our 2nd baseman, Angel Garcia. The ball hit the grass thirty feet in front of me and took a big hop. Too bad I was off balance and all muddled in the head from thinking about Homer. I reached out but the ball skipped by me in a flash. I turned and chased it down. It rolled, like I said, all the way to the wall. By the time I picked it up and threw it in a run had scored and I looked and felt like a damn fool.

But despite my error we hung on and notched a victory. After the game the team celebrated at home plate. We screamed and jumped into each other's arms. No one, not even Coach Kinum, mentioned my lousy play. We'd survived and made the playoffs. The next day we'd face the Watchung Hills Warriors in the first round.

The celebration over, I wandered into the parking lot where family and friends had gathered to welcome the ballplayers. I saw Mom and Amy and, sorry to say, Homer hanging out by Homer's Hummer. Amy right away rushed up and gave me a hug and a wet kiss and told me I'd played great. Mom gave me a hug and a wet kiss too, a bright red lipstick kiss right smack on the cheek. Homer, playing it cool, made us wait a few seconds before he offered his assessment of the game. "Yup," he finally said, "the team played reasonably well. Well enough to win anyway."

I felt like telling Homer where he could stick his attitude, but I didn't have the guts. So I just stood there and took it. Amy gave me a peck on the cheek, said she had to get home to study for finals, and so steered in that direction.

Mom started talking to one of the other moms so I found myself standing with my best bud—Homer O. Homer moved a step or two closer to me and in a soft, sick voice said, "Yo, Josh, have a little trouble with that line drive? Looked from where I sat like you spooked on it. Damn near gave the ballgame away with that move, kid. What the hell were you doing out there? Playing with your noodle?"

So you see what I mean? Understand now what I've been driving at? The guy was a sadistic whack job. I mean, can you believe he said that to me? Like, could I have felt worse about the whole stupid error without him spitting it in my face?

I stood there red as a beet with my mouth hinged all the way open.

Homer beamed like a peacock, like he'd just hit the game-winning grand slam.

And then he said, in a sick voice barely above a whisper, "As for the convertible, you deviant little prick, first chance I get, I'm kicking your scrawny little ass from here to Boontown. Not a chance that move's going unpunished."

Then, right on cue, Mom, all smiles, came up behind me, put her arm around my waist, and said, "Joshua, you must be starving. Let's go to Dill's for hamburgers."

I thought that sounded like a swell idea. Only I had one small problem.

"Homer going?"

"Of course," Mom answered, innocent as can be. "We'll all go."

Mom knew better than to try and set this up. She knew how I felt about Homer. This was no new game. It had been going on for a couple years. A thousand times I'd begged her to break up with him, send him down the road. I refused to do anything at all with the SOB. It'd been a year or more since I'd stepped foot inside his mansion on the hill. But still, Mom persisted. She wanted to pretend like we were one big happy family.

So no way should she have been surprised when I said, "Tell you what, Mom, if Homer goes to Dill's, I'll pass. I'm hungry, but not that hungry."

Mom right away got all pissy with me, demanded to know how I could be so rude.

But Homer—he kept his cool. Squeezed Mom's arm and said, "You know, babe, I have a board of adjustment meeting in Stockton. I think I'll skip Dill's."

So me and Mom went to Dill's Hamburger Haven across the river in Upper Black Eddy, PA, not far from our old digs. We had burgers and fries and I added a black and white shake so thick you had to pull like mad to draw it through the straw. But believe me—it was no carefree and pleasant meal despite the juicy burgers and thick shake and the Delaware sweeping by just a few feet from our picnic table. Especially after Mom had the gall to say, "The next time you see Homer, Joshua, I want you to apologize."

I squirted out a sarcastic little laugh. "Oh yeah, that's gonna happen, Mom. Sure thing. Homer deserves my fist in his mouth, not my apology in his ear."

"Let's not be ugly, Joshua."

"Right, Mom. Let's all be nice and live in Fantasy Land."

And so it went—me and Mom—communicating.

Mom took a short break, then came back with a softer touch. "So," she asked, "the game tomorrow is at four?"

Through a mouthful of half-chewed fries I answered, "You got it."

"I'll be there, of course, but I might be a little late. I have a showing at three."

Mom had about the same interest in baseball that I had in antique jewelry. Which is to say, none. But still she'd been coming to my baseball and soccer and basketball games practically since I could walk. But she'd missed plenty of games too, and so, being an angry teenager from a broken family, that's mostly what I chose to remember.

I said, "Come to the game or not. Makes no difference to me."

I spewed these cruel words despite the fact I'd recently wrecked her new car and oh yeah let's not forget I definitely wanted her at the game. Every kid wants at least one parent in the stands watching and cheering in case he sinks the winning free throw or drives in the winning run. But I'd lived long with disappointment and so had erected some pretty strong and sturdy walls.

More silence followed. And then, the burgers and fries gone, the sun all but set, Mom said, "There might be someone else at the game also."

"Oh yeah? Who's that? Scumbag Homer?"

She ignored me. "Your father."

That got my attention. "What! You're outta your mind."

"No I'm not."

"You're full of crap."

"Actually, no. I spoke with him earlier. He's going to try and make the game."

Now I got to tell you, Mom might've uttered these words without fanfare, but believe me, a call from Big Jack was a pretty exclusive event. I doubt he'd called half a dozen times in the past couple years.

"You talked to him?" I demanded. "Where is he? Is he in town?"

"He's in New York at the big auto show. He said he'd definitely be out to watch your game tomorrow."

"But how would he even know I had a game?"

"I don't know, Joshua. Maybe he reads the New York Times sports section."

"That's rich, Mom. I'm in stitches. You should write for Letterman."

"Maybe I should." Mom was always on the lookout for new career opportunities. Mom, by the way, was thirty-six at the time. Year after year my buddies voted her Hottest Mom in Town. Though personally I thought she had scrawny legs and bony knees.

Right away I could feel the walls start to rise. I wanted to tell Mom I didn't give a damn if Big Jack came to the game or not. Of course, this was a stinking lie.

"So what do you think," I asked, sounding like a six year old, "you think he'll really come?"

On this point Mom couldn't just say yes or no, couldn't keep it simple, tell me what I needed to hear. Their relationship was way too screwed up for that. Her rancor for my father ran deep. She had to stick the double-sided serrated knife into his belly and slowly twist and turn the blade.

"I hope he does, Joshua, I really do. But your father's track record over the years has not been good. I mean, how many times has he let you down? Lied to you? Told you he'd be there and then never showed? More times than I care to remember."

Mom couldn't help herself. She had to take a couple cheap shots at the old boy. I didn't really blame her, though I got to tell you her comments pissed me off. Despite his long and silent absences, Big Jack was still my father. The only father I had. So I didn't appreciate Mom running him down.

"Why don't you close the trap?" I suggested. "Cool your heels?"

She shrugged. "Who knows? Maybe your father will show for the game. I mean, it's not absolutely impossible."

It's never a good idea to run down a boy's father. He'll only hold it against you.

"Okay," I told Mom, "you can wrap it up now. We all know how you feel about Dad. It's the Gospel according to Lisa Anne."

"Go ahead, Joshua. Go ahead and defend him like you always do. Ignore what he's done. Just remember who's here with you day in and day out, taking care of you, making sure you have a warm and loving home."

Probably I could've softened then, muttered a kind word or two, maybe even gone around the table and given Mom a hug. But me and Mom had been at each other for a long time, a lot of years.

I'd turned way too hard to suddenly grow soft.

I stood there, thought it over, then turned facetious. "Geez, Mom, I didn't realize parenting was a competition. But hey, as long as it is, let's go ahead and declare you the winner. Congratulations! You win an all-expense paid trip to Disney World!"

And with that bit of nastiness sweetening a perfectly spectacular

June evening, I turned my back on my mother and stormed off. Over the years me and Mom had fought and argued so much that it felt perfectly normal and natural. In the end almost all the fuss and bother came back to Dad. If Big Jack had stayed home where he belonged, taken care of his family, not flown the coop, then maybe me and Mom would've gotten along better and sadistic bullies like Homer never would've entered our lives.

I left Dill's and walked out onto the bridge back to Bridgeton. Halfway across I stopped. I put one foot up on the rail and spit over the side. The hamburger/milkshake loogie turned end over end, then splashed into the Delaware and instantly got sucked under the bridge by the current. The current got me thinking about Jake, and that got me rolling on Mom and Dad, then on to Homer and the school psychologist who a while back had tried to tell me how I projected my feelings about my father onto my mother's boyfriends. Well I just wanted to enjoy the river, not start reflecting on all that projection jive. But I couldn't shut the psychobabble off like a spigot, no way, my brain had to wash it through the system.

"You see, Josh," lectured brown-haired, brown-eyed Child Psychologist Anita Krebs, "because your father left the nest under unpleasant and difficult circumstances, you have unresolved feelings. Undoubtedly you have quite a lot of animosity for your father because he left. But since he's not here, you project that animosity onto others who are here. This, of course, would include any men interested in your mother. Does any of this make sense to you?"

It didn't right off, no, but standing there on the bridge I figured Psychologist Krebs was trying to say I hated Homer's guts when really I hated my father's guts. My brain right away declared this a lot of crapola. Big Jack might've left, sure, abandoned me and Mom, but he was still one of the coolest dudes on the planet. Homer was nothing but a bully and a snake and if I ever got the chance I'd slice the bastard in two. I'd already wrecked the Mellow Yellow VW convertible he'd given Mom; I'd go after him next. Which hey, meant what? That I'd squashed the bug on purpose? Taken aim at that drainage ditch in a premeditated kind of way?

Jesus. Maybe. Though I didn't think so. That kind of babble seemed a little far-fetched to me. I thought the crash mostly had to do with the booze and the weed.

More of Psychologist Kreb's mumbo jumbo spilled out of my head, ran down my spine, dribbled off my heel, and dropped into the Delaware. She claimed I was, "avoiding conflicts and denying problems. This whole father/son/broken family cycle," she insisted, "reeks of chaos and turmoil. It's dirty and complicated, Josh, dirty and complicated."

I plugged up my ears and made a run for it. I had places to go and ball games to play and final exams to study for. Get a little hole in your shirt and the psycho docs will find a loose thread and start pulling and pretty soon they'll have you entirely unraveled.

I made my way home. I slipped through the back door of the old Victorian. Gram was in the kitchen washing dishes and whistling an old Big Band tune. Stompin' At the Savoy by Benny Goodman.

"Joshua, you're all out of breath."

"Been jogging," I told her. "And thinking."

"That sounds like a good combination."

I crossed the tiled floor and gave her a hug. Gram gave me one back.

"Where's Mom?" I asked. "I didn't see the Civic."

Gram let out a little sigh. "I suppose at Homer's."

"Well," I said, "isn't that swell."

Gram, the queen of tact, kept quiet, but she gave me a look. She hated the SOB same as me. Of course, she'd never been real fond of Big

Jack either. She thought her girl deserved better, someone like the good man she'd married four decades ago.

"Gotta go study, Gram. Finals coming." I started up the back stairs. Safely up in my third floor room I closed the door and cracked the books. Biology, I think. Maybe algebra. Something big-time boring. I fired up my Mac, downloaded a few tunes. Some Norah Jones and some Stunt 101. I have a wide variety of musical interests.

My focus kept drifting. I couldn't keep my thoughts together for more than a few seconds. Which made it tough to study. I got to thinking about Amy and how it would be cool to lie naked with her. Then I started wondering what Homer would do to me for wrecking the Beetle. Kick my ass seemed like a good bet. And from there my thoughts drifted to Dad and I got pretty worked up thinking he might show for the big game against Watchung. I wondered if he knew about me wrecking the Beetle and about that lumber getting lifted and Police Chief Walters asking questions. Which little by little got me thinking about Mom and Jake and the whole mess of our lives. It was all plenty grim and depressing and for a while my thoughts dragged me down and made me blue.

But I got over it because I always do. I learned early it doesn't do any good to feel sorry for yourself. "You're gonna get your butt kicked from time to time," Big Jack used to tell me and Jake. "That's the way of the world, boys. Best thing you can do is dust it off, crack a smile, and carry on. Never let on it hurts. Never let on like you give a shit."

The Passage

The Snag

We ran through the streets of Rawlins, showered, ate breakfast, then got back on the road. All the while me and Retro and Bones, cohorts in crime, kept our mouths shut. I mean, what were we gonna say? "Yo, Big Jack, what's with the heavy cache of weapons in the trailer? Plan on doing some big game hunting out in the Rockies?"

Nah, me and the boys played it cool, like a pack of coyotes. While we waited to see what would happen next.

An hour west of Rawlins we crossed the Continental Divide at 7000 feet. Big Jack told us all water flowing east of the Divide ultimately wound up in the Atlantic and water flowing to the west of the Divide worked its way into the Pacific.

What I noticed was the land west of the Divide had big-time Ugly written all over it. We drove down off the Divide into wide-open and cratered country. Like country you might see on the moon. Brown and dry and pockmarked. But fenced in, every square mile of it. We didn't spot any animals though, not wild or domestic. Nothing could, or would, live out there, except maybe snakes and scorpions. And I don't know they'd choose it but maybe have it forced upon them.

In tighter to Rock Springs the scenery began to change again. Tall white buttes looking like earthen skyscrapers punched the landscape. We spotted a large flock of birds flying out of the west. Big Jack pulled over so we could all hop out and get a look through the binoculars.

I took my look and declared, "Canada geese."

"Sandhill cranes," corrected Big Jack, still scoping the birds with his naked eye.

And sure enough, they flew closer and I saw they weren't geese at all but bigger, sleeker, more graceful aviators. All of which irked me since it meant he was right and I was wrong. I wanted to tell the big fella I'd called the cops or maybe ATF and informed them Big Jack Tailor had a trailer filled with automatic assault rifles and rocket propelled grenades. But instead I stayed silent and simmered.

In Green River we stopped to refuel. It was my turn to pump the gas. Retro and Bones went into the convenience store to use the can and get some snacks. Big Jack, as was his habit during these pit stops, walked the perimeter of the service area. "Just stretching my legs," he'd tell us. "Keeps the blood flowing."

I watched him walking out of the corner of my eye. And wondered if he might be a dangerous man.

For a minute or so I lost sight of him as he disappeared behind the trailer. Then all of a sudden he showed up at my side, practically right in my face. "How's it going, kid?"

"Going good," I told him, after I'd jumped, literally, several inches off the ground.

"Problem?" he asked.

I topped off the tank. "Nope."

He kept his eyes tight on me. "Good."

I hung up the nozzle and said I needed to pee.

Big Jack said, "A man has to take care of his needs."

I nodded and headed for the bathroom.

Half a minute later I stood all alone in the men's room doing my thing when the big guy suddenly showed up at the next urinal. He prided himself on only peeing like once or twice a day, so I was surprised to see him there.

"Hey, Finnegan Tailor. Fancy meeting you here."

"Yeah," I replied, my stream interrupted by his appearance.

Big Jack got his stream flowing, a forceful gush I could hear loud and clear, like something you might use to put out a fire. After a few seconds, without even bothering to give me a glance, he said, "So what's the deal, kid? The Three Musketeers get a sudden and uncontrollable midnight desire to visit the inside of the trailer?"

I just about soiled my L.L. Bean ripcord hiking shorts. "Huh? What are you talking about?"

"Well now, let's see," he remarked, his powerful stream practically punching a hole in the porcelain, "what am I talking about?... What am I talking about?... Oh, right, about a wide variety of interesting tidbits actually. I'm talking about the dings and dents on the trailer door. I'm talking about the lock I suddenly can't open. I'm talking about kicking some sorry ass right here in Green River, Wyoming unless the guilty cat, who will go nameless, confesses pronto, and I mean before he finishes bleeding that miniscule English lizard of his."

Normally I would've at least smiled at his barrage, but not this time, no way. My face looked like an undertaker's. I considered confession, momentarily contemplated spilling my guts right there in that Conoco crapper. But then I came to my senses. I gave my lizard, which is actually of an adequate size, a couple tugs, zipped up, assembled all my cool, and steered for the exit. "Sorry, big guy," I said, sweet as can be, "but I don't know dick about that trailer or its dings or dents." My voice cracked some, but I got it out.

I figured he'd grab me, probably by the neck, and maybe hold me up off the floor against the wall until the truth spilled out. But it didn't happen. Big Jack didn't lay a hand on me. He just laughed. And laughed some more. A big rolling laugh that sent a chill rippling down my spine. I could still hear him laughing even after I got back to the van, climbed inside, and closed the door.

"We're snagged," I informed the guys.

"What do you mean?" asked Retro.

"He knows."

"Who knows what?" asked Bones.

"Big Jack. He knows all. But don't let on. Hang tough. Don't give an inch."

Oh yeah, Big Jack gave us some looks upon returning from the head and settling into the driver's seat of the Town & Country. Some wild and scary looks. Looks that had the three boneheads from Jersey shivering in our skivvies.

Half an hour west of Green River we turned off I-80 onto US 30, the same Route 30 we'd been on back in Pennsylvania and again in parts of Iowa and Nebraska. But out here in western Wyoming US 30 had a whole different feel. No cities or towns. Very little sign of human habitation. Nothing but sagebrush and chaparral. Finally we reached the town of Opal. Population 95. Elevation 6660 feet. Out beyond Opal we could see snow-capped mountains.

"Bridger-Teton National Forest," Big Jack told us. "Salt River Range."

"How high?" we wanted to know.

Big Jack thought it over. "They got peaks in that area top ten thousand."

"Ten thousand feet!"

"Yup."

We were plenty impressed. In Jersey the highest peak rises to the dizzying height of 1803 feet.

"But farther north," Big Jack informed us, "where we're headed, they got peaks reach up over thirteen thousand feet."

We could only sit in awe.

The scenery pretty much blew us away all the rest of that day. We drove up and over high rolling hills through Kemmerer and Sage and Cokeville. Just north of Cokeville we peeled off onto Highway 89 and headed due north. A few miles later we entered a broad valley bordered on both sides by low lush hills. We'd early in the day been in country as arid and dead as the plains of Pluto, but no more. This valley ran green and smooth. Small farms grew wheat and corn and peaches and apples. In the crossroads town of Freedom an elk the size of a VW bus sauntered across the street easy as ice cream. Big Jack stopped. Bones got a photo. That big bull moose had a 12-point rack as high as a house.

Dead ahead but still plenty distant loomed the high peaks. We drove straight at them. The valley began to narrow. The hills grew close. It was like a funnel growing smaller and smaller, sucking us up like a straw. Soon we had nothing but steep canyon walls hemming us in as we entered the Snake River Valley. We swung briefly back to the east, then north again up along the Snake—a wild, rock-strewn stream raging with white water. At times the road hugged so close to the Snake I could've reached out the window and rinsed my hands. I tell you that river was so beautiful it made my eyes hurt.

Big Jack knew it too and so took his time. He never rushed when life dazzled.

But of course it all ends. Eventually.

Including that slow ramble along the fast-moving Snake. The river vanished into an impenetrable canyon. The road swung away to the northwest, and us too, on up into the tourist mecca of old Jackson.

Big Jack had a couple rooms reserved at the Red Lion Wyoming

Inn in the heart of town. The Red Lion was plenty posh, easily our poshest digs to date. And for the first time since D.C. Big Jack informed me I'd be bunking with him, not with the boys. Retro and Bones would take the room across the hall. This didn't suit me one little bit, not after our run-in back at the Conoco can in Green River, but what could I say? Nothing, that's what. So I dropped my bag and made haste for the exit.

Big Jack, sitting on his bed, phone already in hand, told me to be back at the Inn for dinner by eight sharp. Then he added me and him would be getting up early to take care of some business.

I didn't ask him what kind of business.

For the next couple hours me and the boys cruised Jackson.

All three of us called home. I called Mom but got Gram. She wanted to know if I was behaving myself, if I was having a good time, and if I was getting enough to eat. I answered yes to all inquiries but didn't mutter a mouthful about those one hundred and forty-four automatic assault rifles or the stacks of rocket propelled grenades in Big Jack's trailer. Mom was out and about with my favorite sicko, Mr. Homer Otis, so I didn't get to mention the guns or grenades to her either.

For dinner we ate steaks as thick as phone books with baked potatoes the size of footballs. Big Jack ordered a pitcher of beer and encouraged us to partake of the brew.

"Hell, you boys are men now," he told us as he poured a round and chinked our glasses. "Or at least you think you are. And I guess that's halfway home."

Back upstairs Jack herded the three of us into his room.

"Josh and I are getting up early for a little father-son adventure," he told us. "Carl and Pete, you're on your own for a few hours. Do as you please, just keep yourselves under control. You know the drill. As for me and Josh, we'll be back around noon. We'll head north after that, up into

Montana. Any questions?"

None we dared ask, so we just shook our heads. Retro and Bones said good night and in a flash darted across the hall, happy to escape.

Within seconds of their departure Big Jack had his shirt and pants off and his lean muscular body stretched out on that king size bed. He put his arms behind his head, looked me over, and asked, "So, kid, you ready?"

"Ready for what?"

"Ready to do some business with the old man?"

"What kind of business?"

"A business like any other, Josh. A money-making business."

"Gun-running business?" I wanted to ask but didn't.

"Look, kid," he said while he lay there and scratched his prodigious privates, "we can fart around with this trailer jive if that's what you want. Hell, denial can be a whole way of life. I know because I lived one with your mother for a lot of years. But see, I don't do denial anymore. I drive straight on. I go with the flow and the facts. The new lock, the dings and dents, the screws removed and replaced from the boxes…"

The old boy had my attention now.

He caught my eye. "Here's how I read it. You decided to mind my business, even after I ordered you to stay clear. And now your fingers are dirty. Which is okay. That's what happens in life. Nobody but a dullard stays clean. So tomorrow morning, bright and early, I have a little transaction to make. And I figure, what with you being a man and all now, maybe you got the need and the desire to accompany me on this transaction."

He paused and waited for my response. But when I remained motionless and entirely mute he pushed on. "Of course, if you don't wanna come with me, no sweat. You can always hang here, kid, and play grab-ass with your pals, call your mommy and your girl. I won't make you go. You can't make a boy be a man."

He left that last dig hanging there in the air while time slipped away.

I had questions, a million questions. How did he know so much? How did he know what thoughts I had in my head? And what did he have in store for Mr. Homer Otis? Big Jack hadn't mentioned Homer's name even once since the one mention way back east in Pennsylvania or Ohio.

But it didn't seem like a good time to ask about any of that stuff. Asking Big Jack anything at all, even what time we'd be rising in the a.m., seemed weak, unmanly. So I kept my mouth closed up like a trap.

Big Jack said, "You know, kid, it's ironic. The only reason your mother and your grandparents gave the green light for this little trip is because of all your recent screw-ups. They actually thought spending time with me might help straighten you out. They must've been at their wit's end. And over what? You cracking up that crappy little tin Volkswagen? Hell, if you'd driven the VW like you drove the van the other day no one would've been the wiser. The way you drove that van you could limousine the President from the White House to Camp David. And as for that caper down on Bull's Island, who gives a rat's ass about a few sticks of lumber? Sure, I'm your father and I'm supposed to tell you not to wreck cars and steal property. I'm supposed to tell you to be a good little boy and respect your elders. I'm supposed to tell you to be a law-abiding, politically correct little American. Well sorry, kid, that ain't my style. Life's mostly about screwing up from time to time, driving off the bloody road. Sure, if it looked to me like you were on some crazy-ass path, hell bent on a life of crime and thuggery, I'd step in and try to right the listing ship. But you're a good kid. With a conscience. Just trying to figure out how to take care of yourself. Because, boy, if there's one thing I know, you got to take care of yourself. I've been doing it since I was sixteen, so I know. A man gets in your way and won't move, you got to move him. You can't be waiting around for someone else to do the job. Not me. Not your mother. Not your grandfather. Not God Almighty."

Big Jack wound down then. Some more time passed. I stood there, frozen.

Big Jack put me on the spot. "So, kid, what do you say?"

"About what?"

"About tomorrow. You in or you out? Going or staying?"

Before I had time to think I heard myself say, "I'm... I'm in... I'm going."

Big Jack nodded. "Glad to hear it, kid. You know why? Because this business is about you. In a few short years your skinny little ass is going off to college to get properly educated so you can make a difference in the world. It's my job to pay for that education. That's what's in the trailer, kid. A goddamn first class Ivy League education."

I could feel my heart trying to explode through my chest. I didn't know what to say or do. I could hardly breath. I thought I might cry. Before I did I quick shed my clothes and slipped between the sheets. Where I lay trembling till dawn.

The Ballgame

Mom had it figured wrong. Big Jack showed for the game, though I can tell you he made me wait. He made me worry.

We were the home team so we took the field first. I jogged out to right, making sure not to step on the third base line on my way across the infield. Baseball players have a lot of superstitions, and this ballplayer's no exception. Stepping over baselines was at the top of my list. I knew if I stepped on the line I'd for certain make an error that same inning. It had happened a time or two already and no way did I want it to happen again. Especially not in a game as big as this one.

I played catch with our center fielder, Rodney Luster, while our pitcher, Clem Tucker, a southpaw with a vicious curve, warmed up. Clem had excellent stuff but I hated when he pitched. He'd watched way too many big league ballgames and had developed this excruciatingly slow style. Clem would walk around the mound, rub the ball, leave the mound, knock dirt off his cleats, rub the ball some more, and then, maybe, if the stars were all aligned properly, he might actually deliver a pitch. Usually a wicked curve the batter would miss by a mile. Or if the batter did make contact the ball usually dribbled out to second or short with no zip at all. I'd played a couple games with Clem on the mound and never once touched the ball in right field. Which was good for our won/loss record, but dull as dead dynamite out where I waited.

So the game got underway and it took like an hour to get through the first couple innings. The pace of play dragged. I had plenty of time out in right to observe the crowd. Our team occupied the dugout along the third base line. Behind the dugout was a set of bleachers where families, friends, and fans sat and rooted for the Owls. Even before the first pitch was thrown I spotted Gram and Pop sitting in their usual seats halfway up on the right side. They had a cooler with Diet Pepsi for Gram and a couple of ice cold beers for Pop. You weren't allowed to have alcoholic beverages on the grounds at South Hunterdon High, but nobody, not even Police Chief Walters, would've dared tell Tom Middleton he couldn't enjoy a cold one while watching his grandson play ball.

At the top of the bleachers I spotted Amy with her two best pals, Alison and Karen. Amy shouted constant encouragement to me. When I came to the plate in the 3rd with no one on and no one out, Amy hollered loud enough for everyone in the county to hear, "Come on, Josh, knock one out of the park!"

Which I tried to do but instead whiffed on three straight sliders.

Clem hit next. He whacked a hard shot into left. It looked like it might clear the 7-foot wall that wrapped around the outfield. The wall wore an excess of advertisements, including a bright red one where I played in right: MIDDLETON OIL SUPPLY. Pop had sprung for the ad after I made the club.

The left fielder for Watchung went back after Clem's shot, all the way to the dirt track beneath the wall. The crowd stood and roared. Clem rounded first and headed for second. The left fielder held high his glove. And splat! The ball landed in the pocket and disappeared—nothing more than a long out.

At the end of three it was Warriors zip and Owls zip.

Mom arrived in a flurry in the top of the 4th.

I say flurry because she had to say hey and have a little chat with everyone in the bleachers before she finally settled next to Gram. She worked the stands like she was running for Mayor. I would've been embarrassed only I'd years ago grown accustomed to her ways.

All through the 4th and 5th innings I kept my eye peeled for a couple of dudes. Mr. Homer Otis for one. And Big Jack Tailor for another. Neither showed.

The 5th inning came and went. So did the 6th. Still no sign of Homer or Jack. Not much action in the game either. At the end of six we still had a tie ballgame. No runs, no errors, just a few scattered hits.

I really had no reason other than a boy's optimism to think my dad would show for the game. History certainly said he wouldn't show. I nevertheless kept a steady eye on the stands hoping to spot him. But pitch after pitch, out after out, inning after inning, Big Jack failed to show. By the top of the 7th I'd pretty much given up on the old boy.

But sure enough, in the bottom of the 7th, I stepped out of the dugout, grabbed a couple bats, and walked into the on-deck circle. And son of a sister there he stood—Big Jack Tailor—behind the backstop, his arms up over his head, his fingers laced through the chain link fence.

"Hey, kid," he said, easy as can be, like we'd just shared breakfast together that morning, bacon and eggs, like a year or more hadn't past since he'd last showed up out of the blue.

But hey who was counting? Not me, not now, now was now and that's all that mattered.

"Hey," I said, my heart charging like a tiger and a lump bigger than a baseball lodged in my throat.

He locked eyes with me. "So you gonna give us a little bingo, kid? Get us a base runner, steal second, score a run, put the Owls on the board? Hey? Huh? What do you say? You can do it. I know you can. Got no doubts at all."

I nodded but couldn't speak and then Angel Garcia struck out and it was my turn to hit. The brain's sometimes capable of an incredible amount of stimuli and this was definitely one of those times. On my way to the batter's box about a zillion bits of data zapped around my head like insects swarming an outdoor lantern. I thought about the last time Big Jack had seen me play ball. It had been a while, several years, maybe all the way back to my Little League days. Then I remembered no, it'd been more recent, he'd showed up at a game a couple years earlier but he'd been soused and noisier than a bent fan, badgering Mom and calling the ump a bum after the ump called me out at a close play at the plate. Big Jack had come right out onto the field ranting and cursing. It took half a dozen fathers to calm him down and drag him away. And then Chief Walters pulled up in his squad car and threw Big Jack in jail for a night to teach him some social skills and decent manners. All in all it had been a rough go and I'd done my best to erase the whole mess from memory.

Then, still on my way to the batter's box, I got to thinking about my little brother Jake, and how he'd died, and how Big Jack had cried and cried for days and days till I began to think he'd never stop, maybe he'd cry till his tears flooded the house and washed us all straight into the Delaware. But then he got into a bottle of Jim Beam to no doubt take away the pain and the tears, but the booze made him mean as sin and he got in a big fight with Mom and busted up some furniture and just about everything in the house made of glass. But he never busted Mom up, never once, never laid a mean hand on her ever, except of course for that Toyota Sell-A-Thon debacle. After he sobered up Mom did what she always did—she took his head in her hands and kissed him on the forehead and on the cheeks and finally on the lips, and sure enough, you got it, they both commenced sobbing like babies over the loss of little Jake. I was just five years old at the time but I watched it all through the rails of the banister at the top of the stairs. And thought this was the normal ways of the world.

An emotional thunderstorm every goddamn minute of it.

And finally I reached the batter's box and I heard Mom and Gram and Pop and Amy shouting my name, urging me on, cheering for me to make something happen for the South Hunterdon Owls. I could hear the whole crowd yelling and I could see the pitcher on the mound rubbing the ball staring in at me trying to get in my head. And out of the corner of my eye I could see Big Jack, calm and cool, over against the fence, his fingers still laced through the mesh. Even with all the noise and chaos he spoke low. "A little bingo's all we need, kiddo. Relax, it's a game. Just a game. A base runner. A man on first. Just put the bat on the ball and use your speed."

I didn't dare look at him, but I gave a quick nod anyway. Then I stepped into the box and took my stance. I went through my normal routine—knocked the dirt off my cleats, adjusted my batter's glove, made sure my helmet was secure.

And then, practically before I knew it, the first pitch, a fastball, was by me for a called strike.

The crowd groaned.

"Come on, kid," came the low voice, "see it. Feel it. Focus."

Strike two.

"Whattaya," the voice asked, "up there to make a goddamn out? To go down without a struggle? Life's for swinging, kid. Make something happen."

The pitcher wound up. And delivered. Right away I knew it would be low and outside. Way outside. But Big Jack had me jazzed up. No way did I want to strike out, to go down without swinging. So despite the pitch diving toward the dirt I felt my feet and legs twitch into action. I crouched lower. I reached out and down and put the bat in motion. A split second later bat and ball made contact. The ball dribbled off the bat but at least it was in play and headed down the third base line. I dropped the bat and fled for first. Speed's my best weapon so I knew I had a chance.

"Pour it on, kid," encouraged the voice. "Give it all you got."

The third baseman picked up the slow roller, wheeled, and threw to first. But a fraction too late. I'd already hit the bag and crossed into foul territory. The Owls had a base runner.

Clem stepped into the batter's box. I looked into the dugout to get the sign from Coach Kinum. He wanted me to stay put. No stealing, at least not yet. My eyes moved out of the dugout and fell upon the tall sturdy looking dude leaning against the fence. The dude in the tight gray tee shirt. The dude with the thick 'stache and the penetrating blue eyes and wavy dark brown hair. The dude, my old man, Big Jack. His head gave a quick nod toward second base. And I remembered what he'd said, "A little bingo, steal a base, score a run."

I took a good lead and on the first pitch sprinted recklessly for second. Clem swung and missed but I easily made it in safely when the catcher's throw reached the shortstop high and wide.

Coach Kinum cheered and applauded along with the rest of the crowd but I knew he'd chew me out later for disobeying his signs. Too bad Coach didn't know the big man off to his right was in charge of the show now. I'd do whatever Big Jack told me, just like I'd always done, no questions asked. He was, after all, despite everything, my father, the Lord of the Jungle. A boy needs to listen to his father and no one else no matter what.

A couple more pitches and Clem, like Angel, struck out. So now we had me on second with two down and our leadoff man, Pete Gruntfest, at the plate. A base hit and I'd score, putting us on top 1-zip.

Coach Kinum again gave me the sign to hold my ground. He chased that up with a hard stare.

I didn't allow myself even a glance Big Jack's way.

The Passage

But then Pete, usually our best hitter, swung at the first pitch and missed by a mile. The Warriors' pitcher had a wicked slider.

I couldn't stop myself. I glanced over at Big Jack. He hadn't moved a muscle. But now he gave me a subtle nod toward third. I shook my head—no way, Coach'll kill me if I get bagged. Big Jack narrowed his eyes and gave me another nod.

Pete swung again during all this and once more missed by a mile. I could see he had no confidence at all.

I made up my mind and took a big lead.

The pitcher wound up and threw high, hoping to get Pete to chase a bad one. I right away took off. The catcher leapt out of his crouch, caught the ball, and threw down to third. Just by the thinnest hair I slid in under the tag. Safe! The crowd went berserk. I jumped up and with heart pounding dusted myself off. No way did I look in the dugout. I could feel Coach's eyes burning holes in my back.

I glanced at Big Jack. He smiled, gave me a thumb's up. The fact I was bucking Coach Kinum, spitting in the face of authority, I think made it all the more entertaining for my old man.

Pete fouled off the next pitch. And the next pitch after that. He hung tough.

The crowd continued to cheer. The pitcher looked rattled. I danced around on the third base line. He did his best to ignore me. He wound up, reared back, and threw the next pitch with everything he had. He overthrew. The ball dove, hit the ground in front of home plate, took a nasty hop, and skipped by the catcher all the way to the backstop.

I didn't hesitate. I sprinted down the line.

The catcher threw aside his mask and went after the ball. The pitcher flew off the mound and raced, same as me, toward home. The catcher picked up the ball, whipped it to the pitcher. In a split second I had to decide if I should barrel into the pitcher or slide into home.

"Slide, Josh!" I heard Coach Kinum shout. "Slide, slide!"

But another voice reached me too. "Cream him, Josh! Show him who's boss! Knock him on his ass!"

We all reached home plate together—me, the pitcher, and the baseball. The ball smacked into the pitcher's glove with a loud thwack! The pitcher turned to put the tag on me. But Jack Tailor's boy was ready. I folded my arms across my chest and barreled full speed into the Warriors' pitcher like a pulling guard leading the charge down field on a last gasp drive. I hit him legally, but with everything I had.

The pitcher went flying. The ball did too.

I stepped on home plate. The umpire gave the safe sign.

Owls 1, Warriors 0.

I hadn't scored many runs that season, but I'd scored a big one on a cheap single, two steals, and a wild pitch. The crowd went crazy. Big Jack gave me his easy smile on my way to the dugout. Coach Kinum gave me a stare and shook his head but patted me on the back as I headed for the bench and the adulation of my teammates.

Not much happened after that till the top of the ninth. That's when the wind picked up. It had been as calm as Gram's disposition, but out of nowhere it started to blow a dusty gale just as we stepped out of the dugout to take the field for the final inning. As I approached the third base line that wind grabbed my cap and tore it loose. I went after it, but lunging forward I inadvertently stepped on the foul line. Right then and there I mulled over asking Coach Kinum to take me out of the ballgame. I knew nothing good could come of me stepping on that chalk. But I took my position in right field, all the while praying no ball would come my way.

Fortunately, the first batter for the Warriors popped up to short and the second batter grounded out to third. And just like that we were one out away from advancing to the next round of the playoffs. But then Clem, who must've been dog tired by that time, walked the next batter on four pitches, sending Coach Kinum on a slow stroll to the mound. Out there in right, miles from the action, I wasn't privy to their conversation. But I learned later Coach wanted to pull Clem but Clem convinced Coach he had enough left in the tank to finish the job. Coach thought it over, then told Clem he could have one more batter. Clem nodded and Coach made the long walk back to the dugout.

Well, it didn't take long for matters to grow troublesome. Less than a minute by my account. Clem wound up and made his delivery. The pitch had nothing on it at all. It flew straight and slow and right down the pipe. A hitter's dream pitch. A puff pitch. A batting practice pitch. The eyes of the Warrior batter grew wide and happy as that pitch made its way lazily toward the plate. He turned his shoulders, leveled his swing, and CRACK! the sound of ball on bat exploded across the universe. Right away the ball got up into that wind. A wind blowing hard and strong and true. Higher and higher that baseball flew. And much to my dismay she flew straight in my direction.

It had been a long dull day in right field. I'd seen no action, not a single ball had been hit my way. Not on the grass or in the air. But suddenly here came this towering fly ball steering straight for me and my bad luck like a heat seeking missile. She looked almost otherworldly up there. I watched it and for quite some time I didn't think of it as a mere baseball. But a baseball it was and coming rapidly onto my radar screen. I hoped for a second it would sail out of reach, beyond the wall, beyond my responsibility. But that was no good. No good at all. That meant a home run and us suddenly trailing 2-1.

No, I had to get after that ball, track it down, haul it in. But my feet felt stuck in concrete. I couldn't move. I'd stepped on the third base line and now I'd have to pay the piper. The whole situation had big fat error written all over it.

I heard voices. The voices of my teammates. And my coach. And my mom. And my grandparents. And my girlfriend. And the crowd. "Come on, Josh! Come on, you can do it! You can make the catch!"

And finally my dad, Big Jack Tailor, standing on the top row of the bleachers now, legs apart, arms outstretched and in motion. "Move, Josh! Come on, boy, make a move!"

So I did. I moved. I backpedaled. But I quickly realized backpedaling wouldn't get the job done. That ball was higher than a skyscraper. And still soaring. I turned my back on home plate and started running, sprinting toward the right field wall. Maybe, I hoped, just maybe I could run that sucker down.

"You can do it, Josh!" the voice assured me. "You can haul her in, boy!"

I could see the ball—white and streaking across the early evening sky. It began to fall. Finally. All I wanted was for it to fall into the soft webbing of my outstretched leather glove. All I wanted was to make the catch, be the hero. The third string utility outfielder who made good.

"Go, Josh!" Big Jack shouted above the wild roar of the crowd. "Give it your all!"

I listened and did what he told me. I obeyed my father's orders. Forget about being the hero. Forget about the playoffs and getting to the championship game. Just make the catch. Make it for Big Jack. For the old man. It doesn't matter what a father does. It doesn't matter where he goes or how long he's gone. He's still the man. The only real man in a boy's life. The only man in the world you have to impress.

I ran and ran. And while I ran I kept my eyes riveted on that

The Passage

baseball. It fell faster now. The wind had vanished as mysteriously as it had arrived. The world felt silent and still. It was just me and that ball. And Big Jack.

I had a bead on her. Dead aim. All of a sudden I felt like I could make the catch, make it even though I'd stepped on the third base foul line.

"Put yourself out on the edge, Josh! On the edge!"

The ball fell like a stone. I reached out. I reached all the way out. I reached out and ran as fast as I could. The ball dropped as gently as a feather into my outstretched glove. I had it! I had it! I definitely had it.

And then a split second later—WHAM! I ran full speed into the right field wall. I plowed directly into that big red advertisement for MIDDLETON OIL SUPPLY.

And knocked myself out cold.

The Chaneys

Big Jack rousted me even earlier than usual. He ordered me into Levi's, hiking boots, and flannel shirt. I did so without a peep.

Outside I could see my breath—big white billows every time I exhaled. We got in the van about the time the shadows started to lift. Not much talking between us as we pulled out of the parking lot of the Red Lion Wyoming Inn. We drove south through the dead quiet streets of Jackson. After a couple miles we turned west onto Wyoming Route 22. Right away we started to climb. The van strained some against the steep grade and the weight of all those firearms. And maybe me and Big Jack strained some too against the weight of the past.

After a fifteen minute uphill push we hit Teton Pass at almost 8500 feet. The temperature plunged, bottomed out at 28 degrees, but man oh man what a view! Big Jack pulled onto the shoulder so we could take a look. To the north the early morning sunlight glistened off the high snow-capped peaks.

"The one jutting into the sky like a church steeple," Big Jack told me, "that's Grand Teton! Almost fourteen thousand."

I'd never once been to church with Dad (Mom or Gram or Pop always took me), but standing there staring at those peaks made me want to drink from the Holy Grail. Or maybe I was just dehydrated from the beer we'd drunk the night before.

Big Jack pointed out a few more of the Teton Peaks—Moran and Ranger and I think Huckleberry—and all the while I imagined us on a regular family holiday, you know, the Tailors do the Rocky Mountains kind of thing. Too bad Jake was dead and Mom hated Dad's guts. Oh yeah, fantasies are sweet but the truth was this: Big Jack and I drove down off that the pass, crossed into Idaho, and went to meet the militia.

After a long descent we reached the valley floor. We drove through some small Idaho towns—Victor, Driggs, Tetonia. The Teton Range—jagged and snow-capped—loomed high and majestic off to the east.

Feeling the need to know our position, I kept one eye on the map and one eye on the scenery. But when Big Jack turned off the main road, our Rand McNally pretty quick grew useless. It only showed interstates, highways, and a few major byways.

We made a couple more turns, went around some tight bends, and pretty soon I didn't have a clue where we were or how to get back to the highway. And maybe Big Jack didn't either since he kept glancing at directions scribbled onto a pad of paper.

Eventually we turned onto a dirt road. "Remember, Josh," Big Jack advised, "no matter what happens, the key is cool. You gotta stay cool. The low-life scumballs coming to a future near you are like dogs. They can smell fear. So it's best not to ooze any."

Oh yeah, Big Jack liked a life of high stimulation. This we had. I felt sweaty and twitchy all over.

Half a mile or so down that dusty dirt road we came to a high mesh fence with a closed steel gate. Two guys dressed in full camo and high black boots and toting guns similar to the ones in the trailer stood guard.

"This an army base?" I asked Dad.

He gave me that patented Jack Tailor smile. "Not exactly, kid."

A large metal sign hung across the gate: PRIVATE PROPERTY. ABSOLUTELY NO TRESPASSING. THIS INCLUDES ALL LAW ENFORCEMENT PERSONNEL AND GOVERNMENT OFFICIALS. UNAUTHORIZED INTRUDERS WILL BE SHOT.

Big Jack saw me reading. "Don't sweat it, kid. These guys are way more bark than bite. And besides, we'll soon be authorized."

My heart firing like a machine gun, Dad pulled up to the front gate. One of the guards approached. He had a big square face, a shaved head, no sign of a smile.

"Don Rodgers," Big Jack told the guard, "to see Will Chaney."

The guard demanded two forms of ID plus the vehicle registration before he'd consider Big Jack's request. I'd never heard of this Don Rodgers character, but Big Jack, a man of many aliases, must've had the proper credentials. After a couple minutes on his walkie-talkie the square-faced guard swung open the gate and waved us through.

"What we have here, Finnegan Tailor," Big Jack explained as we drove down that dusty road, "is the headquarters and training facility for FIRM. FIRM's the slightly skewed acronym for the Free Idaho Rightwing Militia. Basically FIRM is a bunch of angry white guys who for unfathomable reasons hate blacks, Jews, Muslims, Catholics, probably women, most assuredly the Federal government, and God knows who else. They have themselves a little pseudo army up here in the woods of eastern Idaho and they really, really like guns. Which is why we're here this morning. We have guns to sell and they, supposedly, have the money to buy. We'll see."

A thousand questions popped into my totally naïve brain, but before I could ask even one my attention got diverted by some more dudes in camo in a dusty field off to our left. There must've been a couple dozen of them. They'd set up an obstacle course with old tires and ropes and a log wall and this stupid little puddle of a pond. It was like something you might see in a movie about guys who join the Marines and go through basic training. Only these guys were mostly middle age fatsos who kept stumbling over tires and bumbling over walls and falling on their faces in the shallow and muddy pond.

"Probably some new recruits from the Midwest 'burbs," said Big Jack, his mouth and eyes grinning wide. "The tougher times get, what with war and terrorism and high unemployment and government trampling on our civil liberties, the more angry white guys sick of taking Prozac and Viagra crawl out of the bushes seeking alternative means of entertainment and retribution."

I didn't really know what he was talking about, but I gave a nod anyway.

A little farther along, the van and trailer kicking up clouds of dust on that dry dirt road, we came upon the firing range. About a hundred feet from the road a dozen camo-clad men stood, kneeled, and squatted behind a row of hay bales. They fired at targets in the distance with shotguns, rifles, and pistols.

Dad, still smiling, just shook his head and kept driving.

"Why," I asked, "do you want to sell guns to these idiots?"

Big Jack gave me a wink. "An excellent question, kid. And I can tell you this—I enjoy it. I like all phases of the operation—the acquisition, transportation, distribution, collection. But what really drives me is the same motivation that drives anyone to sell anything to anybody—money. Oh yeah, believe you me, it's not politics with Jack Tailor, son. No way. Couldn't give a toot about the Right or the Left or the right or the wrong. It's the Almighty Dollar. Guns for Greenbacks is an ancient American tradition."

I did my best to process all that while we continued along the dusty road.

A few minutes later we pulled up in front of a large garage with half a dozen bays and doors high and wide enough to house tanks and armored personnel carriers. Off to the left was a regular size door. It swung open. Two men emerged. Like the others, they were dressed from head to toe in full Army camouflage. They came slowly toward us.

"So here we go," said my daddy. "Time to do some wheeling and dealing and hopefully even some selling."

Big Jack stepped out of the van. I didn't know if I should step out or stay in. It took me a while to decide. Finally I stepped out. By the time I did Big Jack was busy shaking hands with those camoed gentlemen from FIRM. All three had smiles on their faces, which I thought boded well.

I came around the side of the van. Dad grabbed my shoulder and introduced me as Don Jr. I didn't make real good eye contact but I shook their hands—big clammy mitts. They were a father/son team too. (Did Big Jack know this in advance? Was this why he'd brought me along? I didn't know and never found out.) Their names were Will and Pat Chaney. They had large square bodies. If they'd been appliances—definitely refrigerators. Despite the boxy physiques Will and Pat had soft baby faces. Smooth and pudgy. I wanted to grab the excess flesh on Pat's cheek and give it a squeeze.

Will was maybe ten years older than Dad, Pat ten years older than me. While Will and Dad talked it over, me and Pat kicked at the dust under our boots. I had on my very cool low-slung Vasque Alpha hiking boots, Pat a pair of high black Army boots. I was just happy I didn't have the cuffs of my pants tucked into my boots the way Pat did. I didn't say a word but he looked like a first class doo-wad.

Will babbled on and on about the Second Amendment and what would happen to those "stinking, murdering a-hole terrorists if they ever set foot in Idaho." He said FIRM would slaughter them like filthy swine, make them wish they'd never left their dirty desert hovels. "And I can say the same," he added, his blubbery face dead serious, "about those corrupt vermin in Washington who continue to degrade the Constitution and mess with my God-given freedoms."

Big Jack gave this barrage an equally serious nod of agreement, but I had my doubts. I think Big Jack was just playing possum, doing his sales tricks, same way he used to do selling Hondas and Porsches and Buicks.

After Will wore down Dad (Don) said, "Why don't we check out the merchandise."

So we all went around to the back of the trailer. Big Jack turned to me. "Say, son, you got the key to the lock?"

The key to the lock? I didn't have the stupid key. I'd never even seen the damn key. Retro must've had the key.

Dad let me sweat for a while on this, then he gave me a wink and reached into his pocket. "Oh, sorry, Little Don, seems I got the key right here."

Yup, even in the midst of a stressful, wet-pit arms negotiation with fat, sadistic militiamen, Big Jack had time to needle me, work me over.

He removed the lock and swung open the trailer door. There sat the gun boxes and the boxes of RPGs, just the way me and Retro and Bones had left them. Big Jack had this battery-powered screwdriver all ready to go. He quickly removed the screws from one of the boxes and lifted off the lid. The Chaney boys, anxious for a look, pressed close at the back of the trailer. They were lathered up like a pair of pooches waiting on their midday kibble. Me, I kept glancing over my shoulder. With all those firearms in tow I thought for sure we'd be ambushed by those portly dudes out on the firing range.

Dad lifted out one of the rifles. Instead of handing it over to the Chaney boys he stepped off the trailer and pretty much elbowed them out of the way. He took a couple strides into the morning sunshine and began his spiel. "You boys are looking at the latest and greatest version of the venerable and incomparable M-16. All the rifles I have for you today are one hundred percent U.S. Army regulation. Manufactured for automatic operation. Not converted. Not altered. This baby will empty a full clip faster than you can say 'Run for your life or die, greaseball!' All rifles are fresh from the factory. Neither used or abused. One hundred percent guaranteed for your satisfaction!"

All the while Big Jack gave his spiel he displayed the formidable looking rifle at various angles. It definitely looked like a lethal killing machine. Cold black steel. The barrel, wet with oil to keep away any hint of moisture or rust, glistened in the sunlight.

"You boys know the deal," Big Jack (Don Rodgers) continued. "One thousand one hundred and eighty-eight dollars a piece for these babies. A steep price, I know, but one we agreed upon some time ago. And to be honest, well worth the money for this kind of superb quality delivered covertly to your doorstep. Any questions?"

Will Chaney had a hint of spittle on his chin. I think he might've been drooling over the goods during Big Jack's presentation. Will said, "No, Don, no questions. The merchandise looks exceptional. But we may have one small problem."

Big Jack rested the barrel of the rifle across his shoulder. "A small problem, Will? At this late stage? I don't like the sound of that. Oh no I do not."

"I know, Don, but—"

Big Jack held up his hand. "Will, I hate to interrupt, but do you have any idea what I go through to get these weapons? The contacts I have to make? The risks I have to take? I'm not delivering pizza pies or Baby Ruth bars here, Will. I'm delivering illegal firearms I toted across a dozen state lines. So let's not stand around talking problems. I have no time for problems. You ordered forty-five rifles—that's fifty-three thousand four hundred sixty dollars worth of M-16s. Here they are, and now I want my money."

By the time he slowed up Big Jack had swung from cool and smooth to hot and rougher than three-day stubble. Oh yeah, the old boy was plenty riled. Or at least he sounded so. It could've been an act. Either way I thought him one brave dude. I mean we were hard on enemy terrain. But there stood Big Jack—on the offense, attacking, all guns a-blaze. The man had cojones as big as baseballs.

Will Chaney moved immediately to appease. "Look, Don, we want the rifles. In fact, we could use a few extras. That's not the problem."

"What's the problem, Will? Your briefs too tight? Your boy here need braces?"

This crack caused Pat Chaney to grow a furrow as deep as a ditch between his eyes. He took a couple steps toward my dad. Big Jack didn't budge an inch. Will Chaney put out his thick hairy arm, stopping his son's advance.

"Now come on," Will insisted, "let's all just settle down."

Big Jack said, "Alrightee, Will, lay your problem on me, but be quick about it."

Will Chaney nodded. "It's really just a logistical issue, Don. Most of the men who ordered a rifle have requested the opportunity to handle the weapon, fire a few rounds before forking over the cash. Think of it as test-driving a new car. Or maybe—"

"You gotta be bullshattin' me, Will!" Big Jack had his decibels up now.

I guess bravery's a combination of arrogance and stupidity but clearly Big Jack possessed it. He walked right between the baby-faced Chaney boys and stepped back into the trailer. He laid that rifle carefully back in the storage box, covered it with an oil-soaked cloth, then replaced the screws in the lid with his battery-powered screwdriver.

I felt pretty sure fat Pat would climb in there after him, but father Will held his boy at bay. "Don, be reasonable. We're talking major dollars here these boys are spending on these weapons. They just want to handle the goods. They need to—"

"Not a chance, Will," Big Jack announced. "Absolutely no way. The possibility's not even open for discussion." Then he turned to me. "Let's roll, Little Don. We're outta here." Cool as a cougar he stepped out of the trailer, locked her up, and steered for the driver's side of the van. I made a quick dash for the passenger side.

Will pursued. "Dammit, Don, would you hang on a second."

But Don (Dad) wouldn't hang on. He climbed into the van, slammed the door, and started the engine.

Will Chaney stepped up to the open window. "Don, come on, we don't want this deal to fall apart. We've been months putting it together."

Big Jack let out a noisy sigh. "We had a deal, Will. The details were simple: I bring you guns, you hand me cash. I'm not hanging around while these morons play with their new toys. My ass is on the line here. I got enemies on all sides. I got the FBI. I got ATF. I got local law enforcement. I got you guys trying to intimidate me. So the answer's no. No way! You militia boys know the M-16 is a first class piece of equipment, the best money can buy. That's why you want them. So hear me, Will: I'm leaving, getting the hell off the Ponderosa. You got two hours to get my fifty-three grand collected into one small bag. And I'll be counting it so I want plenty of large bills. If you don't call within two hours the deal's off."

Big Jack wrote a number on a slip of paper. He balled the paper up and tossed it out the window. It landed on the dusty ground.

Will Chaney looked at the ball of paper for a second or two, then he bent over and with a grimace picked it up.

Dad put the transmission in gear. He swung the van and trailer in a tight circle and headed back down that dusty dirt road.

I had a profusion of sweat pouring off my face. And not because it was hot but because I was scared shitless. I asked my dad, "You think they'll stop us? You know, at the gate? Prevent us from leaving?"

Big Jack looked over at me, real serious. "You know, Finnegan, they just might do that. What do you think we should do?"

I shrugged. How was I supposed to know?

"Maybe," he suggested, "we should pull over. Grab a couple of those M-16s out of the trailer in case we have to blast our way outta here."

This scenario caused even more sweat to pour off my brow. It came in great torrents. "Really? You mean, like, we could have a shootout?"

"Yeah, a shootout, kid. Like in the movies. Shootout at the OK Corral. The Outlaw Josey Wales. But hey, I ain't worried. You're a tough guy. You can handle yourself."

I swallowed hard. "I don't know. I mean, I've never fired a gun or anything."

Still serious as a monk, Big Jack gave me a nod. "Well, kid, there's always a first time." He slowed the van to a crawl just beyond the driving range.

Panic setting in, I said, "Maybe we should gun the engine and break through the gate."

"You think?"

"Yeah."

That's when Big Jack accelerated and allowed a big bad-ass smile to spread across his face. And I knew right off I'd been had. He'd cornered me, seen me yellow, then backed off and left me hanging.

"Just messing with you, Finnegan. Playing you like a git-tar. These jackasses wouldn't have the guts to move on a pack of stray dogs. Besides, it's just business."

And sure enough, a couple minutes later we passed through the front gate of FIRM untouched and unfettered.

I felt bad that Big Jack had seen me yellow, but what could I do?

Really nothing but vow to myself to act brave in the hours and days and years ahead. Act brave and be a man.

Big Jack had no problem finding his way back to the main road. He didn't need to study those directions even once.

"So," I asked, after wiping myself dry, "will they call?"

Big Jack didn't take his eyes off the road. "Does a bear crap in the woods?"

I supposed they probably did.

Twenty minutes later we were back in the small town of Driggs cozied up to the counter at Tops Diner with a few slow-moving locals. It had been a long and stressful morning. I was hungry as a wolf in winter. I ordered eggs over easy with toast and home fries and a side of pancakes. Dad ordered coffee, black.

Before any of it arrived his cell phone rang. "Yeah?"

Pause.

"That's right."

Pause.

"I don't see why not."

Pause.

"Alrightee then. One hour. No problem."

Big Jack ended the call. He winked at me again, then made a clicking sound with his mouth. "The Chaney boys have decided to be reasonable."

I nodded, even though I'd been hoping not to hear from the Chaneys. If they'd stayed mute we could've enjoyed our breakfast, moseyed back to Jackson, fetched Retro and Bones, and been on our way to Montana.

My breakfast came. Three platefuls.

Dad drank his coffee, threw a ten on the counter, and got up to go. "I'll be next door at the used car lot when you're done, kid. Take your time."

Used car lot? I hadn't noticed a used car lot? What, I wondered, did Big Jack want to go there for?

I ate my eggs and sopped up the runny yolks with the toast and gobbled down the home fries and pancakes in a flash. Nevertheless, by the time I got over to Owen Baker's Used Car Emporium, Dad and Owen Baker were in the final stages of cutting a deal. My dad loved to cut deals, especially car deals. Owen, a slim dude with a thick well-waxed moustache, looked pretty pleased with whatever deal they'd just cut.

So did Big Jack. "Yo, Josh," he called, "come check out our latest procurement!"

A jet-black Ford Excursion stood there looking massive in the middle of Owen's lot. I mean huge. A monster. Biggest SUV on the planet, I think the ads claimed, with the exception of the super-sized Hummer like the one Homer owned.

"She's almost ten years old but only sixty-two thousand miles on her," Dad told me. "Triton V-10 engine. Enough torque to pull a house. Every option under the sun."

I took a look at that beast and wondered how Owen Baker out here in Driggs, Idaho had come by it. Before I could ask Dad said, "Me and Owen have a few details to hunker over, Josh. We'll be inside. Shouldn't be but a few minutes."

I climbed up into the Excursion. And I mean climbed. A stepladder would've been helpful. Behind the wheel I felt like the pilot of an

18-wheeler. The cockpit was high and wide. The side-view mirrors stuck out halfway to Wyoming. Inside she could only be described as plush. Comfy leather seats. 12 shot CD. Power everything. The boys, I knew, would be mighty impressed with this new ride. They'd mostly kept their traps shut about the Town & Country, but I knew the minivan had been a major disappointment.

But why, I wondered, did Dad want to get rid of her? She was practically brand new, had like a hundred miles on her when he'd picked me up back in Bridgeton. Why buy this behemoth right in the middle of the trip? Just for fun? Or was it some kind of a strategic move? A way to throw off the FBI, the ATF, local law enforcement? I didn't know and felt pretty sure Big Jack wouldn't be a fountain of information.

I climbed back to terra firma just as Dad came out of Owen's office—nothing but a ratty looking construction trailer up on concrete blocks. "Hop in the van, kid," Big Jack ordered. "We got work to do and we gotta be quick about it."

Dad pulled the van and trailer behind Tops Diner. We folded the second and third row seats into the floor of the van making a long flat surface. Next we opened the trailer and moved four boxes of M-16s into the van. Those boxes were plenty heavy. I had to struggle and strain to hold up my end of the operation. The boxes fit like a fine Italian suit into the back of the van. Big Jack closed the rear hatch on the forty-eight M-16s.

We locked up the trailer and drove back to Owen's Used Car Emporium. Big Jack pulled up in front of Owen's office. "Follow me," he ordered. We hopped out of the van, me for the last time, and met at the back. Dad disconnected the trailer from the van.

"Okay, kid," he told me, "here's the swing. Your job's to stay here and watch over the trailer and our new Excursion. Mr. Owen Baker has some wiring to do, then he's going to hook up the trailer to the truck. He seems like a straight shooter but I want you to keep an eye on him. Make sure the hitch is secure and the brake lights work. Very important those brake lights work, Josh. Hate to get pulled over by a state trooper for a malfunctioning brake light. That could cause all kinds of hell to break loose. Okay? Got it?" He slapped me on the back, hopped back into the van, and peeled out of Owen's gravel parking lot with the pedal to the metal. I didn't have a chance to say a word.

Big Jack, let me tell you, got back a whole lot quicker than I thought he would. In less than an hour and a half. While he was gone me and Owen hooked up the trailer to the Excursion, then filled the Excursion's twin tanks with fuel. Owen, you see, offered a free fill-up with every purchase.

Big Jack arrived back at the Emporium in a cloud of dust. I crossed to the van and right off knew he'd made the deal because the back of the van was dead empty. Nothing in there but air. Which meant Dad's pockets must've been stuffed with cash—over fifty grand!

We quick snapped to it. Big Jack went into Owen's office where he and Owen put the finishing touches on their vehicle swap. They came out of the office together. Jack, screwdriver in hand, removed the license plates from the Chrysler and attached them to the Ford. Then we both shook hands with Owen, climbed up into the truck, got ourselves settled, and made for the exit.

That Excursion was quite a beast. It took a while to get her rolling but with that Triton V-10 she moved along at a nice clip once she had some momentum. We drove through Victor, then swung east into Montana on Route 22. The big Ford had plenty of power to pull us and the trailer up into Teton Pass.

Big Jack pulled over at the same place we'd stopped in the

morning. I got out and once again enjoyed the view while my daddy ever so slightly altered his license plates with the application of a few strips of black electrical tape.

His plates had read: C7I-99F.

Now they read: O7T-88E.

Then he changed the trailer plate entirely. He took off the old Jersey plate and put on a new Idaho plate.

We got back on the road to Jackson. Along the way we had a little chat. Actually, Big Jack chattered and I listened.

"And now here, Josh, is a little fact about those rifles you might find entertaining: the government knows I have them. Yup, that's right. At least one small segment of the government knows. See, the government's a colossal animal. Millions of folks on the payroll. And the one and only way to pay all those folks is to collect taxes. Taxes and more taxes. Taxes out the wazoo. Which is why selling guns on the black market is such a fine and dandy idea. There's no record of sale so I'll never pay any taxes on the dough I got in my pocket. It's one hundred percent tax free."

I considered pointing out the whole enterprise was illegal, but Big Jack beat me off the line. "So here's the thing about the rifles. The FBI, actually one secretive branch of the FBI that concerns itself with fringe groups like FIRM, is in cahoots with the US Army. The US Army has millions of M-16s. More than they know what to do with. So with the FBI looking on they let a few boxes slip through the cracks into the hands of guys like me. They know I'll sell them to the militia boys and other malcontents. Which is exactly what they want. See, the FBI allows my little operation for a couple reasons. First off, it allows them to keep track of the weapons these militia groups possess. And second, any time they feel like cracking down on these crazy whack jobs, they know they can get a warrant, bust in on them, discover large caches of stolen government property, and bring down the long and limber arm of the law. Pretty neat trick, huh?"

I nodded, even though he'd mostly lost me along the way.

"But just because a few G-men know what I'm up to doesn't clear the way. Oh no. I still have other branches of the government hot on my trail. Especially those hard-driving boys from ATF."

"What is the ATF?" I asked.

"Bureau of Alcohol, Tobacco, and Firearms."

I nodded. "I'd been wondering."

"Oh yeah," said Big Jack, "what you have here in America is one very powerful government. One of the most powerful and clever governments ever assembled. They have just about all the angles covered. They've mastered the delicate arts of deception and psychology. They control three hundred million people of all colors and creeds, and only rarely do they resort to violence against their own citizens. They're too shrewd to use violence. Here and there some intimidation, sure, but rarely violence. Very tough to get the best of these boys. They're always ten moves ahead of you. All you can do is play the edges, change your name, keep on the move, and try to have yourself a good time. Know what I mean, kid? Know what I'm saying?"

I told him I did even though I didn't. Not really.

Then he added, "And oh yeah, when the time comes you got to have the power to vanish." He snapped his finger. "You have to be able to disappear. In a flash."

I nodded, but didn't mention him having a lot of experience in that department.

He gave my thigh a squeeze. "You're a good kid, Josh. And smart too. Despite your old man being a lousy father and a loose cannon you're doing just fine. Folks back home see problems. Your mother and grandparents, they're worried, keyed up. But that's because they lead sheltered lives there in Bucolia. They don't have a clue how truly fucked up things are out in the real world. They need to relax. You're gonna be okay. Better than okay. You're not following in your old man's footsteps. No selling cars or driving a truck for my boy. Something more… I don't know… relevant. You got me, kid? You listening? The dough from the sale of these guns? It's yours. And there'll be more. Plenty more. Harvard. Princeton. Yale, for chrissakes."

I felt a tug in my chest. And no, it wasn't heartburn from how fast I'd inhaled those fried eggs. It was me feeling an odd warmth for my old man. It was my heart pulling itself up into my throat as I thought about me and him being blood, about me and him burying the old hatchets, and maybe, maybe even becoming friends.

I said to Big Jack, "The real problem I got back home is Homer Otis."

And Big Jack said, "Yeah, Homer Otis."

And I said, "What are we gonna do about that son of a bitch?"

And Big Jack said, "Like all of his ilk he needs a dose of his own medicine."

And I said, "I think so too."

And Big Jack said, "I think you and me are just the doctors to dole it out."

I wanted to ask him how but I had something else gnawing at me first. "How do you know about Homer being a free swinger anyway? Mom tell you?"

He shook his head but kept his eyes fixed on the road. "Nah, she'd never tell me about that. Too much pride. Your mother likes to paint a rosy picture. Must've damn near killed her to ask for my help in dealing with your screw-ups."

"So how then?"

"I just know is all. Call me psychic. See, you and your mother, you're my wife and son. Sure, your mom and I are divorced and all, but she'll always be my wife. Just like you'll always be my son. It's a man's job to defend and protect his wife and progeny. I got lazy, yeah, let my guard down, and some marauders—one truly foul marauder in particular—managed to slip over the castle wall. So now it's my duty to inflict some damage upon the bastard for his offenses against my family."

"Yeah," I said, my motor humming, "we need to inflict some damage."

And Big Jack said, "Mess him up some."

And I said, "Mess him up plenty."

And Big Jack said, "Maybe we'll just take out the sadistic SOB all together."

Exactly what, I wondered, did that mean? Did it mean what I thought it meant?

But I didn't have time to ask because suddenly we reached Jackson and a few seconds later pulled into the parking lot of the Red Lion Wyoming Inn.

The Invitation

I woke up in the Hunterdon Medical Center, the same hospital where I'd been born. I'd been out cold for six hours following my collision with the right field wall. It was after midnight, dark in that room except for some vague light coming through the window.

At first I thought I was alone. But then I saw Big Jack. Standing steady and still over by the window. And gazing into the darkness at what I didn't know.

"Hey," I said. My head hurt. Like somebody'd been pounding on it with a hammer.

"Hey," he said and turned. "You awake?"

"Yeah. What happened?"

"You don't remember?" My dad looked like a shadow. Like a ghost. I couldn't see his face, not even his eyes.

"I remember running into the wall."

"Oh yeah, you ran into the wall alright. Bam! People as far away as Jersey City heard you run into that wall, kid. Sounded like a couple freight trains colliding."

I laughed. But not for long. My whole body hurt when I laughed. "What about the ball?"

Big Jack thought about it, considered what to tell me. "Yeah, the ball. It was in your glove, kid. You had it. You'd run it down. An awesome effort. A great catch. Willy the Kid Mays couldn't've done it any better. But it didn't stay in there long enough. It dribbled out. Then you collapsed and rolled over on top of it. While the kid on first came all the way around and scored. Your centerfielder had to literally roll you out of the way to get to the ball. By the time he did and threw it into second and the second baseman fired it home the kid who'd hit the ball was already in the dugout eating a wiener and washing it down with a bottle of pap."

My old man. The storyteller.

"So," I asked, "Watchung went ahead two to one?"

Big Jack nodded. "That's right. Then it took the EMT boys forever to clear you off the field. I could see right away you were okay, just a little groggy, but they insisted on fussing over you like a bunch of old hens. And your mother, she totally freaked out. Went running across the outfield grass in her high heels and skin-tight blouse and that skirt practically up to her navel... What's up with those duds, buddy boy? Your mother still think she's eighteen? I mean, she looks good, but hell, not that good. I think she—"

"What about the game?"

"The game, right. So your mother—she's hysterical and screaming at the top of her lungs, 'Is he paralyzed?' 'Will he walk again?' 'Is his head damaged?' Your mother should've been in soaps. More melodramatic than a romance novel."

"The game?" I demanded. "What about the game?"

Big Jack got down to business. The game, after all, was important. "Watchung," he told me, "did no more damage in the top of the ninth. In the bottom of the ninth your South Hunterdon Owls got the leadoff hitter aboard with a bunt, but he never moved into scoring position. A strikeout, an infield pop up, and a weak grounder to first, and that was all she wrote. Final score: Warriors two, Owls one. But it was still a hell of a fine season, kid. Nothing at all to be anything less than one hundred percent proud."

"Well that's just swell," I wanted to proclaim. "Really super of you to say. And hey thanks for being supportive and coming to all the games and a being a standup guy and a first class dad."

I thought that stuff, had it right on the tip of my tongue, but I didn't mutter a word of it. Nope, instead I said, "Yeah, there's always next year."

And then my dad grabbed a chair and pulled it next to the bed and sat down in a puddle of light slicing through the window. I could see his face good now. He looked the way he always looked—geared up, alert, ready for action, a man in perpetual motion. Big Jack, being Irish, did a lot of emoting. Never a dull moment with Big Jack Tailor.

He said, "I got something I want to talk to you about."

"Yeah," I said, "what?"

"The summer."

"What about the summer?"

"You got plans, kid?"

I shrugged.

"What are you gonna do once school's out?" he wanted to know. "Run wild? Get a job? Go to camp? What?"

I wondered if he knew yet about me wrecking the convertible. I wasn't about to tell him. No way. I wasn't about to share much of anything with Big Jack. After all, me and the old man, we had some problems, some issues. So I kept it brief. I said, "I don't know. Nothing special."

"Well look," he said not much above a whisper and leaning closer, "I got plans, big plans, and I think you oughta think about maybe spending the summer with me. Out west. Montana. Big Sky Country. The Rocky—"

The door swung open. Big Jack heard that door and cut himself off.

It was Mom. And right away I knew I'd have to wait for the details, to hear all the particulars of the trip Big Jack had in store. But clearly he had something up his sleeve. Something big. I knew because he always did.

Some men drink, some men gamble, some men restore old cars, some men collect stamps—my old man had stuff up his sleeve. Rarely did a day of Big Jack's life go by without some scheme or pipe dream to get rich or soak the rich or travel around the world.

"Joshua! You're awake! Thank God." Mom right off switched on the light. Mom hated darkness. "Why are you two sitting here in the dark? What's going on? What are you up to?" These questions she aimed directly at Dad because, well, because Mom knew from copious amounts of experience that he was always up to something.

"Nada," he answered cooler than an Italian ice on a hot summer day. "Nothing at all, good lookin'. Just talking things over. Mano y mano."

Mom scowled at him and crossed to me. I received the full blessing of maternal devotion. "How's your head, baby? Do you have a headache?" Mom put her hands on me like Jesus healing the sick. She rubbed my forehead, massaged my shoulders. She probed here and there, I guess, for broken bones, torn ligaments, dislocated joints. Mom liked to see herself as a nurse, though more the Hollywood Florence Nightingale variety than someone actually administering to the truly wounded and bloody.

I told her I felt pretty good, but she didn't hear me. Mom was mostly working the crowd. Sure, she cared about her boy, loved him, wanted to make sure he was okay, but the real lovey-dovey hands-on stuff was primarily for Dad's benefit.

She bent over the bed still wearing those high-heeled shoes, short skirt, and tight shirt. Maybe it was my eyes going goofy on me but I felt pretty sure Dad had his eyes fixed on Mom's backside. And I knew he did when he said, "Hey, Lisa, what's up with that skirt, girl? Looks like half of it's missing. You really wear that thing in public?"

To which Mom answered, "Amazing, Jack. All these years and you still haven't learned to keep your mouth shut."

Dad, never a very tactful guy, laughed and replied, "Your cheeks are sticking out like a couple of ripe melons."

"If you don't like the view, buster, avert your eyes."

"Oh, I like the view just fine. Always have. I just wonder if it should be so readily available for public consumption."

"Well," announced Mom, "I don't really care what you wonder. It's none of your business. Now why don't you go sell something or steal something? I want some time alone with my son."

Dad stood. He gave Mom a big smile. "And it's all about what you want, daughter of the divine. Always has been and always will be. Daddy's little girl."

Mom shook her head and made a little dismissing noise with her mouth. "I won't even dignify that with a response."

I felt sure Big Jack would fire back another salvo and we'd soon have a raging war on our hands. This was their modus operandi after all, and had been for a mighty long time. But much to my surprise Big Jack stayed mute. Gave me a quick wink and I knew he had bigger fish to fry and saw no immediate advantage going into battle.

"See you tomorrow, kid," he said and squeezed my shoulder.

"When?" I asked.

"Oh, hard to say. I'll be around." He pointed his index finger at me and made a clicking sound. "Count on it."

"Okay," I said, even though I doubted he'd show. Plenty of times in the past he'd departed with similar promises to return soon or sooner only to vanish without a trace.

Then he turned to Mom and said, "And oh, by the way, Lisa, I have to say, you still got it, girl. In spades. You look hot. Though just between you and me, I'd go a little lighter on the makeup and maybe rethink the whole teenage outfit thing."

I saw Mom's face go crimson. I heard her blood boil.

But before she could curse at him or throw a bedpan at him, Big Jack slipped out the door and fled into the night. Only to return a few seconds later. "And hey, what's up with the ongoing romance with that sadistic loser Homer Otis? I always thought you liked a real man who knew how to treat you sweet."

And then, again, he was gone.

Night arrived. Darkness fell over the train. There was no news, only rumors, all bad and dangerous, and more rain.

    Josh and I closed our eyes and did our best to sleep.

    Neither of us was able.

    And so, after a time, he told me more of his adventures…

The Ramble

We left Jackson in the morning and soon found ourselves in Montana.

"Montana!" shouted Big Jack. "The Treasure State! Big Sky Country!"

We drove up through Bozeman and on into Helena, the state capital. We cruised along the main drag—Last Chance Gulch. Bones took some photos, including one of me and Big Jack standing side by side on the granite steps of the statehouse. I keep that photo on the table next to my bed. Shoulder to shoulder, Big Jack Tailor and his boy.

After lunch we made the long pull north to East Glacier where we checked into Glacier Park Lodge, a massive three-story hotel made of logs and mortar that stood in a wide clearing surrounded by high mountain peaks. We had two rooms on the third floor, one of which I shared with Big Jack.

Before going to bed, Big Jack said, "I'm up and gone early, Josh. Business."

I looked over at him. "You want me to come?"

"I don't think so, kid."

"Why not?"

"I tell you, Josh, these guys are some tougher hombres than the lightweights in Idaho. The Chaney boys were cub scouts compared to these dudes."

I wanted to say, "Then maybe you could use a hand," but despite my best efforts I was still a boy, so I didn't. Instead I said, "Okay."

"Tomorrow's just talk," Jack added. "A lot of strutting and

posturing. Be boring for you. Probably take all day. I suggest you boys take a tour of the park on one of the old red tour busses. There's a road through the mountains to the west side of the park called Going-to-the-Sun. Incredible stuff. Not to be missed."

So that's exactly what me and Retro and Bones did. We took a tour. Had a good time seeing the sights, talking to some folks. The Going-to-the-Sun Road went places few roads dare to go.

When we got back to the Lodge we found Big Jack sitting in the sun with his shirt off sipping a Coors and smoking a cigar.

At dinner Big Jack ordered a pitcher of beer. The waitress gave us a look but Big Jack gave her a smile and off she went to fetch the suds, and four glasses. We all drank up and after a glass or two agreed being out in the Rocky Mountains together was easily the greatest thing that had ever happened.

By the time we got back to our room I was more than a little wobbly. We got the door closed and our shoes off. And that's when I got the guts to broach a few subjects that had been on my mind a long time.

I said, clear as a bell, "I sure wish Jake had never drowned in the Delaware."

Dad, pulling his tee shirt up over his head, paused a second, then said, "Hey, Josh, I hear you. I feel the same way, kid."

Slurring my words, but not too bad, I pressed on. "I got to tell you, Dad, I wish Jake had never drowned in the Delaware, and I wish you and Mom had never fought ever, not once, and I wish we'd all stayed together, you know, like a regular family, only different of course, better, and I wish right now all four of us—you and me and Mom and Jake—were staying here at the Glacier Park Lodge together drinking beers and riding the bus and seeing the sites."

And Dad, patient as Job, said, "I hear what you're saying, son, and hey, I wish for the same things, I really do, but you have to go easy. You'll hurt yourself thinking about all that stuff. Make yourself sick. The past's a brain drainer. Folks spend too much time dredging up the past and dreaming of the future. You've got the present, and really that's all you've got." He tried a smile, then added, "You know what you sound like, Finnegan Tailor? You sound like an old sentimental Irish drunk. I know, because I can sound that way myself if I get enough Jamison's in me. But hear me when I tell you, the past's the past and it's best to keep it that way. Pull it into the present and it just pulls you down."

Yeah, sure, whatever. I heard my old man and I wanted to believe him. But I was just a kid. I didn't have a past yet. My past wasn't all that long ago. It was still all tangled up with right now, with the present. I felt like only a week or two had passed since Jake had drowned in the Delaware. And in my head his Drowning and his Death were all my fault. I was to blame. I'd dragged him down to the water's edge. I'd dared him to test his toes in the cool river. I'd encouraged him to take a plunge.

Oh yeah, all that on my mind and the tears started to flow and I couldn't stop and Dad came over and sat on the edge of my bed and gave me a hug—the first hug he'd given me since before… hell, since before Jake had died—which made me wail even louder. But I got myself under control and used the back of my hand and my tee shirt to dry things up.

Dad, sitting on the bed and looking down at me soft and tender like he'd do when I was a kid and he still loved me, said, "You okay?"

"Oh yeah," I told him, "swell," and then I did that little whimper thing you do after you've been wailing.

"Good," and he gave my shoulder a squeeze.

Soon enough I quit my crying. And then I needed to get away from all that, so I bucked up like a man and asked, "Did it go okay today?"

He thought it over for a couple seconds. "Yeah, you know, I held my own. Like I told you last night, this is a rough group—ornery, radical, and meaner than snakes. An ex CIA op runs the show. A real control freak. And his sidekick/bodyguard—this guy really gave me the spooks. You could see the madness in his eyes. If he's the face of the Militia for a Free Montana I'd just as soon turn the show over now to the Chinese. I tell you, Josh, if I had any smarts at all I'd head for the hills on this one. But, well, there's a nice paycheck due, so I guess come morning I'll get this done. After that our vacation begins in earnest. No more business after tomorrow. Just fishing and hiking."

"Sounds good," I said. "So tomorrow you sell the rest of the guns?"

Big Jack nodded. "That's right." He looked serious, but also happy not to be talking about Jake and Mom anymore.

I said, "I want to go with you."

Big Jack shook his head. "I don't think so, kid. Not this time. Your mother'd kill me if I brought you along. But I'll be back early. After that we'll—"

"I want to go," I insisted. "I want to be there."

"That's the beer talking."

"No, it's not." Probably it was.

He gave me a long look. "You really want to go?"

I nodded. "Absolutely. I don't think you should go up against these goons alone."

This brought a smile to Big Jack's face. "I'm not going up against anybody, Finn Tailor. Like I keep telling you, this is just business."

"Okay, then. No reason why I shouldn't go."

He thought it over, then gave a little shrug. "Alrightee then. We'll do it. The Tailor boys. We'll do it together, kid. Me and you."

"Dad?"

"Yeah?"

"Don't call me kid. And no more of that Finnegan crap either. The name's Josh, Josh Tailor."

"Right on, Josh Tailor. I hear you loud and clear."

We went to bed soon after that, and for a time I just lay there in the dark thinking things over but not saying my thoughts out loud. I heard Big Jack breathing steady. I felt pretty sure he'd fallen asleep.

But nope, the man was as awake as me.

"Just lying here remembering the night you were born, Josh Tailor."

"Yeah?"

"Your mama was overdue. Just a few days, you know, but enough to make us anxious. The doc wanted to make you come, force the action, but I said no dice, we'll let nature do its work. And sure enough, the very next morning, your mom felt those first contractions. That was you inside, deciding the time had come to get on with things."

"You were there?"

"Of course I was there. But let me tell you, your mother did all the work. She was unbelievable. Strong and steady. Almost twenty hours she was in labor. She complained some about the pain, but not much, even though I could see it on her face. It unsettled me plenty. Made me feel pretty useless. But finally, around eleven o'clock at night, her cervix fully dilated, the doc told her to start pushing. He said it would probably take an hour or two so she had to conserve her strength. But Mom pushed you out just minutes later. I know. I watched the show. Took my breath away your arrival into the world."

"Just before midnight, right?"

"Yup, just before midnight with a full moon shining through the window. Oh yeah, your mama was spectacular, Josh Tailor. Delivered you all by herself. The doc and the nurses offered nothing but encouragement. Nine pounds seven ounces. A regular giant among mortals. You looked big enough to send off to kindergarten. And then there you were resting on your mama's belly with Lisa crying and me wailing and—"

"You were wailing?"

"Like a fountain, my man. Like an open spigot. But that's not what I got to say. I brought all this up because of what you said a few minutes ago about your mom and about little Jake. Your mother gave birth to you two boys. Carried you and bore you and nurtured you and loved you. She's one tough girl, your mama. Tough but sweet and filled with love. I was a crappy husband and a mediocre father, but you're still a winner, Josh Tailor. You're a winner because of your mother. Never forget that. And never fail to give that girl her due. She deserves all the love and respect you can muster. Now go to bed, boy. We got work to do in the morning. It's men's work, meaning it's mostly bullshit and charades, but hey, it's what we do."

I had questions and tried asking them, but Big Jack hushed me up, told me enough and then some had been said.

The Collapse

And now I need to take a minute to tell you what happened to me after Jake drowned in the Delaware.

Like I told you earlier, Dad found Jake's body washed up on some rocks down by the Frenchtown Bridge. Dad swept down the river splashing and shouting, wading and swimming—a man on a mission. Me and Mom brought up the rear, Mom screaming Jake's name over and over like a woman possessed.

Finally Dad reached Jake and swept the little guy up in his arms. Dad waded ashore and scrambled up onto the bank. He laid Jake in the grass. And blew into his mouth. And pounded on his chest. All while me and Mom splashed through the river and climbed the bank. Mom, freaking out, hysterical, pushed Dad aside and fell upon Jake's limp body. She shook him. And hugged him. And begged him to live. Begged his lifeless little body not to die. While me and Dad stood there, empty and dead too and unable to change anything.

God, I tell you, it was awful. Close too unimaginable. A mother with her dead son in her arms. My mother. My brother. Worst thing by far I ever saw. Even worse than Big Jack getting shot in the chest. Especially after Mom started crying—wailing—at the top of her lungs. She broke down I tell you, and stayed that way—broken—for days. Weeks. Months. Years. Even, I guess, to this day.

At Jake's funeral Mom got herself so worked up she blacked out. Collapsed right on the floor at the foot of the altar of the Episcopal

Church.

After the funeral Mom and Dad tried to pull their lives back together. Dad moved home and away we went. But the very event—Jake's death—that had brought about their reunion, in pretty short order blew them into a million pieces.

People who keep track of this kind of thing claim few marriages survive the death of a young child. Mom and Dad proved no exception. Dad was ready to move on sooner than Mom. I don't mean he wasn't depressed and all about Jake's death, but he needed to at least try and pretend life was normal. Not Mom. She needed to mourn. And mourn she did, day in and day out. On a good day she looked glum. On a bad day she looked like death. She rarely spoke.

When she did speak it was usually to cast blame. Most of it fell on Dad. If he'd been a better husband and a better father Jake never would've drowned. But a time or two Mom blamed me. Which made me feel swell since I already blamed myself. Right away she apologized, of course, assured me it was not my fault, but the psycho damage was already done.

Jake drowned in July. Dad, after many exhausting battles with Mom, took off the following spring. He left just before my seventh birthday. I didn't see him again till right around my eighth birthday. All that time Mom told me he was away on business. Which didn't make much sense—him being a car salesman up in Clinton and all just half an hour away—but what does a second grader know?

Several times during that year Mom left me with Gram and Pop at the big old Victorian in Bridgeton. For three or four days she'd disappear, then return. I never knew where she went. Later, of course, I found out she'd run off looking for Dad. She couldn't live with him or without him.

And then Dad came back. To live with us. For a while. Hey, I'm not making this stuff up. These people—my parents—they were crazy people.

They tried living together in the house on the Delaware. I was glad to have my dad back. In spite of everything I still loved him, worshipped him even. He was, after all, my father. And for a while, let me tell you, life was good. Dad made things fun. He pulled me away from Mom's funk. He took me fishing and hiking and to the movies. He must not've had a job because he'd put me on the school bus in the morning and be waiting for me at the bus stop when I got off in the afternoon.

At first Mom and Dad got along great. Lots of hugs and kisses. Dad would put on the rock and roll—Layla, Moondance, Mustang Sally—and swing Mom around the living room. Sometimes Mom would forget herself and smile, even laugh, yuck it up. But then she'd cut herself short and go back to mourning. It was like, with Jake dead, she had no right to enjoy life.

Little by little, day by day, the arguing crept back into the house. Inevitable, I know. Arguing turned to fighting and fighting to screaming. God knows what it was all about. I crept down the hallway to my bedroom and closed the door. I plugged up my ears with my fingers. I hummed. Slowly I drifted into childhood neurosis.

And then, sure enough, one day after six or eight months I got off the bus and Dad wasn't there. I knew right away he'd taken off again. I could feel him gone. At dinner I asked Mom, "Where'd he go?"

"That bastard," she answered, her defenses entirely broken down, "went straight to hell. He's gone, Joshua. And you know what I say? I say good riddance to bad rubbish."

Yup, that's what Mom said about Dad. Good riddance to bad rubbish. Made quite an impression on me.

After that I didn't see Dad much. I wouldn't see him for months, even years at a time. He became like a non-person, a ghost, an almost dead man, a ship on a lost and forgotten sea. When I did see him he'd blow into town, cast a powerful shadow over me, block out the sun for a day or two, and then, like smoke, vanish into thin air.

When I was in fourth grade Mom and I moved in with Gram and Pop. The move didn't bother me much since I had the whole third floor to myself. Plus Gram was a much better cook than Mom. And I could count on Gram being home after school and serving supper at seven sharp exactly fifteen minutes after Pop got home from work.

The four of us—me, Mom, Gram, and Pop—settled down mostly peacefully to watch the seasons come and go.

The Devil

We got up before the sun. Which means we got up mighty early in northern Montana during those early days of summer. So early I didn't feel like I'd slept at all. I splashed some water on my face and pulled on jeans and a fleece jacket to beat back the chill.

We exited the Lodge even before the bellboys had manned the front door. We made our way through the darkness to the Excursion, but before we could shove off we had a couple chores to do. First we had to reattach the trailer to the truck. Big Jack had taken it off the day before to make himself more mobile. Then we moved all the camping gear from the trailer into the back of the Excursion. Big Jack didn't say why.

Finally we hit the road. We drove through East Glacier. The town was dark and deserted. We drove due east. I don't think we saw but a couple cars.

In the town of Browning we stopped at the Java Shack and got large coffees and buttered hard rolls to go. "Breakfast of champions!" declared Big Jack.

We sat out in the Java Shack parking lot, that big Triton V-10 idling away. A few pickups rolled in and out. The drivers were mostly small and dark-skinned.

"Mexicans?" I asked.

Dad shook his head. "Nope. Indians. Blackfeet."

"Seriously? Indians?"

"Would I kid you, kid? I mean Josh. Josh Tailor."

I shrugged. "You might, yeah."

A police cruiser pulled into the Java Shack. Big Jack's antennae popped up. He watched the cop exit the cruiser and walk toward the Shack. As soon as the cop passed through the door Big Jack slipped the Excursion into gear and got us back on the road.

A few miles to the east we passed the Museum of the Plains Indians. Big Jack said, "Yup, Blackfeet Indians. We're in the heart of the Blackfeet Indian Reservation. It's a big chunk of land, nearly the size of Rhode Island. But the Blackfeet don't really own it or run it. It's a Federal show. The Blackfeet just get to live here in modest poverty. But if you want to commit a crime—rob a bank, sell some firearms, rub somebody out—this ain't a bad place to hide. Much tougher for Federal law enforcement to nail you on an Indian reservation than out in the general population."

We pushed east. The sky began to glow orange. The sun splashed over the horizon.

Big Jack had the truck flying now—seventy-five, eighty miles an hour along that deserted stretch of Montana highway.

"An eye for an eye, Josh. An eye for an eye."

"Say what?"

Big Jack just shook his head and stared straight ahead.

Was he talking about Homer? I didn't know and didn't ask. It didn't matter what Jack was talking about. Homer was the dude who popped into my head. Homer and the whole notion of retribution.

"The Montana Militia, Josh. The Militia for a Free and Independent Montana. A very intense bunch of sickos. Ex skinheads, jarheads, neo Nazis, all variety of assorted convicts and psychopaths."

I must've looked worried because Dad glanced at me and added, "No sweat, Josh. Today we're just dealing with the head honcho and his psycho sidekick. No big deal. They just want the weapons."

I nodded and did my best to wipe the worry off my face. I wanted to look cool and tough, not worried and stressed.

In the town of Cut Bank, on the eastern edge of the Blackfeet Indian Reservation, we turned north. Five or six miles later we drove into the small backwater burg of Santa Rita. It had a boarded-up gas station with a couple rusty pumps, a general store that looked like it hadn't been open since the Civil War, and a bar called the Leisure Club. It, too, was closed. Big Jack pulled into the gravel parking lot anyway. He drove around back, stopped the Excursion, got out, and had himself a look around. I got out too. The Leisure Club was a squat single story building made of concrete with a flat roof. It looked about as inviting as a bunker.

Big Jack said, "This is where I met with the Montana Militia. The Leisure Club's their private hangout, where they drink beer, play pool, and plot the subversion of the government and the elimination of all non-white Protestants."

I didn't know what to add to that, so I added nothing at all.

We climbed back into the truck. Dad said, "We'll do the deal here."

He then reached into the center console's storage compartment and pulled out a very lethal looking firearm. "This baby here is a three-fifty-seven Magnum. She weighs four and a half pounds, has a ten-inch barrel, and fires nine rounds in a clip. She makes an excellent deterrent. And she's pretty good, too, at stopping aggressors in their tracks."

"But I thought you said not to worry?"

"And I meant what I said, Josh. But that's no excuse for being unprepared."

We pulled out of Santa Rita and continued north. We made a few turns. As always, Big Jack seemed to know exactly where he wanted to go.

We reached the wide-open high plains. Back to the west I could see the Rockies, high and fierce, but north and east nothing but flat. The road ran straight like the lines on a notebook. Big Jack didn't say much. I didn't either.

Fifteen minutes out of Santa Rita, out in the middle of absolutely nowhere, we pulled off onto the side of the road. Just pulled off without a car or house or human anywhere in sight. It had been a couple hours since we'd left the Lodge, but it still wasn't even 7 o'clock in the a.m.

At 7 sharp a black Jeep Wrangler pulled up next to the Excursion. Big Jack rolled down his window. The driver was a white guy with a shaved head, a pockmarked face, and a scar at the corner of his right eye that ran clear down to the corner of his lip. He wore a well-trimmed black goatee that he stroked constantly with the thumb and index finger of his left hand. He right away gave me the willies. I thought with some certainty he might be the Devil or his kin.

The Devil didn't smile and say, "Hey, how's things?" Or, "How was the drive over?" Or "Top of the morning to you."

No, he said, his voice like the cutting edge of a stiletto, "Who's the kid?"

"My son."

"I thought you'd be alone."

"You thought wrong, friend."

The Devil narrowed his eyes—vacant black eyes that looked plenty evil.

Big Jack said, "Don't worry, he's a good kid. Smart too. I'm learning him the business."

The Devil thought it over. He stroked his chin, then growled, "Follow me." And he hit the gas of his dusty black Wrangler.

We followed. Big Jack said, "This one's a real charmer. Trained by the military to kill. Best not to turn your back on him."

The Devil swung his Wrangler into a gravel lane and under a tall arch of lodge pole pines. Atop the arch was a sign: FREEDOM RANCH

We followed the Wrangler down that gravel lane for a quarter mile or more. The Jeep kicked up clouds of dust. Dad stayed well back. Split rail fences lined both sides of the drive. Horses grazed in the pastures set off by the fences.

"I'm not anticipating trouble," Big Jack told me, "but if it comes, best keep a clear head. Make quick, sharp decisions."

Off to the right was a large barn. A Chevy Blazer, a Chevy pickup, and a big green John Deere tractor sat parked in front. Straight ahead stood a ranch house—a rambling single story log structure with more stone chimneys than I have fingers.

The Wrangler stopped near the barn. We pulled up behind the Jeep.

The front door of the ranch house opened. A large thick-chested man appeared in the doorway. He held something in the crock of his left arm. It took me a second to realize it was a child, a baby, just a year or so old.

"What do you think of that?" asked Big Jack.

"Think of what?"

"Looks like a peace offering to me. Maybe this'll go easier than I thought."

"I don't get it."

"The guy in the doorway," Big Jack explained, "is Conrad Gibson. Ex CIA man I mentioned. He's the brains and the dough behind the Militia for a Free and Independent Montana. I figure that's his grandchild he's holding. I also figure our buddy in the Jeep called Gibson while we drove here and told him I had you along. So Gibson's showing me he can do the family thing too. It's a nice touch."

A young woman appeared in the doorway. She took the baby from Conrad and retreated into the house. Gibson stepped off the porch into a wash of early morning sun. He wore cowboy boots, Levi's, a denim shirt, and a real slick, low-cut black cowboy hat. He ambled in our direction like a man in no hurry at all.

Big Jack opened the driver's door of the Excursion. Before he stepped out he handed me the .357 Magnum.

The revolver was plenty heavy, the steel as cold as ice. "What do I do with this?"

Big Jack smiled. "Anything funny happens, start shooting."

"What? Are you serious?"

Big Jack exited the Excursion, then leaned in the open window and said, "Keep it out of sight. Stay put. Listen up. Try and learn something."

Big Jack Tailor and the equally big Conrad Gibson met at the left front bumper of the Excursion. They shook hands and locked eyes.

Conrad Gibson said, "That your boy?"

Dad said, "Yup."

Conrad Gibson gave me a smile and a wave. He looked like a nice enough guy, kind of like Retro's grandfather back in Bridgeton. Only I knew looks can deceive.

"So," Gibson asked my father, "you have the goods in the trailer?"

"I suspect so," answered Big Jack.

Conrad Gibson nodded.

The Devil stroked his chin.

Big Jack stayed cool.

I began to sweat inside my fleece.

Conrad Gibson said, "What I'd like to do is, swing on over to the barn and unload around back. Out of sight of the family, you understand?"

"Sure," said Big Jack, "I understand. Only I have a different idea. I'm on foreign soil here, Conrad. Me and my boy, we're making the haul back and forth to Great Falls. I don't know a soul up in these parts. So if it's all the same to you, I'd like to finish the deal on more neutral turf."

Great Falls? Why was Big Jack telling Gibson we'd come from Great Falls? Great Falls was due south. We'd come from Glacier—due west.

Conrad Gibson did not look happy. Clearly he was a man used to doing things his own way. "What do you have in mind, Boyd?"

Who, I wondered, was Boyd? Another of Dad's aliases? How many did my old man have? Just when you thought you had a hold on him he spun away.

The Devil stroked his chin with his left hand. He kept his right hand buried in the pocket of his denim jacket. I figured he had a gun there.

Big Jack asked Gibson, "You got a truck with a hitch?"

"Pickup and Blazer have hitches," answered Gibson. "Why? What's the deal?"

"I propose we head down the road, away from your spread here, where I can have a little breathing room. This is the first of hopefully many transactions between us. I'd like it to go well. Smooth, you know. Out behind the barn, well, that makes me a little nervous. My daddy used to tan my hide out behind the barn."

He did? They had a barn in Jersey City?

Conrad Gibson smiled. "So, Mr. Boyd, you don't trust me?"

"Sure I do, but in this business, better to trust no one."

Conrad Gibson nodded. "Okay, so we leave the ranch. Then what?"

"We have a look at the merchandise, you hand me some cash, and I move the trailer from my truck to your truck."

"You're giving me the trailer?" Conrad Gibson looked dubious.

"That's right. This way, to anyone watching, it looks like I'm selling you a trailer. We can't help the contraband that might be aboard."

Conrad Gibson thought it over. "Not bad. Not bad at all. But leaving the ranch seems risky. We're out of sight here. Inconspicuous."

"Don't worry," said Big Jack. "We won't go far."

"The thing is, Boyd," countered Gibson, "if I wanted to steal these guns from you and cause you harm, I'd've done it already."

Big Jack threw off a big smile. "I don't think so, Mr. Gibson. Not with your wife and daughter and grandkid over in the house looking out the kitchen window."

Conrad Gibson no longer looked like Retro's grandfather. He looked more like a Gestapo SS Colonel on vacation at a western dude ranch. "Watch your step, Mr. Boyd."

"I'm just watching out for my health, Mr. Gibson."

Conrad Gibson took a couple breaths and said, "I don't like your plan."

"Fine," said Big Jack, tougher than any linebacker who ever played in the NFL, "I have no problem with that. We can agree to disagree."

"What does that mean?"

"Just means me and my boy will be leaving."

"What are you talking about?"

"I have a long list of individuals who'd like this merchandise."

And then, sporting balls as big as moons, Big Jack, God-like in his aura, defied his own advice—he turned his back on the Devil. Turned his back and strolled oh so leisurely toward the Excursion.

The Devil started to pull his hand out of his pocket.

I felt my palm sweaty around that big cold Magnum.

Big Jack reached the driver's door of the truck.

Conrad Gibson grabbed the Devil's wrist. And stopped the Devil from doing whatever the Devil had in mind to do.

Big Jack climbed into the Excursion, gave me a wide smile. "How we doing, kid?"

I managed to nod but not speak.

"You got a death grip on that weapon, boy. Relax."

I relaxed. Sort of.

Conrad Gibson approached the truck.

I shoved the Magnum under my seat.

"All right, Boyd," said Gibson, "we'll do it your way. Where to?"

"I got a place in mind."

"But you're not saying where?"

"It's less than fifteen minutes from here. But do me a favor and leave your chum behind. He doesn't really add much to the party."

Conrad Gibson laughed. "That's good, Boyd. You're a real card. We'll follow you. Anything out of the ordinary, I'm gone."

Big Jack (Boyd) nodded. Gibson backed off.

With Gibson and the Devil glaring at us we swung our rig around and headed back down that gravel lane. We reached the road and waited for them to come up.

I said, "I don't like these guys."

Distracted, Big Jack replied, "Tough to like everyone, son."

"Yeah, but these guys seem like bad dudes. Real bad."

"They do, don't they." Big Jack kept his eyes on the mirrors.

I thought we should just skedaddle, start driving and keep driving, but Big Jack, I could tell, was in action mode. "Okay," he announced, "here they come."

I turned around and took a look. They were in the Chevy Blazer. The Devil drove, Conrad Gibson rode shotgun.

Dad pulled out onto the asphalt road. The Devil followed close behind.

Big Jack said, "Okay, Josh, here's the drill. If we find trouble there won't be time to talk it over. First thing I want you to do is have a good look at that Magnum."

I pulled it out from under the seat.

"Right now," Big Jack told me, "she has a full magazine. Nine rounds. To fire just snap off the safety—there—aim, and pull the trigger. Probably all you'll have to do is hand me the gun. But if you gotta fire, don't hold back. Aim and fire like a man. Got me?"

Heart accelerating, I nodded.

"Good. Now with the safety on I want you to slip the gun into the deep pocket of your fleece. It won't be visible there, but it'll be plenty handy, just in case."

I slipped the Magnum into my pocket, half fearing it might accidentally fire and shoot off my pecker.

Big Jack checked his mirrors. "Okay, when we get to the Leisure Club I want you to stay in the truck till me and Gibson and the psycho go around to have a look in the trailer. Then get out and ease your way around behind us. I want you back there with me while the loonies inspect the goods. Covering my ass, you know, in case of trouble."

For the first time I sensed Big Jack didn't feel real good about the situation. But he didn't need me squawking or turning yellow, so I just gave him another nod.

"After they inspect the guns we'll do the cash transaction. It'll take a few minutes to count the dough. Then we unhitch the trailer from the truck. While I do that you get up here behind the wheel. Soon as I get the trailer unhitched you pull forward. Just pull up out of the way. But keep the engine running and the transmission in gear. Listen up, kid, because this is key. I want that engine running and the transmission in gear. Keep your left foot on the brake and your right foot easy on the accelerator. Got it?"

I could feel my heart pounding. "I got it."

"You sure?"

"I'm sure."

"Good. If anything happens I want you to mash that accelerator and go like hell. Don't wait for me. I'll get out on my own." He looked over at me. "You hear me, Josh?"

Oh yeah, I heard him. Loud and clear.

"You drive, boy. You drive and you keep driving till you reach a safe place."

I nodded but didn't say a word.

A mile or so later we entered the small ghost town of Santa Rita, this time from the north. It looked the same as before—dead. Dad pulled into the parking lot of the Leisure Club and drove around back. The tavern was still closed. Which didn't surprise me since the clock on the console read 7:33. I couldn't believe it was still that early. I felt like we'd been up and at it for hours.

Dad shut down the engine and stepped out of the Excursion. Through the open window he said, "Stay cool, kiddo. And remember to come on out nice and easy once we move to the back of the trailer."

For the next few minutes I could see but couldn't hear Big Jack and Conrad Gibson and the Devil. They moved around some, but mostly they stood between the Excursion and the Blazer, talking it over and kicking at the dusty gravel.

When they moved around to the back of the trailer I swung open the passenger door and climbed out. Slowly, and plenty nervous, I made my way back to the action, .357 Magnum pushed into the pocket of my fleece and banging against my hip. I took a roundabout route, so as to look nonchalant and not arouse attention. By the time I reached my position they had the trailer open and the lid off one of the M-16 boxes.

Nobody paid me any mind. I doubted either Gibson or the Devil thought for a second I had a loaded handgun in my pocket..

One by one they took the lids off the boxes and inspected the M-16s. Then they moved on to the boxes of RPGs. It all took time. Dad kept glancing out the back of the trailer. He'd started to look like I felt—plenty nervous. Probably he figured Gibson would want to move fast out there in the open—cut and run—but nope, the man acted like he had all the time in the world.

Nothing happened. The Devil inspected the rifles and played with a few grenades while Big Jack and Conrad Gibson sat on the back of the trailer and dealt with the money phase of the operation.

Conrad had a thick black briefcase. He set it down, unlocked the two latches, and opened it up. It was full of cash—stacks of one hundred dollar bills. College money.

"It's all here, Boyd. Every nickel we agreed to."

"I'm sure it is," said Big Jack, "but I'd feel better with a quick look."

Gibson swung the briefcase toward my father. Big Jack right away began to count the money. I thought everyone looked reasonably relaxed. I started to believe everything would turn out hunky dory.

Dad rifled through those stacks of hundreds faster than a black jack dealer in Atlantic City shuffles cards. I don't know if he kept a tally in his head or if he was just making a show of it, but either way he looked impressive with his lightning fast fingers ripping through those bills.

Seconds after Big Jack finished his count, the Devil stepped off the back of the trailer. He scowled at Big Jack while wiping gun oil off his hands with a rag.

The Devil turned to his boss. "We gotta a problem, Mr. Gibson."

That got my attention. That got everybody's attention.

"What kind of problem?" Conrad Gibson asked.

"All RPGs accounted for, but I count only ninety-four M-16s." The Devil's voice sounded like something rumbling from the bowels of the earth.

"Ninety-four?" questioned Conrad Gibson. "You sure? We contracted for ninety-six."

"Ninety-four," repeated the Devil. "Definitely ninety-four. I counted twice. You want I'll count again."

Big Jack stepped forward. I feared he might say what I was thinking. That being whether or not the Devil had enough brainpower to count to ninety-six. But instead Big Jack sounded ticked off. "Now hold on, gentlemen. I packed those rifles myself. I know for a fact I had ninety-six. I know…" He cut himself short.

"What is it, Boyd?" Conrad Gibson demanded. "Why the discrepancy?"

"Actually, now I think on it, there's no discrepancy. It's my error." Big Jack turned to the Devil. "Your count's right—ninety-four's the number. I forgot I sold a couple extra units down in Idaho last week."

The boys from the Militia for a Free and Independent Montana looked suspicious. They stood tall, arms folded across their chests, awaiting an explanation.

Jack pulled a wad of hundreds out of the briefcase. "Here's twenty-four hundred bucks to make us square."

Gibson reached out and grabbed the wad. He stuffed it in his pocket, gave my father a long look, then asked, "So, Boyd, you trying to pull a fast one? We don't take kindly to cheats up in this neck of the woods."

Big Jack stayed cool. He didn't kowtow, nor did he get the hairs up on the back of his neck. He closed up the briefcase and latched the latches. Then he said, "Mr. Gibson, we both know in this business you don't cheat.

You cheat someone and you're soon outta business. Or dead. Let's just chalk it up to what it was—an honest mistake."

"An honest mistake, huh?"

"That's right. Now what do you say we move this trailer onto your Blazer so we can all get on with our day."

Big Jack didn't waste time. He picked up that briefcase and walked around the side of the trailer to the back of the Excursion, once more defying his own advice by turning his back on the Devil.

I was left back there with the two militiamen. They exchanged glances. I don't know what those glances meant, but definitely nothing good. Then they both turned and stared at me. My heart just about jumped out of my chest. How, I wondered, do you get brave in a hurry?

I made haste to join Big Jack. But Big Jack didn't want me back there. He wanted me behind the wheel. His eyes pushed me in that direction while he opened the back of the Excursion and tossed the briefcase on top of the camping gear.

A couple seconds later Conrad Gibson and the Devil arrived at the back of the Excursion. They watched Big Jack uncouple the hitch from the truck. I watched in the rear-view mirror and thought for sure there'd be trouble.

But no, Gibson instructed the Devil to help Boyd with the safety chains. They removed the chains, then Big Jack used the built-in jack to lift the hitch off the ball. Once the hitch was clear he called to me, "Okay, son, move the truck up and out of the way."

I turned the key, put her in gear, and rolled slowly forward. I stopped where I had a straight shot out to the highway. My brain reminded me to turn south, go down to Cut Bank, then turn west onto US 2. I watched the action in the rear-view mirror.

The Devil crossed the parking lot. Conrad Gibson had a lot to say to my father, but I couldn't catch a word of it. The Devil climbed into the Blazer, pulled forward, then backed up to the trailer. The deal, I thought, was nearly done. With any luck we'd be gone and on our way in a couple minutes.

Big Jack, in fact, was moving toward the Excursion already. Maybe we'd be gone even sooner.

But with Big Jack just a few feet from the truck Conrad Gibson asked him to help with the trailer. Dad turned and went back.

The Blazer obstructed my view so I couldn't see exactly what went down. For like five minutes they messed with the hitch and the chains. Then all of a sudden Big Jack and the Devil came out into the open, both of them full of piss and vinegar. They stood chin to chin, their voices loud and tough. The Devil gave Big Jack a shove. Big Jack shoved right back. The Devil shoved again. Back and forth the shoving went.

I thought about hopping out of the Excursion, drawing that Magnum, and putting a slug right between the Devil's eyes. But thinking is easy, actually doing is a whole lot more commitment.

Gibson stepped between the two men. He ordered them to cool down. He wanted them to shake hands, but neither man would do it.

"Pull on out of here, Boyd," he advised, "before we have real trouble."

Big Jack saw the wisdom in that. He nodded and headed for the Excursion. He came up along the passenger side. "Hey, kid."

"Hey," I said. I had one foot on the accelerator and one foot on the brake pedal, just like my father had told me. I thought we were home free. "Come on, let's roll."

Big Jack pulled open the door and stepped onto the running board.

In the rear-view mirror I saw Conrad Gibson and the Devil climb into the Blazer, the Devil once again behind the wheel.

Big Jack gave me a smile. He had a trickle of blood on his chin. "Enjoying the show, kid?"

"Not really. I think I'll enjoy it a whole lot more once we're safely back at the Lodge with Retro and Bones."

"Relax. People get testy during these transactions."

"Get in," I ordered.

Big Jack ignored me. "You got the Magnum?"

"Yeah, in my pocket."

"Hand it over. It might be time for a little show of force."

I reached into my pocket to get it.

The Blazer began to roll forward, trailer in tow.

I pulled out the Magnum and set it on the passenger seat. "Okay, now will you please get in the damn truck?"

Big Jack reached for the gun.

The Blazer came up alongside.

Big Jack turned to have a look.

The Devil's face filled the world. "Hey, Boyd," he called, voice thick with hate, "I got something for you."

Big Jack reached back for the Magnum. But too late.

The Devil raised his left arm and stuck it out the window of the Blazer. Attached to his hand was a gun not unlike the Magnum. He pointed it at my father.

Conrad Gibson shouted, I'm sure of it, "No, you moron! Don't do it!"

But an instant later the Devil's gun roared. The muzzle flashed. An explosion echoed back and forth between the two trucks.

Big Jack flew backward into the Excursion, across the passenger seat, and up over the console, practically right onto my lap.

I screamed. And looked up. Straight into the wicked evil eyes of the Devil.

He had his gun pointed directly at my face.

Either a rush of adrenaline or the existence of God made me mash down on the accelerator. The Excursion lurched forward.

The Devil's gun roared again. But caused no damage.

Big Jack, groaning and bleeding from his chest, dragged himself off the console and onto the passenger seat. "Drive, boy! Drive!"

I peeled out of the parking lot and started south. Big Jack grabbed the wheel. He swung it in the opposite direction.

"Don't we wanna go south toward Cut Bank?"

He shook his head and held his chest. "North. And then west."

Already he looked plenty pale. "Son of a bitch," he moaned. "Son of a sorry bitch."

I turned north and pushed the accelerator to the floor. The Blazer pursued, but none too swiftly with that trailer laden with M-16s and RPGs.

I felt like we could easily outrun them.

But then Big Jack, bleeding to beat the bandit, picked up the Magnum off the floor where it'd fallen during the melee. He turned to me. His face was ghost-white. "I want you to slow down, kid."

"Slow down? Are you crazy? We gotta move! Get you to a hospital!"

Big Jack, mustering his rapidly fading strength, pulled himself into the back seat of the Excursion. "I said slow down, boy. Let the bastards come." Then he crawled into the far back with the camping gear and the dough.

The rear window, I noticed, was still open.

I slowed from seventy miles an hour to fifty miles an hour. And then down to forty miles an hour.

The Blazer came over a low rise. No other vehicles in sight. The world had us in it and no one else. That's when it dawned on me what Big Jack had in mind.

"Let 'em come, goddammit!" he shouted, his voice loud but creaky.

I slowed to thirty miles an hour. The Blazer closed to within two hundred feet, one hundred feet, fifty feet. I could see the two militiamen clear as bells.

So could Big Jack. He made his move. With the Blazer bearing down on us, no more than thirty feet from the rear bumper, Big Jack hauled himself onto that pile of camping gear. He stuck the big .357 Magnum out the back window and squeezed off half a dozen rounds in rapid succession.

In both the rear-view and the side-view mirrors I watched the results of Big Jack's fine marksmanship—first the windshield of the Blazer shattered and then both front tires exploded with a hiss of air.

The Devil fought to control the wheel. But he couldn't do it. The Blazer—trailer fishtailing wildly back and forth—swerved onto the shoulder of the road and then went careening off the smooth asphalt altogether. It crashed through a split rail fence and down into a drainage ditch.

Conrad Gibson and the Devil quickly exited the vehicle. The Devil sprinted back to the road. He dropped to one knee, drew his pistol, and began firing. But this time his bullets proved harmless. Petal to the metal I pushed the Excursion out of range.

We crossed a low ridge and rolled out of sight. I took my first decent breath since the roar of the Devil's fire. But then remembered Big Jack in the back in a bad way. I saw him pulling at his shirt, messing with his wound. I started to pull over.

But Big Jack, his voice weak, still gave the orders. "Keep moving, boy. Another mile. Then left on Highway 213. Don't miss it. We gotta get onto the Blackfeet Indian Reservation. We gotta find..."

His voice trailed off so bad I couldn't hear the last. But sure enough, a minute later I saw the small Montana highway sign: 213. I made the left without taking my foot off the accelerator. The tires squealed.

213 was all busted-up, pot-holed asphalt. I could see my dad back there bumping up and down on those sleeping bags with every dip and crown in the road. He held his arms tight across his chest. Save for his moaning he could've been dead.

First my little brother and now my father. My father who I was just getting to know again. Know and like and maybe even respect. I even had it in mind to forgive him for his sins. But now this bloody mess. What the hell did God want from me?

I slowed. I needed to get back there and check on him. But I didn't get us halfway stopped before he called, "Keep rolling, Josh. We got a-ways before the next turn."

I kept rolling, and did my best to avoid the deepest potholes.

We might've been on an Indian reservation but I sure didn't see any Indians. Or anyone else for that matter. No one and nothing out there but low rolling hills and lush green grass waving gently in the morning breeze. It would've been a tranquil scene if not for the old boy moaning and groaning and bleeding maybe to death in the back.

Half an hour slowly passed. I tried hard not to think. Not about the past. Or the future. Or about Big Jack dying or what I'd do if he did or how we'd get home or what I'd tell Mom. No, none of that. I just shut myself down. And drove.

I stayed, like Big Jack'd told me, in the present.

I pulled the atlas out from under the seat. Steering with my knees I opened to the Montana map. It took a minute but I found 213 in the northeast corner of the Blackfeet Indian Reservation. Before long we'd be up in Canada. Maybe that was Big Jack's plan. Escape across the border before seeking medical attention.

A while later his voice reached me again. "Gonna make a turn soon, kid. Keep your eye peeled. We're looking for 666. It'll be a hard left. There won't be a sign. But don't miss it. We don't wanna wind up in Canada. That won't work for us at all."

How, I wondered, did he know all this? Had he been up in this beautiful but remote neck of the woods before? And if so, when? And why? The man was a constant source of mystery and amazement.

Like a hawk on the hunt I watched for 666. When it finally showed I nearly missed it. 666 was nothing but a beat-up old path. Still, I followed orders and made the turn.

213 was a road of pure gold compared to 666. I couldn't do much over twenty miles an hour without pounding the Excursion, and probably my father, to pieces.

"Don't worry," he called out, as if reading my mind. "A few miles of this is all we got. Then we'll pull over. And get the old man some water. I'm plenty parched."

Fifteen minutes later that washboard dirt track narrowed even further. It couldn't have been six inches wider than the Excursion.

Big Jack must've been watching out the window because suddenly he said, "Up on your right, kid, you'll see a turnout. I want you to pull the truck in there nice and easy and shut her down."

Sure enough, half a minute later I spotted the turnout. It was just a place where the road widened for fifteen or twenty feet. I steered for it and pulled the Excursion off the road. Not that I really had to pull off. I hadn't seen a single car since Santa Rita.

I slowed, stopped, and shut down the engine. In the back Big Jack stayed way too quiet. For just a second I wondered if he might be dead.

I pushed open the door and stepped out. I saw green fields and rolling hills. I heard birds singing and water trickling. There was a stream banked with cottonwoods. The sun felt warm, the breeze cool.

In a split second I convinced myself Big Jack would be okay. I'd give him some water, patch him up, then haul him off to the nearest hospital where he'd get some R&R before we all headed back to Jersey. My little fantasy even had the elimination of Homer Otis and the reconciliation of Mom and Dad and the three of us living happily ever after along a wide river somewhere, maybe the Delaware or the Potomac or the Snake or the Missouri. Amazing, absolutely incredible, what the brain can conjure up in the time it takes to snap your finger or draw a breath.

Then I took a good deep breath and went around to the back of the Excursion to find out what life really had to offer. Heart pounding like a pile driver, I pulled open the big rear hatch. Morning sunlight splashed across my father's face. His skin had no color at all.

His lips were dry and bone white. I got him some water out of the cooler. At first I didn't think he'd take a sip. He just lolled his head back and forth. The moaning and groaning wouldn't quit. Clearly Big Jack was in a bad way. And half out of his mind with pain and probably blood loss.

I kept asking him what I could do, how I could help. I don't think he even heard me. I wet his lips with water. They soaked up moisture like desert sand.

Briefly he rallied. He pushed himself onto his left elbow and took a long gulp of water. "Get me outta this damn truck, Josh," he mumbled. "Out onto the ground."

No easy chore, but careful as I could I slid him out the back and over into the soft grass. I brought the sleeping bag he'd been lying on. It was wet and sticky with blood.

I kneeled at his side. He didn't move much, just a few strained twitches. But then he sat up on his elbow again, asked for more water. I brought the bottle to his lips. He drank. And then he lay back down.

I heard a vehicle coming along the road. I could see it a-ways off—an old pickup, rusty and dented.

My father, his voice barely a whisper, said, "Josh?"

I bent down. "Yeah, Dad?"

The old pickup drew closer. It came up next to the Excursion and stopped.

Big Jack squeezed my arm. "You did good today, kid. You handled yourself like a man. You're ready to take your place in the world."

And then Big Jack's eyes fell closed.

The door to the old pickup creaked open. An old man stepped out. He must've been a hundred years old. He carried a long wooden stick, like a staff a shepherd might use in the hills. He was an Indian, a Blackfoot Indian, I assumed, as we were on the Blackfeet Indian Reservation. He stood no more than five feet tall, weighed no more than one hundred pounds. He had brown skin, deeply creased, and long gray hair braided in a ponytail hanging halfway down his narrow back. He watched us for a time, and then headed our way. He walked slower than any man I'd ever seen.

The old Indian kept coming till he hovered over us. He stood at my side and in a low, gruff, gravelly voice said, "I had wheat to thrash and sheep to shear, but the Great Spirit called."

"It's my dad," I said. "He's hurt. Bad. I'm afraid he might die."

The old Indian studied Big Jack for a moment and then said, "This is not the valley of death."

"What?" I asked.

"This is not the valley of death," he repeated. And then the old Indian said just above a whisper, "What in this weary world have you done now, Jack Tailor? Gone and gotten yourself shot?"

The Blackfeet

You should've seen the hands on that old Indian. I tell you, they looked like a couple of mangled claws. Withered and gnarled with fingers bent and crooked. But the old Indian had magic in those fingers.

Right there on the side of that rutted road, right there in the grass, the old Indian used those fingers to poke and probe Big Jack's wound. First he tore away Big Jack's bloody and tattered shirt. Then he dipped a reasonably clean white cloth in water and wiped away the dry and crusty blood on Big Jack's neck and chest and arms.

I'd feared the Devil had blown open my father's chest, maybe shot him straight through the heart. But upon closer inspection I could see the bullet had penetrated up higher where the chest muscles wrap into the shoulder. There wasn't even that big of a hole, about the size of a nickel. The bigger hole was on the other side, where the bullet had blown out the back. That hole was as big as a silver dollar and all jagged and rough and black. The old Indian stuck his fingers right in the hole. It made me wince to see him do it. My whole body shuddered and my eyes looked the other way.

The old Indian, who had a clear, soft voice, said to me, "We'll need to carry him to the house."

I looked around. "House? What house?"

"My house. I have medicine there. And bandages."

I nodded.

The old Indian said, "How did this happen?"

"The Devil shot him."

He looked at me with hard gray eyes. "The Devil? The Devil did not exist in these high plains or in these mountains until the white man swept down upon us with his greed and his black powder."

"Is that right?"

The old Indian smiled. He had a few yellow teeth. "Are you strong enough," he asked, "to help me carry him?"

I must've been twice the old Indian's size and a hundred years younger. "Hell yes, I can carry him. I'll carry him all the way back to Cut Bank if I have to."

"Good," said the old Indian. "Let's go."

The old Indian had the strength of a man half his age. Together we carried Big Jack across a green meadow dotted with small red and white wildflowers. My old man, let me tell you, was plenty heavy. I had to rest every hundred feet or so.

The old Indian sighed and shook his head every time I called for a blow. He was some Indian.

And of course I wanted in the worst way to ask him how he knew my father.

We started up a long hill. It was steep with slippery lush green grass. I kept losing my footing. I kept stopping to rest. I kept complaining. I demanded to know how much farther. The old Indian just sighed and muttered under his breath.

We reached the top of the hill. The land leveled. Across another meadow of red and white wildflowers I saw a small wooden cabin. Beside the cabin was a huge garden filled with corn and other crops. Beyond the garden the land rose into a series of rolling hills. And beyond the hills—the Rockies, tall and majestic.

Several small children came running across the wildflower meadow. "Gus!" they shouted. "It's Gus! It's Gus!"

There must've been nine or ten of them—small Blackfeet Indian children between the ages of maybe three and eight. They jumped on the old Indian, dragged him playfully to the ground.

Then some other Blackfeet came out of the cabin, five or six young adults in their twenties and early thirties. They, too, came across the meadow. They were followed by another generation of three Blackfeet, two women and a man in their fifties. Bringing up the rear was an old Indian woman who looked a lot like the old Indian. They could've been brother and sister but turned out to be husband and wife. All of those Blackfeet were their progeny—children, grandchildren, great grandchildren.

I was pretty well blown away.

Especially after they carried Big Jack the rest of the way to the cabin, cleaned him up, dressed his wound, put him in a narrow bed with clean sheets, and fed me a bowl of chicken stew with corn, potatoes, carrots, and turnips. I'd never eaten turnips. They were good. I ate like a starving dog.

The old Indian and his great grandchildren sat around me while I devoured my meal. I didn't know it, with all the stress and strain, but I'd been plenty hungry.

"So," I asked, after wiping my bowl clean with a slab of brown bread and saying thank you like a million times, "are we going to take my father to the hospital? Is he going to be okay? Will he live?"

"Don't worry, young Tailor," answered the old Indian, "he'll live. Your father has the nine lives of a puma. He lost a lot of blood but the wound is clean. There is no need for a hospital. They will only ask questions. He needs rest. He can get that right where he is. It would be best if he stayed put for at least a few days. But your father is an antsy man. We will see how long he can stay still."

"You think after a few days he'll be able to move?"

"Maybe. We'll have to wait and see. I assume there might be trouble on your rear."

"Trouble?"

"Someone shot him. I assume you had trouble."

I nodded. "Yes, we had a run-in with the Devil."

"Right," said the old Indian. "The Devil."

I ducked away from that and asked, "How do you know my father?"

The old Indian took a moment to think.

So did I. I'd crossed the country with Big Jack, had half a dozen strangers call him by half a dozen different names. And then, out of the blue, in the middle of the Blackfeet Indian Reservation, my old man lying in the grass bleeding to death from a bullet wound, an old Indian steps out of a rusty pickup and calls my father by his real name. Go figure.

"You know, son," answered the old Indian, "I think I'll let your father tell you how he and I met."

After a while I went into the small bedroom at the back of the cabin and sat next to Big Jack. He lay stretched out on that narrow bed, filling it from side to side and from end to end. He had no shirt on. The clean white bandage went over his shoulder, across his chest, down under his armpit, and up over his shoulder again. The old Indian said he wasn't going to die. I believed him. What else could I do?

Big Jack slept. His breathing was shallow but steady. He looked white but not as white as he'd looked earlier back in the Excursion.

Outside I heard the great grandchildren playing some kind of Blackfeet Indian game. Through the window I could see them knocking a ball around with sticks. I could also see several of the adults working in the garden, picking crops and weeding between the rows. It was some garden, the biggest garden I'd ever seen.

The sun hung high in the sky. A nice breeze swept through the window.

The old Indian came into the room. "How is he?"

"Sleeping."

"The more he sleeps the better."

Our voices woke Big Jack. He needed a minute to come around. "Josh?"

"Yeah, Dad?"

"What the hell? Where are we?"

The old Indian stepped forward. "Hello, Jack."

My father needed another minute to get focused. "Gus! I had hopes I might see you." Big Jack tried to push himself up but the wound put a strong grimace on his face and drove him back into the bed.

"I heard you coming," said Gus the old Indian, "from a long way off."

This brought the hint of a smile to Big Jack's tortured face. He turned to me. "I want you to step up, Josh. This old-timer here, in case you haven't met formally, is Mr. Augustus Roland Witherspoon. Also known by his Blackfeet name of Sways With the Wind."

A crooked smile crossed the old Indian's face. I didn't have a clue what history these two had, but clearly they had a past.

I shook Gus' hand, then said to my father, "I asked Gus how you two met. He told me to ask you."

"He did, did he?"

I nodded.

"Well, me and Gus met up in the mountains a few years back. More than a few now, come to think of it. I was running from something or someone. Old Gus was just sitting on a rock, his days of running over. I sat down to rest. Gus right away began to rant in my ear. 'White man is the scourge of the earth. He has no respect for the earth. No understanding. He believes in conquest, not compromise or cooperation.' I believe I said something like, 'Huh? What are you yapping about, old man?' And old Gus said, 'The Blackfeet lived on these high plains and in these mountains for a thousand years before the white man arrived. We had a way of life that existed for many generations without change or disruption. We lived close to the earth. We did not strive except for life's essentials. Then the white man came with his ambition and his ammunition and in one generation he decimated the Blackfeet because the white man feels alienated from the earth and so must use his power to destroy. The earth is round. The universe is round. Life operates on a cycle. Hopefully the white man's arrogant and impatient dominance of earth will cycle into oblivion.' Oh yeah, I didn't ask old Gus what he was yapping about after that. No way. I listened hard to what Gus had to say. And let me tell you, kid, I'm listening still."

I needed to shake my head a couple times to keep all that in motion. Even for Big Jack that was a mouthful.

He leaned back into the bed and took a couple deep breaths. "Sorry, boys, but I think I'm gonna fall out again. Blew my load with that little speech."

"You rest," said the old Indian. "I'll look in on you later."

Big Jack asked me the time.

I glanced at my Timex Explorer. "Almost three."

"You need to hightail it back to Glacier," Big Jack ordered. "Those boys are gonna wonder where we are."

"Can we call them?"

"Not from out here. No phone. No cell service. This is the boonies, Josh."

"So you want me to go back? By myself?"

"Can you handle it?"

I thought that over for as long as I dared. "I guess so."

"That's what I want to hear. You saved the old man's hide out there today. Saved me from a painful and certain end at the hands of that sick psycho. First chance I get I'm gonna put a bullet through his head. But enough of him. You need to get back to Glacier and take control of those two knuckleheads."

"Right," I said, working up to it now, "I gotta roll."

Big Jack nodded. Then he grimaced from all the effort. After a couple seconds he lowered his voice and said, "There's a pile of money back in the truck. And another pile in our room at the hotel. Take good care of that dough, kid. It's for your future."

"I'll take good care of the money," I assured him. "But just till tomorrow, then we'll be back to pick you up."

He nodded. "Better make it day after tomorrow. I'll need a little time."

"Take all the time you want," I told him, "but me and the boys will back tomorrow."

Big Jack took my hand, gave it a squeeze. "It'll all work out fine, Josh. Better than fine. Just remember you're a man now and a man does what he has to do."

His head rolled to the side. And out he went.

I watched him for a minute or two, then, happy he was going to live but plenty nervous I was on my own, I took my leave.

The Storm

After thanking and saying so long to the Blackfeet I made my way back across those meadows to the Excursion. For a few minutes I stood around in a befuddled stupor, then I did the only thing I could think to do—I got behind the wheel and started driving. I drove in the direction the truck was already pointed. The compass on the overhead console said SW. Southwest.

Yup, me, Finnegan Joshua Tailor, was driving a Ford Excursion southwest in northwestern Montana. Alone. A solo flight. On the Blackfeet Indian Reservation. 2500 miles or more from home. It was 84 degrees outside the Excursion, 73 degrees inside the cabin. The battery was charging. I had half a tank of gas. I had the Excursion's big potent Triton V-10 engine under my command. But I had no driver's license, no official driver's training, no right, really, to be piloting that bulky ship. But what could I do? Park the beast along the side of the road and start hitchhiking?

Nope, I kept driving. But only for another mile or so. Then I pulled off onto the narrow shoulder of that rutted lane. I needed to take a few deep breaths, get a grip on myself, a grip on reality.

Those jobs reasonably well done, I reached under the seat for the atlas. I opened to the Montana map and got my bearings. If I kept moving south on 666 it would take me to Route 2 about halfway between Cut Bank and Browning.

I thanked Big Jack for fine-tuning my navigational skills. And also for putting me behind the wheel back in Nebraska. I felt like I had the confidence now to get this done. To get back to the Lodge. To do whatever needed doing. I just had to stay cool no matter what jive flew my way. I had to be Big Jack.

I left the map of Montana open on the passenger seat. Then I stepped out of the truck and walked around back. I opened the rear hatch. And located the .357 Magnum where Big Jack had dropped it after blowing the Blazer off the road. I came up with the weapon heavy and cold. I wanted to throw it into the nearby creek, never lay eyes on it again, but no, that wouldn't do. Not yet.

I carried the gun forward and climbed back into the driver's seat. In the center console I found a fresh clip of bullets. They were long, nasty, deadly looking things. I shoved the clip into the .357, then buried the gun in the console underneath some papers. For good measure I locked the console up tight. No way did I want Retro or Bones rummaging around in there looking for gum or Lifesavers and coming up instead with that cold piece of steel.

The gun safely stowed, I returned to the back of the big Excursion. I pulled out all the camping gear, laid it on the ground, and inspected everything for signs of Big Jack's blood. Mostly he'd bled on one of the sleeping bags. That bag was back in the grass. But I also found blood on one of the other bags, so I dragged it into the underbrush off the road. No chance of anyone spotting me. That road was as deserted as the moon.

I reloaded the camping gear, then took care of one last detail—the briefcase. I picked it up, popped the latches, and took a look inside. My eyes went buggy at the sight of all those hundred dollar bills. I grabbed a thick wad, stuffed them in my pocket, then closed and locked the case.

I placed the case under the camping gear, walked back to the driver's door, and climbed up into the seat. I slipped on my shades and baseball cap and headed down the road. Plenty quiet on 666 in the heart of the Blackfeet Indian Reservation.

Half an hour later I reached US 2 and a whole lot more traffic. I waited till the road was clear for as far as I could see before pulling out. That big V-10 had no trouble getting up to highway speed. Without a trailer filled with M-16s and RPGs the Excursion accelerated like a sports car.

I settled in right smack on the speed limit—65 mph.

In Browning the traffic was stop and go. I grew plenty nervous, especially after a Montana state trooper pulled out of a gas station and took up a position just two vehicles behind me. Sweat formed on my brow even with the AC blowing cool on my face. But after half a mile or so the trooper pulled off onto a side street.

I quit my hyperventilating and relaxed some.

Not too much later I reached East Glacier. And soon after that I drove under the big WELCOME TO GLACIER NATIONAL PARK arch.

I found Retro and Bones out on the big sweep of lawn behind the Lodge playing touch football with two guys about our age.

Retro spotted me and jogged over. "Josh, where you been? It's been hours. Me and Bones were starting to think you and Big Jack had flown the coop."

"Sorry," I told him. "I got back as soon as I could."

Bones came over with the two footballers. Their names were like Sam and Stan from Tulsa, Oklahoma. I didn't catch it all.

They wanted me to get Big Jack so we could have a game of 3-on-3. I wanted to tell them what had happened over in Santa Rita. I wanted to tell them about the guns and Conrad Gibson and the Devil and Big Jack getting shot and me driving him to safety and the old Indian. But I didn't. I kept quiet. I said, "I don't think so."

"Why not?" demanded Retro.

"'Cause Big Jack wants us up in his room for a little powwow."

"Who's Big Jack?" one of the boys from Oklahoma wanted to

know.

"Big Jack Tailor," Retro told him. "Coolest hombre west of the Mississippi. Also Josh's dad. Walks the world like he owns the place."

Hearing my buddy Retro say it made me certain I'd keep him as a friend forever.

I heard him add, "It's Big Jack who's taking us around the west."

The football game broke up. Me and Retro and Bones headed back to the Lodge.

"What's with the powwow?" Retro asked as we passed through the lobby.

"Let's wait till we get to the room," I answered.

"We pulling out?"

"Pretty soon," I told him. "Probably tomorrow."

I couldn't get up to the room fast enough. Luckily, before we got to the room and got the door closed, I brought myself under control. And then I managed to give the boys a reasonably calm and coherent account of what had gone down since me and Big Jack had left the Lodge in the predawn hours. It took time but I got the story told. It came out, you know, in fragments—bits and pieces—but my buddies hung with me.

After I wound down the boys still had a thousand questions. They wanted all the details. We must've talked it over for a couple hours.

Eventually Bones asked, "So what are we going to do now?"

"We're going to hang here at the Lodge till tomorrow," I told him. "Then we'll go back to get Big Jack. Hopefully in a day or two he'll be able to travel."

Bones thought it over. He looked a little spooked. "Don't you think we should maybe call the police? I mean, this guy you call the Devil shot your father."

"I got strict orders: no cops."

"What about our parents? Or at least your mother? Shouldn't we tell someone what happened to Big Jack?"

Retro stepped up. "Yeah," he said, "maybe we should. But we're not gonna. You heard what Josh said: no cops."

In the morning I woke early, way before dawn. I packed my gear first, then Big Jack's gear. He carried his stuff in two old leather satchels. In the larger satchel I found clothes and shoes. In the smaller satchel I found an assortment of driver's licenses, passports, and a slew of credit cards. All with different names. But all containing photos of my father, a broad smile on his face.

All those fake IDs made me wonder about the life my dad led. A wild one, that's for sure. Definitely not like the lives fathers led back in Bridgeton, NJ.

Also in the smaller satchel I found a black nylon bag. Inside the bag was another pile of money—probably the money Big Jack had made off the Chaney boys. There were stacks of hundreds. I didn't count it, but clearly I was in possession of a pretty fair stash. Along with the Montana militia money I figured in excess of a hundred grand.

The packing done I carried everything down to the truck. A quick look around assured me I had the parking lot all to myself. I shoved the briefcase and Big Jack's small leather satchel deep inside one of the sleeping bags. I put the money-laden bag on the bottom and packed the rest of the camping gear around it. Short of a bank vault, this was as safe as I could make the money for the time being.

After stowing the gear I popped the hood and checked the fluids—oil, coolant, brakes, transmission. Big Jack had taught me what to check. "A few minutes now," he liked to say, "will save you some major hassles later."

Back in the Lodge I rousted Retro and Bones. "Rise and shine, birds! Up and at 'em! We're burnin' daylight. Time to put away the bedrolls and move those cattle."

In reply they cursed me and threw pillows at me and suggested I take a long hike off a short pier. I told them to shake a leg, the Excursion train, passengers aboard or not, would be pulling out of the station lickity split.

Half an hour later we hit the road. We made it over to Browning no sweat. But just west of Browning, the needle fast descending toward empty, we decided we had to get gas. Throughout the trip pit stops had always been welcome reprieves from the endless driving, but now the chore loomed as a real hazard to our independence. We knew folks would be able to get a good look at us while the Excursion sat idle at the pumps.

Fortunately, out west, you pump your own gas. No curious pump jock comes out and does it for you. Which meant we could remain relatively incognito.

I swung the Excursion into a Chevron station and steered for the most distant set of pumps. I had my shades on and my baseball cap pulled low over my brow. Soon as I shut off the engine Retro hopped out and started pumping. Bones did the windows with a squeegee. Especially the windshield. You had to be diligent washing the windshield at all pit stops on account of the dead bugs that piled up thick and gooey.

I stayed quiet behind the wheel, hid my face inside the atlas.

The Excursion had two fuel tanks. It took some time to get them filled up. Several minutes. And nearly forty gallons. Over a hundred bucks. I handed the money to Bones as soon as Retro quit pumping. He headed for the cashier's counter.

A couple minutes later Bones returned, climbed into the back, put the change on the console between the front seats, and said, "I asked the girl at the cash register about driving in Montana. She said you can get a special farm license at fifteen."

Me and Retro exchanged glances. Retro said, "Come on, Bones, you asked a girl a question? All by your lonesome?"

To which Bones, shy as a mouse around girls, replied, "Blow me."

Which brought on belly laughs from the pilot and copilot.

The banter and the successful pit stop lightened our mood some, made us feel downright frivolous. We'd been stressing pretty strong over our predicament.

Behind us, coming hard and fast out of the Rockies, pushed black clouds and bolts of lightning. Retro and Bones climbed into the back of the truck to watch the show out the rear window. I had to content myself with glimpses of the storm in the side view mirrors. At least I did till we put some distance between us and Browning. Then, out on US 2, at the 666 turnoff, I swung down that dirt lane and shut off the engine.

Over the next twenty minutes we saw more bolts of lightning than I'd seen in my entire life. They came flying out of the black sky one after another. We climbed out of the Excursion and watched the show and oohed and aahed like we were back in Bridgeton watching the 4th of July fireworks display over the Delaware. The sky directly overhead grew dark, then darker, then as black as a moonless night. The rain—great gushes of it, sheets of it—swept over us, driving us back into the truck. Drops the size of Junior Mints pelted the roof and windows like machine gun fire.

Bones said, "I wish Big Jack was here to see this."

Retro said, "Yeah, me too."

No doubt about it—Big Jack brought a level of comfort and security to sticky situations. I'm not saying we were scared or anything, oh no, but had Big Jack been there we probably would've enjoyed that storm even more and feared it less.

"He's not far," I told the guys. "Just half an hour or so up this old dirt road."

I headed up 666. I didn't do much over 20 mph with all the potholes as big as foxholes. The boys kept demanding to know how much farther.

Finally we reached the turnoff where I'd unloaded Big Jack the day before. I saw the old Indian's rusty pickup. I shut down the engine. We stepped out.

"Looks to me," said Retro, "like the middle of nowhere. Where's Big Jack?"

"Follow me." I led them across that wildflower meadow and up into the hills. I was plenty excited to see my father. Yesterday he'd told me I'd saved his life. Imagine what that did for my ego and self-esteem. It swelled me up some, that's for sure. And now I wanted to hear him sing my praises again, this time for taking care of business at the Lodge and for successfully hauling me and the boys back to the old Indian's homestead.

Across the meadow the cabin came into view. I expected a whole band of young Blackfeet to come running through the grass to greet us. But none came. Not a one.

We made our way up the hill toward the cabin. Things looked plenty quiet. I saw no one and heard no one. Not on the porch or out in the garden.

Retro said, "Yo, Josh, where are all the Indians?"

"I don't know. They were all here yesterday."

We stood in front of the cabin. "Gus!" I called. "Hey, Gus! It's me, Josh Tailor."

No reply.

I went up onto the front porch and through the front door without bothering to knock. I headed straight for the room off the back where I'd left my father the previous afternoon. He wasn't there. The bed was empty.

The whole house was empty. Not a Blackfoot in sight.

We hung around and waited for a couple hours. We sat on the front porch. We kicked a ball around the front yard. We speculated as to the whereabouts of Big Jack and that band of Blackfeet.

It was pretty weird, I tell you, plenty strange.

My mind settled on the possibility that Big Jack had taken a bad turn and Gus had hauled him to a hospital. But then why was the old pickup sitting out by the road?

I didn't know. I didn't have a clue.

The boys started grousing. They said they were hungry but I think they were mostly scared. Big Jack had vanished. We were out in the middle of nowhere. Dusk looked not too far off.

We hiked back to the truck. I'd left the headlights on. The battery was dead.

Retro cursed me out.

We had oranges and Devil Dogs for dinner. Night fell. No one said much. We got out the sleeping bags. I made sure to take the one with the money. We spread the bags on some flat ground.

And a few minutes later, the stars—unbelievable! That vast western sky held so many stars I swear to God there couldn't have been room for many more. You couldn't find the Big Dipper or the North Star so dense was that blanket of twinkling white lights.

We lay in our bags, hands behind our heads, and stared up at that amazing sky.

Retro said, "Makes you feel kind of, I don't know, small. Insignificant."

"And those are just the stars emitting light," added Bones, our resident genius and amateur astronomer. "There are planets revolving around every single one of those stars. Like our sun. Which is actually a relatively minor star. Yet it has a dozen planets. So we might be seeing billions of stars tonight, but there are trillions of planets out there we can't see."

That got us all thinking about the infinite size of the universe and our small role in it. As well as I can recall, no one said much after that. I mean, our predicament—no Big Jack and a dead battery and so far from home—seemed pretty significant and all, but was it really? In the big scheme of things?

It took me a while to get comfy with those kinds of thoughts in my head and all those hundred dollar bills pushing for space. Finally I dozed. But I don't think I'd slept more than a few minutes before the strange sounds of that Montana night startled me awake. And kept me awake pretty much straight through till dawn.

I heard owls screeching and either wolves or coyotes calling to one another in long, mournful howls. I heard what sounded like monkeys fighting to the death over their last banana, but Bones insisted it was foxes preparing to mate. To top it off we heard, and sort of saw, this large wooly mammal (bear? elk? antelope?) charge up the road in one direction, then, a minute later, charge by again in the other direction.

The enormous beast nearly stomped on Retro, turning his head to mush.

All this and those stars provided little time for shuteye.

But I guess I slept some because when I finally opened my eyes again the sun had lifted into the sky. My watch claimed it was nearly 7:30.

The boys woke up. We argued for a while about our next move. They wanted to hike out, find someone to help us get the truck started. I said I was going back up to the cabin to look for Jack. Before they could grouse I moved off. Across that meadow of wildflowers and up the hill.

The boys followed, a ways back.

The Passage

And this time when the cabin came into view I was not greeted with silence. The old Indian's great grandchildren raced across the meadow to meet me. They grabbed my hands and pulled me toward the cabin. I slowed them down long enough for Retro and Bones to catch up. The old Indian's entire clan came to welcome us. They offered us food and cider. It was like a party.

I said to Gus, "We came by yesterday. The place was deserted."

"Yes," said Gus, "we had to move north. To avoid the agents."

"What agents?"

"From the government."

"I don't understand."

"Looking for your father, you see."

I didn't see. "What are you talking about?"

The old Indian took my arm. "Come inside. Your father left you something."

"What do you mean he left me something? Where is he? Is he okay?"

"So many questions for such a young man. Better to wait and watch."

Gus led me into the cabin. We went into the back bedroom. The bed was made up with fresh sheets. Big Jack was nowhere in sight. He'd vanished. An old trick.

On the simple wooden dresser was an envelope with my name on it. Inside was a letter written on unlined paper. I unfolded it and read:

> *J. Finnegan Tailor,*
> *Hope you're well, kid. We got word in the middle of the night ATF was prowling around the reservation. So we lit out for Canada ASAP, your old man stretched out on the back of a cart pulled by an ATV. Quite a show!*
> *Hiding out now along the Milk River up here in*

The Passage

Alberta. The chest and shoulder hurt like hell. But gimme a few weeks and I'll be skinning rabbits. Probably deserve what I got dealing for with those sick bastards.

Here's the deal. I can't risk coming back across the border for a couple months or more. Sorry about fouling up the trip but you boys will have to get yourselves home. Old Gus will haul you down to Great Falls where you can use the dough to catch a plane or a train. Or, if you're feeling ballsy, just climb up behind the wheel of that big old Excursion and start driving east. You got money, maps, and big brass cojones. That's all you need. But hey, if you choose the driving option, don't tell your mama it was my idea.

I love you, kid. Take care of yourself. And take care of that a-hole Homer Otis too. Or wait for me and I'll help you out. Soon as I can I'll be floating back to Jersey.

Your old man, Jack Tailor

I read the letter twice. And then I turned to Gus. "You were with my father?"

Gus nodded. "Until last night."

"And he's okay?"

"He's plenty tough, son," Gus told me, "for a white man."

"He'll recover from his wound?"

Gus nodded again. "He'll recover."

"So then, that's it?"

"Your father asked me to drive you to Great Falls."

I shoved the letter in the pocket. "I'll need to confer with my buddies."

Retro and Bones were outside kicking a ball around with the great grandkids while the rest of Gus' extended clan looked on. I took my buds aside and explained the situation. As you might expect, Bones voted for a ride to Great Falls followed by the first flight home. Retro wanted to cruise, wanted the three of us to pilot the big Excursion back to Bridgeton.

And me, well, I wasn't about to have my best bud in the world call me a yellow so I sided with Retro. We'd drive home. All the way to Jersey.

We said our goodbyes to the Blackfeet. Gus never once tried to talk me out of driving home. All he said was, "Your father knew you'd drive. He said it was in your blood and that it would do you good. Give you time to think."

Gus walked back down to the road with us. He helped us jumpstart the Excursion off the old pickup's battery and then he sent us on our way.

The Rednecks

We drove and drove. No one said much. We needed to get comfortable inside ourselves for what lay ahead.

We turned onto US 2 and just before we got to Shelby we stopped to have a look at the map. At first we thought we'd take US 2 all the way across northern Montana. It looked like a good, safe, out-of-the-way route, a route Big Jack might've chosen. But it also looked to me like a long and lonely way to go.

I had another reason for changing my tune—cops. On US 2 we'd pass through one small town after another—Joplin, Rudyard, Glasgow, Wolf Point. Which meant a lot of small-town policemen getting a good look at us. But if we stuck to the interstate in that high black truck at 70 mph we'd be a whole lot more anonymous.

So we turned south onto I-15. An hour later we reached Great Falls. Two hours after that we hit Butte where we headed east onto I-90. Another couple hours and we pulled into Bozeman. We stopped for gas at an enormous station that must've had a couple dozen self-serve pumps. One by one we went inside to use the head and buy junk food. Within ten minutes we were back on the road.

Less than an hour later I started to wear down. I'd been driving about six hours but it felt more like six days. The neck and back felt stiff and tired. Tension rippled along my spine, probably a result of my hyper focused driving style.

I said to Retro, "What do you think? Wanna drive?"

"Just waiting for the word, boss."

I set the cruise control at sixty-five, then climbed out of the driver's seat while Retro climbed in. We switched positions without even slowing down. Probably sounds dangerous, but we did it no problem, slick and easy.

"Not more than a mile or two over the speed limit," I ordered.

"You sure? They'll pass us like we're standing still."

"Let 'em pass."

Me and Bones switched positions. He moved up front, I sprawled in back. "Wake me when we get to Billings," I told him. A second later my batteries died.

Before I could dream Bones shook me awake. "Coming into Billings, Josh."

I glanced at the clock: 4:47. I'd been asleep almost two hours.

I sat up and opened the atlas, turned to the map of Montana, and showed Bones our location. The time had come to make him a navigator. "I-90," I told him, "will take us south into Wyoming and then over into the Black Hills of Dakota."

Bones spent a couple minutes studying the map. "Josh?"

"Yeah, Bones?"

"How long you think before we get home?"

"Depends where we go and how long we stay. Straight through we could make it in a couple days. Three at the most. Why?" I asked. "You in a hurry?"

Bones gave the question some thought. Finally he said, "No, not really. I don't know. Maybe. It'll be good to get home. But this is good. This is cool."

"This is the way Big Jack would've wanted it."

Bones nodded. "I should probably call my parents. It's been a while."

I hesitated a second and then said, "We'll call next stop."

The Passage

Next stop came an hour later down near the Montana/Wyoming line. A big truck stop with a dozen pumps, a couple restaurants, even a place to shower. We all called home.

I dialed the house on Cherry Street in Bridgeton. Mom answered on the first ring.

"Hey," I said.

"Josh!"

Never in my life had I felt so glad to hear Mom's voice. Of course I didn't tell her how happy I was. Oh no, I had to play it cool.

She right away wanted to know where I was.

I wanted to tell her about Dad. I wanted to blurt out every last gruesome detail about our battle with the Devil. But I didn't. I held it back. I held it in. Didn't say a word.

"On our way, Mom. Still in Montana but now heading east."

"Montana? My God, Joshua. When will you be home?"

"I'd say... in a few days. Maybe—"

"Where's your father? I need to talk to him. You're way overdue, Joshua. I told you before you left I wanted you back by—"

"I love you, Mom."

"What?"

"I said I love you."

Caught off guard, Mom needed a second to recover. "I love you too, sweetie."

"I just wanted to tell you that, and, you know, tell you I miss you, and that, like I said, we'll be home soon and I'll be real happy to see you because you're the best mom a kid could ever have."

"Joshua, you'll make me cry. You're so sweet. I miss you too."

That was all the mushy stuff I could take. I said I had to go and hung up.

At dusk we pulled into the wild west town of Sheridan. After a search we secured ourselves a room at a fleabag called the Frontier Motel. Our first motel without Big Jack. The front desk clerk, a stick thin woman immersed in her National Enquirer, didn't even look up at us. All she wanted was $112.83, cash, before handing over the key.

The room was not only pricey but small, hot, and fetid. It smelled like someone had died under the bed. But what could three young outlaws on the run do? Complain?

Nope, we showered, caught our breath, then went looking for food. We'd eaten nothing all day but cakes, chips, candy, and Coke.

The scarecrow at the front desk told us about a Mexican place down the road.

I asked, "How far?"

She said, "Not far. A few blocks."

We decided to walk. Too bad in Sheridan, WY a block stretches for like a mile.

Not only did we have to walk forever but then this old convertible Pontiac GTO filled with Sheridan's finest young rednecks thought it would be cool to hassle us. They drove back and forth along the wide boulevard, taunting us with each pass. They said nasty stuff about our mothers and heaped upon us every curse word known to man.

"You stupid small-brained rednecks!" shouted Retro. "You're dumber than prairie dogs!" He hurled back their profanity curse word for curse word.

Which of course caused those rednecks to slow their GTO and threaten to beat us to bloody pulps. Luckily we'd been in training with Big Jack so soon as they slowed we sped up and sprinted down the sidewalk. We got through the front door of Pedro's Mexican Palace just before those

Sheridan boys caught up with us.

We ate tacos and burritos, several each. The dudes in the GTO waited for us across the street. The four of them leaned against the Pontiac, their arms folded tough-guy style across their chests. They looked like real jackasses. Too bad we were afraid of them, scared little boys. Big Jack would've laughed his ass off.

We spent the whole meal discussing how best to get safely back to the Frontier Motel. A taxi sounded like a good idea, but the Mexican kid waiting our table felt pretty sure Sheridan didn't have taxis.

Then all of a sudden something started to pelt the front window of Pedro's. It sounded like stones being tossed against glass. I assumed it was the GTO boys.

The Mexican kid saw us worried and laughed. "Dust storm," he explained. "Fifty mile an hour winds blow down off the mountains and clear across the desert. Makes a grain of sand sound like a stone."

The dust storm was good for us. It drove away those rednecks. They wanted to get that GTO undercover before all that flying debris wreaked havoc with the paint job.

We took the opportunity to pay and bolt. The Mexican kid hadn't been messing with us—fifty miles an hour, minimum. And us plowing straight into the teeth of it. Heads down, eyes covered, shoulders hunched—we pushed and shoved our way back to the Frontier. By the time we finally got there I had sand and dirt and grit in my eyes, ears, teeth, and nose.

We went to bed, dog-tired, but no one could sleep. We flopped around like fish out of water, restless and damp, on those mushy, moldy mattresses. It was, I have to tell you, the smell of Death. And the Devil. And for me Homer Otis. And the Heat—the air conditioner poured only hot air into our luxurious digs. And that damn Wind—it rattled the windows and shook the door and blew dust through the cracks and disturbed our already disturbed minds.

Where, I wanted to know, was Big Jack? He'd never have us sleeping in a dump like this. Was there any chance he'd ever come back?

I knew he would, eventually. He'd show up one day, unexpected and uninvited. And I'd want him to stay. And he would. For a while. He'd lay some of his philosophy on me. Make me change my thinking on this and that. And then, like air, he'd vanish again. Disappear.

Yeah, it was a long and terrifying night. I had nightmares about the Devil coming out of his Jeep armed and dangerous, about those rednecks driving that GTO through the front window of Pedro's, running us down like armadillos on the highway, about Chief Walters arriving at the old Victorian in his Crown Vic and arresting me for crashing the VW and stealing lumber and for the murder of one Mr. Homer Otis.

Oh yeah, it was bad. Very bad. A bad night. A couple times I woke up sweating and screaming for my mama. Thank God I had my buds there to calm me down and tell me to quit acting like a fool.

Manhood's all well and good but boyhood doesn't fade easily. It's a rough passage.

The Passage

Deep into the night young Josh kept talking. I wanted to tell him I needed a break, I needed some sleep, but his story was riveting, and of course I wanted to know how it would all turn out.

I wanted to know if they made it home. I wanted to know about Homer.

Throughout the night more rumors flew. The news was not good. But I didn't pay it any mind. There was nothing I could do about any of it anyway. I was warm and dry and for the time being safe.

And I had this story, Josh's story, to entertain me. To sustain me.

And maybe to give me hope…

The Badlands

We got up and out of Sheridan pretty early in the a.m. We took cold showers, stuffed coffee and donuts in our bellies, and pulled back out onto I-90. Almost immediately our itinerary became the major topic of conversation.

Bones, sitting up front with me, the atlas open on his lap, said, "We can take 90 all the way to Chicago where it hooks up with 80. 80 will take us straight back to Jersey through the Water Gap. If we pull hard we could be home maybe by tomorrow night."

"Tomorrow night? You gotta be kidding me, Bones," I said. "We still got a couple thousand miles to go. When'll we sleep, eat, take a leak?"

"You sleep while Carl drives and he sleeps while you drive."

"What about when we both sleep? You gonna drive?"

"I'm not driving."

I turned to Retro. "What do you think of Bones' plan?"

Retro was sprawled out across the back seat. "I say, what's the hurry? Nothing back home but a long hot summer and a lot of nothing much to do. Out here we're free to do as we please."

"I want to get home," insisted Bones.

"I want to get home," mimicked Retro.

"Back off," said Bones.

Retro laughed and backed off.

On the whole home thing I fell on middle ground. I felt Bones' desire to get home—both to see Mom and to deal with Homer—but I also wanted to make Big Jack proud. He'd been everywhere, seen everything, and believed you had to make the most of time. "You only get so much of it," he preached like a mantra, "so don't be a fool and waste it." Then we'd pull off the highway to watch a hawk circling overhead or to help an old couple fix a flat tire or to just smell the evening air. "Enjoy the moment, boys," he'd tell us. "It's the only one of its kind."

So I decided to ride the middle road between Bones and Retro while pondering my own haziness about getting home or staying on the road. I did, however, suggest we beeline for the Black Hills of Dakota and a visit to Mt. Rushmore.

It took us till early afternoon of another sweltering hot day to pull ourselves out of Wyoming. We passed out of the Cowboy State into the Mount Rushmore State. Bones, studying the map, said, "Not too far ahead, right on the road to Mount Rushmore, is a monument to Crazy Horse, the Lakota Chief who took out Custer at Little Big Horn."

From the back Retro said, "I dig Crazy Horse. Both the Indian and the band. Let's stop and check it out."

Half an hour later we reached the Crazy Horse Monument. We could see it from a mile off, this enormous white stone face jutting off the end of a mountain and gleaming in the afternoon sun. It was here because Crazy Horse had spent his entire adult life fighting to keep the white man out of the sacred Black Hills only to die a violent death at the hands of those same white men at the ripe young age of thirty-three.

The colossal sculpture had been started more than fifty years before me and Retro and Bones arrived. Fifty years but still not finished. Crazy Horse's shoulders and torso still had to be chiseled out of the mountain. The problem was money. The Indians didn't have the dough to finish the job. They asked the Federal government for help, but Crazy Horse was considered a nuisance and an enemy of the state, definitely not a hero worth preserving in stone, so the government told the Indians to pound salt.

We took a good long look at Crazy Horse from the visitor's center in the valley at the base of the monument. All through the visitor's center were glass boxes where you could stuff spare bills that would be used to keep the project going. Fascinated by Crazy Horse, saddened by the plight of the Plains Indians, and grateful for the assistance of old Gus and his Blackfeet clan for taking care of Big Jack, I stuffed several hundred dollar bills into one of those boxes. I figured it was what Big Jack would want me to do.

After a while we shoved off for Mt. Rushmore. Rushmore definitely had the glitz and glamour over Crazy Horse. It had a far slicker and more professional feel. From the glass and granite visitor's center to the various viewing platforms to the gargantuan granite faces up on the rock wall—Mt. Rushmore swallowed you whole. Plus you had the comfort and familiarity of George and Tom and Honest Abe and Teddy gazing down on you. Crazy Horse had looked wild and maniacal, an untamed warrior ready to slit your throat and steal your scalp. But the Presidents—they made you feel right at home—safe and secure, just the way Willa had said they would.

I stood and stared for quite a while at Washington and Jefferson and Lincoln and Roosevelt. And I'll admit I was moved by the whole show. Changed even. The way Pop had told me I'd be. But I also got to tell you that, thanks to Big Jack, I had some dubious attitudes running through my brain. Big Jack demanded you take a longer, closer look at things, not just buy into the sweet facade. He wanted you to glance at the other side of the story. Like the way he'd given us a peek into the affluent, slave-driven lifestyle of George Washington back in Virginia. Big Jack had instilled in me the beauty of a little healthy skepticism and the reality the only person you can rely on is yourself.

Late in the afternoon we climbed into the truck and drove on. With

Retro at the wheel I took the opportunity to turn around and take a last look out the back window of the Excursion. The sun, still high in the western sky, hung directly over the stern gaze of General George Washington. I saw him standing out on the front lawn of his lavish Mt. Vernon plantation. I saw him watching the placid Potomac gliding by. I saw a dozen slaves cowering at his feet calling him mastuh. And then a second later the Excursion swept around a wide turn and Mt. Rushmore vanished from view.

An hour later, evening slowly coming on, we reached Wall, South Dakota and the western entrance to the Badlands National Park. Bones, sticking to his hard line, voted to zip right by, but me and Retro voted to swing in and have a look.

At the gate we paid the guy ten bucks and got a map and a pamphlet published by the National Park Service. We didn't have any idea what to expect from the Park but in we went. Just the name—Badlands—was plenty cool. Any young guy would be drawn to a place with a name like that. But for me anyway, more than the name was Willa the waitress back in Nebraska who'd told us not to miss the Badlands, that we had to go to the Badlands and watch the sunset and listen to the wind and be changed forever.

The Badlands is a wild, barren, deranged landscape littered with surreal colors, deep canyons, and bizarre rock formations you might see in a sci-fi flick about other galaxies. It looks more like the surface of the moon than an exit off the interstate in the middle of the Great Plains. Retro thought it looked like a futuristic dream world. Bones declared it closer to a nightmare. And me—I thought the weathered peaks and jutting buttes and shadowy gullies looked like ancient cities. I imagined entire civilizations living out their lives amidst the mysterious ruins. Plus I had this strange ringing in my ears during our entire visit. I asked Retro and Bones if they could hear it. They looked at me like I was nuts and said no.

Half an hour into the park I spotted a turn-off. I told Retro to stop, told him I had to stretch my legs and take a leak. He shrugged and turned into the small parking lot for the Prairie Wind Overlook. No one else was around. We climbed out of the truck and up onto some high ground with a nearly 360 degree view. It must've been close to nine in the evening. The sun hung low on the western horizon out beyond the distant silhouette of the Black Hills. Long shadows spread across the eerie landscape.

Retro, with the eyes of an eagle, pointed to the plains off to the south and said he could see buffalo. I couldn't see them but took a look through Big Jack's high-powered binoculars and sure enough there they were—a whole herd of the enormous big-headed beasts grazing in knee-deep grass. For some reason I decided those buffalo were an optimistic omen for the future.

I continued to hear that ringing in my ears. I went looking for it. My feet carried me away from my buds. Not far. Just a few hundred yards along a dirt path and out onto a secluded overlook facing due west into the setting sun—a huge ball of heat glowing bright orange. The ringing grew louder. And then stopped.

I turned around. And perched up on a rock not ten feet from where I stood sat Big Jack Tailor, my old man. He wore his usual uniform—moccasins, jeans, and a gray tee shirt. He looked a whole lot better than the last time I'd seen him. He looked good: strong and ruddy. A man's man. No wound at all in his chest. All healed up and smiling.

"Hey, kid. How you making out?"

"Pretty good."

"How's the driving?"

I started to relax, to accept the ways of the world. "Fine. No problems at all."

"You can make it back to Jersey?"

"Oh yeah. No sweat."

Big Jack nodded. "Listen, kid, I'm glad we had a chance to do some talking and some traveling together. And I'm glad we buried some old hatchets."

It was weird, standing out in the middle of the Badlands talking to my imagination, but in some ways it was as good as having the real Big Jack at my side.

And then I heard my name. "Josh! Yo, Josh!"

"That's your buddies calling," said Big Jack.

"Yup."

"They're counting on you to get them home safe and give some meaning to all the crazy shit they've witnessed these past weeks."

"Yup."

"Listen," my dad said next, "I need you to do me a favor. Two favors actually."

"If I can I will."

"First favor's this: Live free."

"Live free?"

"That's right, kid. Live free. It's not a cliché. Sounds easy but it ain't."

"I'll do my best."

"Good. And favor number two: love your mother."

"I love Mom."

"I know you do, but I mean really love her. All the way up. You gotta go to the mat for her, kid, each and every day."

"I will. I want to."

"Okay then, that's it. Live free and love your mother. And of course get yourself educated. Ignorance never did anybody any good. And now I gotta go."

"No, wait a second. Don't go. What about Homer Otis?"

"What about him?"

"What am I supposed to do?"

"You know what to do. If he's standing in your way and won't move, you have to move him. You can wait for me if you want, but I think you're man enough now to do the moving yourself."

"You do?"

"Absolutely. And now, like I said, I gotta go. And so do you."

I saw Retro and Bones coming along the trail and out onto the overlook.

"There he is," said Bones, looking relieved.

"Yo, Tailor," said Retro, "we thought you'd disappeared."

I took a look at my two best buddies, offered them a smile, then glanced over my shoulder. The only one who'd disappeared was Big Jack. He'd vanish yet again. Me—I planned on sticking around.

Darkness beginning to fall over the Plains, we left the Badlands. I know it'll sound strange but I had my head chock-a-block with Mom and old Gus and Willa the waitress who'd foreseen it all and of course Big Jack. Did life, I wondered, have meaning? Did things connect? Did they happen for a reason? Was fate real or just a figment of our far flung imaginations?

I didn't know. I didn't have a clue. How could I know? I was just a kid, dazed and confused, but altered.

Through the twilight and into the night we drove. East along Interstate 90 across the broad rolling prairies of South Dakota. Three hundred miles from the Badlands to Sioux Falls. Close to six hours driving when you factor in speed limits, time changes, a late meal at a greasy spoon. It was near two in the morning by the time Retro and Bones had their grilled chesses on rye, soggy French fries, and Cokes at an all-night truck stop. I had coffee, black. But even that simple meal took time and slowed our progress. Then, just east of Murdo, we lost an hour faster than you can say South Dakota when we drove over an invisible line that took us from Mountain Time to Central Time.

On into the Dakota night we drove. Me behind the wheel, Bones riding shotgun, Retro asleep in back. Bones tried to stay up and jawbone with me but pretty soon he fell out also. And then it was just me—wide awake with nothing to keep me company save my thoughts and the high beams dancing on the asphalt dead ahead.

The speed limit on I-90 in the middle of Nowhere, South Dakota was 70 miles per hour. Or maybe 75. I can't just now recall. But I do recall I set the cruise control precisely on the posted limit. Not a mile per hour over or under. It would've been cool to push the truck up to say 85 or 90 or even 100mph—she would've done that and more no sweat—but we didn't need some bored Dakota state trooper playing in our parade.

I had that wide-open interstate just about all to my lonesome. Of course, I got to thinking again about Big Jack and his life as a long haul trucker, out there in the night all alone without his kids or the woman he'd left but still loved. A lonely life, even though he'd tell you it was the life he wanted, the life he'd chosen. And that got me thinking about Mom and what I'd tell her once we got home. You know, about Big Jack getting shot and the Devil and Gus and us driving home on our own. Was it better for her to know all this stuff or was it better for her to remain in the dark?

I couldn't decide what to tell her. How much or how little. Whether to make it up or tell her the truth. In the end I decided the right thing to say would come to me when I stood face to face with Mom and looked her in the eye. I'd magically know what to tell her. Because I loved her and maybe that's what love means.

I had all this stuff racing through my thoughts as I drove through the night. Too much stuff, really, for one kid to handle. Especially when all I really wanted was for Dad to be home, for Jake to be alive, for Mom to love Dad, for Dad to love Mom, and for Mom and Dad and Jake and me to all live together under the same roof and I didn't even care where so long as a river ran nearby.

Hey, I know I've said all this stuff before, probably a million times since I started telling you this tale—but listen to me, it's what every kid in the world from a busted, screwed up, dysfunctional family wants—wholeness. Sweet wholeness.

The Passage

The Last Leg

Just west of Sioux Falls, near the intersections of I-90 and I-29, dawn a faint glimmer on the eastern horizon, I couldn't take it anymore. My eyes felt heavy as lead weights. So I exited the interstate and entered a mega truck stop strewn with 18-wheelers, their diesel engines fouling the sweet morning air while idling noisily in the shadowy light.

I reached back, grabbed Retro by the shoulder, and gave him a shake. "Your turn in the saddle, cowboy. I need some rack time."

We all used the head, then bought fried egg sandwiches and cartons of OJ. After gassing up we got right back on the road. I climbed into the back and stayed awake just long enough to cross into Minnesota, then out I went.

I slept most of the way across the North Star State. A few times I rallied, sat up, and took a look out the windows. Mostly I saw farms—big, wide-open farms sprawling across some of the flattest land we'd traversed yet. It must've been sweet land though because everywhere grew crops tall and green. And something else—the land looked clean and pristine, like something out of a Hollywood feel-good movie.

I must've fallen back to sleep because late in the morning Bones woke me to say we'd soon be crossing the Mississippi River. I pulled myself up and shook the cobwebs off for a look at the Big Muddy. But to tell you the truth, it wasn't much. Where Interstate 90 crosses just north of LaCrosse, the mighty Mississip runs scrawny and languid. The river's all splintered and broken up by rocks and boulders and small islands. We didn't even bother to stop.

The West was over. Just the responsibilities of home remained.

Madison, Wisconsin. Rockford, Illinois. The mess of Chicago. Gary, Indiana.

Outside South Bend we stopped to eat. Denny's—turkey dinners with gravy and all the fixins. At least Retro and Bones ate. I had no appetite. I shoved back my chair and went to find a phone. I called Mom back in Bridgeton. She was surprised to hear from me so soon after my last call. Little did she know I had an ulterior motive.

Like Big Jack, I had something up my sleeve.

After some niceties I asked, "Think you'll be home tomorrow night?"

"I expect so. Why?"

"We should be getting back about then."

"As early as tomorrow night?"

"Yup, though it might be late," I told her. "Maybe not till after midnight. But we're going to keep driving till we get there."

Mom assured me she'd be home waiting. She'd wait up till dawn if necessary.

I returned to my buds, a hint of a smile on my face. The boys were still buried in their chow. Out the window and across the street I spotted a Days Inn. I said I needed sleep. They said they did too. So I walked over and got a room. Paid cash. The woman behind the desk didn't want to know about a car or a driver's license or where I was going or where I'd been or whether or not I'd taken care of the Devil or what plans I had for Mr. Homer Otis or the future. She just made change, handed me a plastic key, and told me to sleep well.

Which we did. Like the dead. I didn't wake up until 9 o'clock the next morning, nearly eleven hours later. One by one we dragged ourselves out of bed, showered, and pulled on any reasonably clean clothes we could find.

By 10 o'clock we were back on the road. All three of us felt rested and ready to pull the final leg back to Jersey.

Retro drove across Indiana over ground we'd covered with Big Jack a whole lifetime ago. No one did much talking. I didn't even do much thinking. I'd done all the thinking I needed to do. I had Homer Otis reasonably straight in my head. Now I just needed to take care of business, move him out of the way.

In Holiday City, Ohio we gassed up. I moved back into the driver's seat and fired up the Blues. The miles, hours, and tunes flew by. Toledo. Sandusky. Cleveland. Junior Wells. B.B. King. Bobby Bland singing I've Been Wrong So Long. Youngstown, and then on into the Keystone State with the sun still high in the sky but evening out ahead of us beginning to come on with a few early shadows.

We had just one more state to cross.

But Pennsylvania's no small player in the state-size game. You need to put three hundred miles on the odometer to cross PA from west to east. And the northern route is no picnic. The Alleghenies might not be the Rockies, but it takes time, and plenty of gas, to push through those ancient hills. From Youngstown practically all the way to the Delaware Water Gap the land rises and falls. Like life itself you climb and descend, climb and descend. Moving downhill the 18-wheelers wiz by you at 80 miles an hour. Then on the steep ascents the big trucks slow down to 50—45—40—even 35 miles an hour and you wiz by them. You have to stay on top of your game or else you'll wind up squashed along the side of the road like a bug or a whitetail deer.

Retro had the wheel. He dragged us up and over those hills.

I rode shotgun, stared out the window, and went over my plan to deal with Mr. Homer Otis. Not that I had to put my plan into action, not right away. I could put things off. Dither and procrastinate. Take all the time I needed to figure things out. But I had no intention of playing the waiting game. I feared if I waited I might never act. I'd find one excuse after another to let that bastard run free.

"There's times in life," Big Jack liked to lecture, "when you got to face the bully on the playground. When you got to take the bull by the horns. Hesitate, for even a moment, and the big sumbitch will gore you to death."

Oh yeah, Homer Otis had gored me plenty. Gored Mom plenty too. It was time for him to get his comeuppance, and then to stand aside, move out of the way.

And for reasons both complicated and I guess righteous the job had fallen to me.

Around eleven o'clock, out near the Pocono Raceway, without slowing down, me and Retro pulled our switcheroo. I took the reins for the final push. We exited I-80 for the last time and headed south on PA 33. Half an hour later we reached Easton. But instead of crossing into Jersey we continued south on PA 611. The Delaware flowed just off to our left. We couldn't see the old river through the darkness, but being Delaware River rats born and bred we sure could feel her and smell her. She smelled like home.

It was late now, after midnight. The river road was mostly deserted. We drove slow through Riegelsville and Upper Black Eddy. We drove past the house where me and Jake and Mom and Dad had lived before Jake drowned in the Delaware.

At Uhlerstown we crossed the river. Halfway across that steel span we reentered Jersey—the Garden State. Pulling off the bridge I spotted a

Frenchtown copper sitting in his patrol car outside the River Café—the same River Café where Mom had worked back before me and Jake were ever born. The cop glanced at the Excursion but made no move to impede our progress.

I blew a sigh of relief. No way after 2500 miles across America did I want to get nabbed just a stone's throw from Bridgeton, just a long fly ball from Otis Hill.

I turned south on NJ 29. Home felt close now, close enough to touch. I drove a couple more miles then turned onto a dirt road that led back to the river. Halfway to the river I pulled over, turned off the headlights, and shut down the engine. The time had come to do a little housecleaning.

Bones right away got himself worked up. "Why are we stopping? We're just a couple miles from Bridgeton."

Before I could say a word Retro jumped in, "Stay cool, dude. We got one more stop on this journey before we can put it to rest."

My head turned quick to have a look at my best bud. Did he already know what I had in mind? If he did he was psychic since not a word had slipped from my lips about Homer Otis. All the way across the country I'd been holding the proverbial cards close to the old vest while weighing whether to proceed solo or call upon my buds for assistance.

Retro gave me a wink.

I asked, "You know what I gotta do?"

"You mean what we gotta do."

"What's going on?" Bones demanded. "What are you two talking about?"

"Just hold on, little man," Retro ordered. "We got a few loose ends to tie up."

"Loose ends? What loose ends?" Our buddy Bones, I got to say, had hung tough through the whole mad trip, but now, finally, he'd started to crack. His voice sounded just inches shy of desperate.

I decided to let him slide. It would be better for everybody.

"Relax," I told him. "We have some tidying up to do is all. We can't just roll into town in the middle of the night driving a giant black Excursion with no Big Jack at the helm. We got to do this right."

Bones liked things rational. My words made him calm. He nodded. "Okay, I get that. So what do we have to do?"

"We're heading over to the shack," I replied. "We'll slide into town on Old River Road. With any luck we won't see a soul. We'll unload the gear and get things squared away. After that, I'll drive you home."

Bones nodded again. The plan sounded sensible to him.

"All I ask," I said, "is for you to lay low till morning. Me and Retro need some time to take care of a few details, you know, get rid of the truck and all."

Bones assured me he understood. That gave me confidence.

"And listen," I told them both, "you got to remember—it was Big Jack hauled us back across the country. In that minivan. He drove us home, dropped us off, then blew Bridgeton for points unknown. He said nada about his next move, so we know nada. No one'll be surprised by Big Jack's disappearing act, so that's our story. Short and sweet. No way in the public telling did Big Jack get shot. And all that stuff with the guns and the Devil and the Blackfeet Indian Reservation—it never happened."

"Blackfeet Indians?" asked Retro. "Never heard of 'em."

"Exactly," I said. And then to Bones, "You got it?"

He had it. At least he said he did. I hoped he did. I knew, under pressure, Bones might give it up. But what could I do? You only got so much control in life.

"Alrightee then," I said, "let's roll."

I started the engine and drove back to 29. We proceeded south till we reached the north end of Bridgeton. Just before entering town I turned toward the river again onto Old River Road. I drove to the end and pulled the Excursion through a narrow opening in a tall bushy hedgerow. Beyond the hedgerow I shut down the engine. The three of us went straight to work without a word. I opened the rear hatch and started handing the camping gear to Retro and Bones. Out went the tent, the sleeping bags, the stove, the lanterns, our backpacks and larger duffel bags. I held my sleeping bag till last. I wanted to carry that myself. No way did I want my buddies getting wind of that bag's weight.

Toting piles of gear, we made our way down the dirt path to the Delaware and the old shack. It was plenty dark, but we could've navigated blindfolded. We'd walked that route a million times.

The inside of the shack looked about the same as always—littered with empty snack bags and soda bottles and old magazines. We piled our gear in a back corner. I made sure my cash-filled sleeping bag was on the bottom of the pile. I knew I'd hightail it back there first thing in the morning to fetch the dough, but till then I felt confident it'd be safe.

I closed the door behind us and we walked back to the truck. Taking our time we combed through the entire interior in search of anything that might connect us to the big Ford. We didn't find much. Any trash we tossed into a plastic bag. The registration and insurance card, both containing one of Big Jack's many aliases, I stuffed in my pocket to be disposed of later, or maybe to be kept as mementos.

We climbed back into the Excursion. I backed the truck through the hedgerow, swung around, and steered for town. I turned right on Water Street and drove half a dozen blocks east to High Street. I pulled over but kept the engine running.

"End of the line, Bones. You're on foot from here."

Bones nodded and pushed open the door. He leaned forward and for some reason shook hands with me and Retro.

Retro said, "Been good traveling with you, dude."

Bones smiled. "Adventure of a lifetime." And then all of a sudden he looked reluctant to go, to leave his buddies behind. "We'll see you guys tomorrow? Right?"

"Absolutely," I told him. "Let's meet at the shack in the afternoon. Around four."

That seemed to reassure him. He nodded, grabbed his small duffel, and stepped out of the Excursion for the last time. "See ya," he said, and slammed the door.

I pulled away. In the rearview mirror I could see him standing there watching us move off along the deserted street.

I drove south through and then out of town. Bridgeton was a tomb—dark and silent and still.

For a mile or so we didn't say a word. Then Retro turned to me and said, "So what's the word, Josh? We gonna kill this son of a dog or just rough him up some?"

I turned and looked at Retro. And offered him by best Big Jack smile.

The Passage

To reach Homer's walled compound we drove south on NJ 29. But not far, less than a mile. I turned left onto Otis Hill Road. The road rose steeply away from the river. Large estate homes, all built by H. Otis Construction, stood back from the road every quarter mile or so. MacMansions folks in town called these enormous houses with their half dozen bedrooms and bathrooms. But by far the largest house in the crowd stood isolated at the top of Otis Hill at the end of Otis Hill Road. It was there behind high brick walls and tall wrought iron gates that Homer Otis lived.

More than a year had passed since I'd last set foot on Homer's Compound. At that time, following a Homer backhand across my cheek, no doubt for some insidious felony like channel surfing, I vowed never to return. But hey, vows are sometimes broken. And so here I was—stopping by for one last visit.

You know why I'd come. We've been all through Homer's domestic crimes and physical infractions against me and Mom. No need to go over all that crud again. Homer had without question earned this middle-of-the-night visit. I just hoped I had the guts to do what needed doing.

The big black wrought iron gate at the head of Homer's driveway was closed and locked. It operated like a garage door opener. Homer never arrived or departed without closing and locking that gate. He had way too many enemies, both real and perceived.

But I'd days ago out on the road in Montana and Wyoming thought through the locked gate and how to work around it. I hadn't been spacing out while we hauled east—I'd been plotting my plan of attack.

I went right by the main entrance without taking my foot off the gas. I drove to the very end of Otis Hill Road, to where smooth macadam gave way to loose gravel. Here Homer Otis had his service entrance. This entrance too was blocked with a locked iron gate, so I just kept driving. I drove another couple hundred yards to where the gravel road turned to dirt and then dead-ended. I parked and turned to Retro. "I think we're about done with the big beast."

He nodded and I shut down the engine but left the key in the ignition. I grabbed the .357 Magnum out of the bin between the seats. We took one last look through the vehicle for any evidence of ourselves or Big Jack. We found nothing.

"Ready to roll?" I asked.

Retro swung open his door. "One question."

"Yeah?"

"I assume you got a plan?"

"I got a plan."

"Then I'm ready."

We stepped out into the night. It was warm and muggy, smelled like rain. There were no stars. It was plenty dark out there at the end of Otis Hill Road.

After removing the license plates and disposing of them in the nearby woods, me and Retro walked back to Homer's service entrance. Both the gate and the wall were too high for both of us to scramble over so I climbed onto Retro's shoulders. He stood as tall as he could. I reached up and managed to grab the top of the wall with my fingertips.

I pulled myself onto the wall, gave Retro a thumb's up, then hung myself over the side and dropped onto Homer's lush green weedless grass. And suddenly I was inside. I was now, officially, a Marauder.

I slipped along the wall, back to the gate. Retro stood there waiting.

"Soon as I reach the kitchen," I told him, "I'll hit the switch to open the gate. Be quick. I'm only gonna leave it open a couple seconds."

"I'll be ready," he assured me.

"If the gate doesn't open in, say, five minutes, it might be best if you shove off."

Retro thought this over for a second or two. "We'll see."

I shook hands with him through the gate, turned, and sprinted into the darkness.

The mansion stood on high ground about a hundred yards away, up through a stand of oaks and across a sweep of finely manicured lawn. Homer spent enough money on his grass every summer to feed a small starving African nation. Oh yeah, Homer was a rich guy. Filthy rich. He had millions. But he wasn't safe. Not from me.

I emerged from that stand of oaks and could see the vast brick and timber house silhouetted against the night. Half a dozen chimneys soared into the sky. Homer, twice divorced, lived in there all alone. Although he often had Mom in there with him. Several nights a week in fact. Nights she wasn't with me. But not that night. That night Mom was home. Waiting for her son to return from his cross-country sojourn.

I raced across the lawn to the detached six-bay garage behind the mansion. I didn't see Mom's Civic. I saw no cars at all save the numerous vehicles owned by Mr. Homer Otis. Homer had a Z8 and the canary-yellow Hummer plus a Porsche Turbo, a Chevy Silverado, a '57 T-Bird, and an Audi A-8. But still he was the uncoolest dude on the planet. Big Jack was cooler by a mile driving a fricking minivan.

I felt confident Homer was inside all by his lonesome. Now all I had to do was get in there with him. Something I'd been dreaming about for a long while.

I went around to the back door. I knew Homer kept a spare key hidden under a rock to the right of the back stoop. If the key wasn't there I planned to ring the bell and tell Homer I'd come looking for Mom. He'd grumble some but he'd definitely open the door. After all, he had no reason to be afraid of me, no reason to think I was on the attack. I'd always been a perfectly submissive little tyke.

But there was no need to ring the bell. A year after my last visit that key, though dirty, was still under the rock.

My next dilemma was Homer's home alarm system. Paranoid to the core, Homer had the finest home security system money could buy. But what Homer didn't know, and what could therefore hurt Homer, was that I knew the code to disarm the system. At least I used to know it.

I shoved the key into the back door lock and gave it a turn. The lock fell open.

I knew as soon as I pushed open the door a timer would go off. I'd have sixty seconds to enter the house, cross the kitchen, and punch the four-digit code into the keypad on the wall, thereby disarming the system. If I failed to execute properly the alarm would sound, both in the house and down at the police station. I'd be in a bind then. I'd have a whole lot of explaining to do. Both to Homer and to Chief Walters.

Still, I made my move. Didn't hesitate. For quite a while now, really ever since Homer had given Mom her first black eye more than two years earlier, I'd been thinking about this, about breaking in and busting his legs or cracking open his skull or maybe even cutting off one of his hands. But to tell you the truth, I never thought I'd have the guts to do it. But now, thanks to Big Jack, I had guts galore.

I pushed open the door and quick crossed the kitchen floor. On the opposite wall the keypad glowed red. The numbers stood out big and bold. Calmly, almost serenely, I pressed the 2, then the 6, then the 9, then the 1—the year of Homer's birth, in reverse.

The keypad clicked several times. The numbers turned yellow, then, after a few seconds, green. Green was good. Green meant my luck was holding. Green meant the system had been neutralized.

I returned to the back door. To the right of the door was a panel with several black switches. The center switch on the bottom of the panel unlocked and opened the back gate. I held this switch down for fifteen seconds. Then I pushed the switch back up, closing and locking the gate.

I stood by the door and waited. Less than a minute later Retro raced out of the shadows. He cruised in silent and up onto the back stoop. "Hey," he said.

"Hey," I said.

He slipped through the door. "Any problems?" he asked.

"None at all," I told him. "Piece of cake."

Retro nodded. We moved off, me in the lead. We went through the kitchen and dining room and into the enormous front foyer. A massive stairway like something out of Gone With the Wind led to the second floor. Me and Retro sprinted up those stairs two at a time. I had the .357 Magnum tucked into my Levi's, cold steel and plenty visible.

Halfway up the stairway was a wide landing. From the landing you could either head left or right. Head left to the guest bedrooms—all nine of them. Head right to the master bedroom suite. That's the route me and Retro took.

All by itself that master bedroom suite was as big as a regular person's house. At the top of the stairs it opened into a huge sitting room with a sofa and a love seat and a giant plasma TV that must've been four feet high and eight feet wide. Beyond the sitting room loomed Homer's personal library. Bookcases full of books Homer had never read lined the walls. Homer had a big cherry desk the size of a small ship in the middle of his library. With a big chair and a big lamp and a big computer monitor.

Homer liked big. Big made Homer feel potent and important.

Beyond the library, through thick double doors, loomed the bedroom. That night those double doors hung wide open. Me and Retro charged straight through the opening like a pair of wild boars. The thick plush deep-pile carpet muted our charge.

Homer's bedroom was as big as a basketball court. Push the already high ceiling up another few feet, put in a couple hoops, and the Philadelphia 76ers could've played the NY Knickerbockers in there.

We moved to the middle of Homer's massive bedroom. I motioned to Carl to take the left flank. I took the right flank. We didn't want Homer slipping away.

Quick as cats we converged on that California king. And there, in the shadowy darkness, lay Mr. Homer Otis, all alone amidst a tangle of navy blue satin sheets. He looked like any middle age American white guy with thinning hair and soft belly. Only this middle age American white guy was suddenly as vulnerable as a duck on a pond on the opening day of hunting season.

I reached down, gave him a shake. "Yo, Homer. Wake up, dude."

Homer woke up all right—in a big hurry and looking mighty spooked when Retro snapped on the bedside lamp.

"Huh? What? Who?" Homer rubbed and blinked his bleary bloodshot eyes.

Me and Retro waited.

"Josh, is that you?"

"I believe it is, Homer."

Homer, foolishly comforted by the sight of his girlfriend's son rather than some drug-crazed burglar or Third World religious fanatic with a bomb duct-taped to his chest, relaxed his tense facial muscles and sat up. My mother's boyfriend, to my surprise, slept in the buff. I would've figured him for a satin PJs kind of guy.

"What's the matter?" he demanded. "Is there a problem? Is it your mother?"

I was moved by his concern, brought nearly to tears. "Nope, it's not my mother."

Homer rousted himself. Reality began to take hold. "How the hell," he asked, looking puzzled, "did you get in? How did you get by the gate?... The alarm?"

"Everything was wide open, Homer. Like a giant black hole."

His brow furrowed as he thought things over. This may have been the moment when Homer began to consider the possibility that something had gone terribly wrong in his sick safe privileged little world. He said, "You know, Josh, your mother's not here."

"That's correct, Homer," I told him. "Mom's not here. She's home, waiting for me. It's just you and me and my good buddy Retro. You remember Retro, don't you, Homer?"

Homer's eyes glanced nervous around the bedroom. And then, without meaning to, he gave himself away. His body shuddered. His eyes showed fear. He suddenly and instinctively knew me and Carl had not dropped by at two in the morning selling TV Guide subscriptions or looking for answers to life's most puzzling questions. We'd come about the past and to discuss the future. And don't think he didn't know it.

Homer did his best to play offense. "You know, Josh, you really shouldn't be here... I mean, can I do something for you?... Is there something you want?... Do you need to call your mother?... I thought you were away... Out west or something... With your father."

I started to say something but then realized it was better to just stay quiet and listen to Homer grovel and watch the sweat beads form on his shiny forehead and his upper lip.

"This isn't right, Josh. I think maybe it's time for you to leave. It is, after all, the middle of the night. I think—" Homer cut himself short. His eyes, already red and puffy, suddenly grew to the color and size of beefsteak tomatoes. "What is that… in your pants? Is that a gun?"

Only men who feel perfectly safe and secure in the world sleep in the buff. Men who understand the world's a volatile and violent place don't sleep naked. They know if the big bad wolf rolls into their bedroom in the middle of the night they'd better have some small piece of cloth covering their private parts.

The Great Real Estate Mogul and Elevator Heir looked pitiful lying there naked and white on his big bed. But I have to say, even in the presence of that .357 Magnum he made an effort to act tough. He told us we were way out of line and if we persisted he'd have to call the police. When we didn't budge or mutter a word he made a move for the phone beside the bed. And that's when Retro upped the ante by swatting old Homer back into that big cushy mattress as easy as he would've brushed away a pesky fly.

Homer right away looked terrified. So terrified I had to wonder if Retro's swat was maybe the first time in Homer's life someone had actually smacked him. He pressed his body against the solid oak headboard and pulled that satin sheet up around his chest.

It was a pretty pitiful display. I couldn't believe how easy it was to terrorize him. To intimidate him.

Did I feel good about that? Did it make me feel powerful? I don't know. Maybe. I know now I wouldn't want it to become a way of life or anything. But right then, I got to tell you, seeing the man who'd pummeled my mom like she was a punching bag cower in the corner like a frightened pup made my heart pound steady and true. Why, I asked myself, had I waited so long to strike back?

I knew now this was my fight, and I was glad I'd come to it.

"I'll tell you why we've come, Homer," I said. "There's a couple things I want. Give them to me without a hassle and all will be well. Deny me and things won't go at all easy for you." I'd been silently practicing those lines all the way across the country.

Homer gathered himself and tried to get tough again. Probably he remembered how easy it'd been to push me around in the not-so-distant past. "What the hell is this, Josh? You spend a little time with that bum of a father of yours and all of a sudden you turn into a thug. You break into my house. You threaten me with a gun. You—"

Retro roared like a lion on the Serengeti, reached across the bed, and thumped Homer hard on the chest with his index finger.

"Homer, my man," Retro lectured, "I'm tired. Tired to the bone. I want to go home, go to bed, sleep for a week. But first I need to deal with the lousy likes of you. It's a sorry business but somebody's gotta do it. So I'd be grateful if you'd KEEP YOUR COTTON-PICKIN MOUTH SHUT! You got me?"

Homer, now nearly part of the headboard, no doubt wanted to rebel against these two young hoodlums bossing him around. But panic had taken a pretty strong hold on Mr. Otis. He managed a mournful nod.

Retro turned to me. "Okay, Josh, let's get on with it. I want out of this bedroom. It smells like fear and death in here."

I nodded, then turned to our host. "May as well get the easy part over with first, Homer. The first thing I want is an apology. A clear, simple, sincere apology for the way you've treated me and Mom. Take a second to muster up some heartfelt words, Homer, because if I don't buy your sentiment, me and Retro might have to beat some sincerity out of you."

Homer took maybe five seconds, then he dove into this whole absurd denial act. He had the guts to say stuff like, "But I love your mother,

Josh," and, "I only ever wanted the best for you," and, "We're a family," and best of all, "If you back off now I'll forgive you and forget this whole episode ever happened."

"Well that's swell of you, Homer," I told him. And then I asked him if he maybe wanted to apologize for those occasions when he'd slapped me upside the head or bloodied my lip or kicked me in the balls or blackened Mom's eye or nearly broke her arm when he shoved her up against the wall.

Homer had the balls to reply, "I think you exaggerate, Josh. I might've slapped you lightly once or twice in an effort to teach you some respect. And as for your mother, well, I think she leveled quite a few more blows against me than I ever leveled against her. I never hit your mother, son. I only really ever kept her at bay."

To which Retro, as impatient as a charging bull, turned to me and said, "Is it time yet to kick this stinking, lying protoplasm's teeth down its throat?"

I told him no, not yet, but man oh man did I feel like pulling that .357 Magnum out of my pants and shoving it hard against Homer's sweaty temple. Fortunately, I heard Big Jack whisper in my ear. "Stay cool, kid. Always keep your cool."

"Homer," I said, "you smacked us and punched us and kicked us, even spit on us. You humiliated us. And lied to us. You kept us apart. You ran us down. You ran my father down. I don't know what's the matter with you. And I don't really care. To me you're nothing but a bully and a coward who hits women and kids. Well sorry, dude, but I'm not a kid anymore. I'm a man now and I'm here seeking retribution. So I suggest we get on with the apology. The time's come for you to hold yourself accountable."

Now I don't have to tell you that human beings have an almost infinite ability to justify their words and actions. Homer Otis was so completely and disgustingly wrong when it came to the way he'd treated me and Mom that it bordered on the absurd. But still he couldn't bring himself to apologize, to mutter two simple words, "I'm sorry." He couldn't do it. Like a nation with the biggest bombs and the largest army, Homer Otis believed might made right.

And so he left me no choice.

"Alright, Homer," I said, "you're gonna be stubborn about this." I turned to Retro and asked, "You ready?"

"Oh yeah. Chafing at the bit."

"What are you going to do?" Homer demanded.

"Sorry, Homer," I replied, "no questions."

Homer rallied. He sat up some. "This is my house. I'll ask all the questions I—"

Homer grew mute when Retro swept in and backhanded him across the mouth. It was a pretty solid swat. Retro had been holding that swat inside for a long time. He knew all about what Homer'd been doing to me and Mom. I'd recounted to him every brutal detail, every smack, kick, and drop of spittle. Retro hated Homer as much as I did. He'd been urging me to retaliate for well over a year. So it gave us both a twinge of perverse pleasure to see the blood dribbling off Homer's lip.

"Homer," I explained, "that's exactly the same way you backhanded me one night after I asked you not to curse at my mother. You recall that night, Homer? You bit her on the arm and called her a whore because she talked to some dude at the grocery store. I asked you not to call her that. For my insolence you whacked me across the mouth."

Homer scowled at me. He wiped the blood away with the back of his hand. His eyes looked both scared and angry.

I made a fist and punched Homer hard in the right eye. I mean I really creamed him. He didn't even see it coming. He cried out in pain, fell back, hit his head against that oak headboard.

I grimaced and shook out my fist. If you've never done it, let me tell you, it hurts when you punch a guy in the head that hard. I didn't let it bother me though.

"Do you recall punching Mom," I asked, "with a right jab similar to the one I just gave you? Do you recall that night, Homer? Because if you don't, I do. Like it was just yesterday. It happened right downstairs in the kitchen. You and Mom got in an argument. About some other guy. You got all heated up. Jealous and crazy. Then, because you're a sick dirtbag, you made a fist and punched my mother right in the face. A defenseless woman. You gotta remember that night, Homer. She had a black eye for weeks. Did her best to hide it with makeup."

Homer made some effort to speak, probably to defend himself, but I had other business. I drew back my arm and walloped Homer hard on the back of the head.

"Hate to sound like a broken record, Homer," I said, "but that's exactly what you did to me one rainy afternoon. I got a little too aggressive with the remote, kept changing channels faster than you liked, so just for the hell of it you reared back and clobbered me in the head. And no, it was no little love tap, Homer. It wasn't you trying to instill a little respect in the girlfriend's son. Oh no, Homer, you knocked me right off the sofa onto the floor. And then, like the piss yellow coward you are, you told me if I ratted you out you'd fill my mouth with concrete. Oh yeah, Homer, I enjoyed watching TV and hanging out with you after that."

All the beatings and beratings Homer had leveled against me and Mom came rushing through me like a storm. I got a little carried away, jumped up on the bed, kicked Homer hard in the right shin. And then, for good measure, I kicked Homer savagely right between the legs. Oh yeah, I kicked him in the balls as hard as I could.

Homer cried out in some pretty severe pain. He instinctively moved to protect his private parts even while a nasty bruise began to swell on his leg.

"Remember those good times, Homer?" I asked, hovering over him, eyes alert and crazy. "Remember the day we were outside kicking the soccer ball. Just messing around, not even playing a game. But you got ticked off because I stole the ball from you. So what did you do? You retaliated by kicking me in the shin. Hard enough to cause a huge purple welt. That's sick, Homer. Definitely the behavior of a very sick individual."

Incredibly, in a low, whiny voice, Homer said, "I didn't kick you on purpose."

"Bullshit. And when we got back to the house—me crying and bleeding—you made sure to tell Mom it'd been an accident. But what about when you kicked me in the balls, Homer? You must remember that? It was just a few short weeks ago. Was that an accident, too, Homer? Was that your leg spontaneously and involuntarily ripping through the air and the toe of your boot unexpectedly making contact with my poor unprotected and unsuspecting testicles?"

Writhing on the bed, doubled up, mostly out of breath, Homer managed a hard response. "You wrecked the car, you little shit. Somebody had to do something."

"I see. Somebody had to do something so you kicked me in the balls. That's truly beautiful, Homer. Now somebody's gotta do something about you, too. And it turns out that somebody's me. I could call the cops, charge you with abuse, assault and battery. I could but you'd use your dough to squirm out of it. The law's against me, Homer, and I know it. So I gotta be my own law. I gotta serve up my own justice."

That little speech over I grabbed Homer by the hair. I grabbed it and pulled it. I pulled on his thinning brown locks harder and harder while he screamed and screamed and tried to squirm away. After maybe thirty seconds I let go.

"How was that, Homer? Fun? I saw you handle Mom that way once. Like she was a rag doll. She'd done something to tick you off. Something awful like arrive five minutes late. Or wear a skirt you didn't like. Or maybe get a fingerprint on one of your precious CDs. So like some ape in the jungle you grabbed her by the hair and started pulling. Twisted, Homer. I mean seriously, man, you need help. You need to find out why you'd treat a woman and a kid so bad. You need—"

I cut myself short. Homer, get this, had started to weep. I swear to God. Real tears. At first I thought the tears had to do with the pain we'd inflicted upon him—you know, the physical abuse—but that wasn't it. Homer, despite his heinous nature, felt bad about what he'd done to me and Mom. Sure, it'd taken a beating for him to discover the error of his ways, but hey, so what? After all, Homer Otis, like most despots, was just another frightened, insecure little boy hiding out in a man's body.

And then—through his tears and sobs—Homer had this to say in a subdued and halting voice, "You're one hundred percent right, Josh, I never should've laid a hand on you. Not in anger. Not you and not your mother. Never. I'm sorry. Sorry's not enough, but I'm sorry nevertheless."

So there you go. An apology. Did Homer mean it? Or was he simply angling to survive? Trying to keep us from knocking his teeth out? Was his apology sincere? Or was he playing to our sympathies so I wouldn't unload that .357 Magnum into his brain?

Tough to say with any certainty. Hard to know.

"Thanks, Homer," I said, "I needed that. We both did. That wasn't so hard, was it?" Then right back on the attack. "And now, what about all the other crap you pulled? All the manipulation and humiliation you heaped upon us? All the times you kept Mom and me apart to satisfy your grubby little desire to exert control over a kid and a woman in a lousy place? What about all that, Homer? Huh? What about it?"

Homer actually took some time to think things over. Finally he said, "I just... I don't know... I didn't mean... Or maybe I did mean..." Homer had his head down. His chin rested against his chest.

He made me sick. I said, "Time for you to put on some clothes."

"Huh?"

"Now. And then we can get down to our final piece of business."

Homer had some dried blood on his lower lip, a puffy eye that would surely be black and blue come morning, and a swelling on his shin fast becoming the size and shape of a golf ball. No telling what shape his gonads were in. He took a deep breath, swung his legs off the bed, and got to his feet. He crossed to his bureau, opened a drawer, pulled on a white tee shirt and a pair of white sweat pants.

White—the color of surrender. "One thing," he said.

"What's that, Homer?"

He pointed to my waist. "The gun. Can we please get rid of the gun? This isn't the Wild West."

You could've fooled me.

I pulled the Magnum from my pants. I removed the clip. The empty clip.

"Look, Homer," I said, "no bullets. Just a prop really. A deterrent. Like the atom bomb. You got it but you know you can't use it."

I tossed the revolver into the air a couple times, then threw it over to Retro, who caught it easy and shoved it into his waistband.

The three of us walked single file into the study. And through the study to the TV room. Homer sat on the sofa. I took the love seat. Retro, fearing Homer might bolt, stood near the door leading to the stairway. I didn't think Homer'd bolt. Homer was no doubt plenty ticked off, but I think he'd also withdrawn into a genuine state of repentance and reflection.

Well, probably not, but if you're going to live it's best to live with hope.

"So Homer," I began, "I'll get right to it. You and Mom—you're finished."

His head came up. "Huh? What?"

"You heard me—finished. I don't want you seeing her anymore. Ever."

He stared at me. He looked confused. Definitely he hadn't seen this coming. No way. Probably he figured his little apology would make things square.

"Now hold on a second, Josh. I don't see why that's necessary. I might've made some mistakes, but I—"

"I'm not interested in talking about this, Homer. It's not open for discussion. It's finished between you. The lies and abuse and humiliation are over. I wish Mom had the strength and the guts to end this mess herself, but obviously she doesn't. So I'm doing it for her. I'm stepping up. I'm drawing the line. I'm calling the shots now."

Homer looked at me like I must've been nuts, totally out of my mind. "You're in no position to tell two adults what they can and can't do. You're way out of line here, Josh. Hell, you're just a boy. You don't—"

"Homer!" I cut him off. "Try to remember—this is man to man. Mano y mano. I treat you with respect. You treat me with respect. Our days of kicking each other in the balls are hopefully over. Okay? Now understand, I only have one mother. She's been through hell. First my dad put her through the ringer. And now you've put her through the ringer. But you're done. Finished. The relationship is sick. Diseased. I don't care what becomes of you, Homer. I don't care if you crawl into a hole and die a dirty death. I don't care if you shoot yourself in the head over the loss of your one true love. But I do care about my mother. And I'll protect her with my life. Do you hear me? With my life. I'll do whatever it takes to protect her from the stinking disgusting sadistic likes of you."

There, I'd said what I'd come to say. Now I was pretty much done.

I stood up and took a couple laps around the big TV room. I'd been in Homer's house maybe half an hour. I'd held myself together pretty well. You know, for a kid. But let me tell you—my armpits were soaked, my heart raced, my head throbbed like it had been split in two by an axe. I was stressing big-time and fast running out of juice.

Fortunately, Homer remained mute while I paced. Had he put up even a small battle, my defenses might've collapsed.

I gathered myself for the final assault. "Here's what I have to do, Homer. I have to threaten you. If you see my mother—romantically, socially, any way at all— I'll be forced to pay you another visit. Only next time it won't be an eye for an eye. It won't be me just shoving you out of the way. I'll shoot you, Homer. I'll put real live bullets in that gun and shoot you right between the eyes. And don't think for a second I don't have the guts to do it. I'll do whatever it takes to keep my mother safe from the likes of you."

Homer didn't respond. He looked spooked, but also plenty mad. He didn't like being threatened, not by some kid who'd busted into his mansion, roughed him up, and read him the riot act. Inside Homer was seething big-time, thinking up ways to take his revenge against me. But I wasn't worried. Not about Homer Otis. Otis was a stinking coward. He smelled yellow. I felt no fear of him at all.

"You're pretty pissed off right now, Homer," I told him, "But you'll get over being pissed off and realize I'm right about all this. Then you'll do the right thing and leave my mom alone. Let her get on with her life. Let her find somebody decent to love her and treat her good. Long as you do that no one'll ever have to know how you beat us and belittled us. It'll be our dirty little secret."

I piped down then, partly because I was spent, but also to give Homer a chance, if he so desired, to say his piece.

Thirty seconds passed. A minute. Two minutes. Homer didn't say a word.

I said, "Okay, Homer, that's it then. We're outta here. I assume you'll let us go in peace. After all, this is just between you and me. Men settle their differences amongst themselves. They don't drag cops and lawyers and armies in to do their fighting."

I motioned to Retro. We both moved toward the door leading to the hallway.

Homer stood. He did his best to stand tall. "Get out!" he ordered. "Get the hell out of my house! Do you hear me? Get out and don't ever come back. Break into my house again, you little shits, and I swear to God I'll shoot you down like rabid dogs."

Oh yeah, I thought, that sounded fine. In fact, better than fine—it was perfect. I wanted to say something like, "Whoa, Homer, I'm shaking in my boots." Or, "Homer, you big bad ferocious man, don't hurt me." But I didn't. I kept my trap shut.

Homer needed the last word and I was happy to let him have it.

The Splash

Retro wanted out of there. ASAP. He pretty much sprinted down those Gone With the Wind stairs and across the front foyer the size of Grand Central Station. I caught up to him and asked him why the big rush? He thought for sure either Homer would call the cops or come after us with a sawed off shotgun.

I tried to tell him no way would Homer make a move.

Retro, feet still moving, rushing now through the dining room, said, "Josh, it's a free country. At least for the time being. If that's your opinion you're entitled to it." Then he pushed into the kitchen, crossed the tiled floor, pulled open the back door, and quick slipped out into the night.

I slowed just long enough to flip the switch that opened the front gate. Then I too exited Homer's mansion, hopefully for the last time. I followed Retro around to the front of the house. Together we started down the long, sweeping, tree-lined drive. We moved somewhere between a sprint and a jog.

I said, "What do you say we ease up some?"

Retro said, "What makes you so sure Homer won't make a move on us?"

I slowed the pace and replied, "Homer's a coward and a bully. No way does he come after us with a gun. And what's he gonna tell the cops? That his girlfriend's kid broke into his mansion and smacked him around? His girlfriend's kid who's an honor student and an athlete at the local high school? He'd look like an idiot. And even if he does call the cops and they do come—so what? Bridgeton's only got six cops. We know them all, Carl.

They like us despite our occasional infractions. They'll ask us what we were doing up at the Otis compound. We'll say we went looking for my mom after our long absence out west with Big Jack. I mean, come on, there's no evidence we broke into the house."

Retro thought it over, then asked, "What about the beating we gave the bastard?"

"What beating? The black eye and the bump on his leg? Maybe the jackass fell out of a tree. It's our word against his. I have no recollection of punching or kicking Mr. Homer Otis. Do you?"

Retro smiled and shook his head. He was beginning to see my point.

We slowed to a brisk walk. We passed through the wide-open front gate and out onto Otis Hill Road. Homer didn't show up behind us. Police Chief Walters didn't show up in front of us.

Retro said, "You think he'll see your mom?"

"Oh yeah, he'll see her. Sure. Once or twice. Just to hold on to his manhood. But he'll be looking over his shoulder for me every two seconds and'll soon enough back off."

We walked down to the bottom of Otis Hill Road and out onto the northbound shoulder of NJ 29. Dawn felt close. The sky had turned from black to gray. You could almost feel the shadows fading.

"Some trip," said Carl.

"Yup," I agreed, "some trip."

We walked a while.

"Hey Josh?"

"Yeah?"

"Thanks for inviting me along."

I smiled at my best bud in the world. "My pleasure."

"I guess we did some growing up."

"I guess we did."

Without exchanging another word we crossed the road, cut through some trees, and made our way down to the riverbank. Retro handed me the Magnum. I took one last look at that cold steel, then threw it high into the sky. In a flash it disappeared into the darkness. Several seconds later we heard the splash! Within seconds, without us even seeing it, that gun sank forever to the muddy bottom of the Delaware River.

We walked toward town. Dead ahead I could see the silhouette of the tall steeple atop the Episcopal Church where I'd been baptized and where my little brother Jake had been laid to rest. I hadn't thought much about that steeple before, but suddenly it looked like a beacon pointing the way home.

I asked Retro, "When we were working Homer over, you know, knocking him around, did you... did you enjoy it?"

Retro needed a few seconds. Finally he shrugged and said, "Only because of all the stuff he'd done to you and your mom. I enjoyed seeing him pay for that. But I hope I never have to do anything like it again. What about you?"

"I didn't like it. Not for a second. Gave me the willies having that kind of power and control over another human being. Made me sick to my stomach when I punched him in the face. I guess I'm just glad we didn't have to kill him."

Retro said, "I never could've killed him. No way."

"Me neither."

We walked on. I thought it over. The whole mess. It all passed through my brain in like a millisecond.

"You know what?"

"What?"

"Being a man," I said, "it's gonna be rough. Being a kid was a breeze. Nothing to it. But I can see manhood's no walk along the river. I see the future and it's a whole lot of being held accountable."

"Hey," suggested Retro, "we can always go back."

"I don't think so. We can screw it up, but we can't go back."

"Huh?"

"Never mind."

I knew what I meant, sort of, but I couldn't explain. At least not right then. It would be too much trouble trying. We'd been through a hell of an ordeal. I needed some R&R and some home cooking before I could make sense of it all.

"Come on," I said. "Let's go see our mothers. Maybe bring them coffee in bed. Do something, you know, decent for a change."

We picked up the pace, made the final push into town. Into beautiful Bridgeton, NJ. Big Jack had called it a petty, provincial place, but it looked fine to us.

Dawn pressed against the shadows. The light of a new day spread across the sky. We didn't speak. Didn't say a word. For the time being anyway there was nothing left to say.

"So what about the money?" I asked.

"The money?"

"What happened to the money?"

Josh smiled. "Ah, the money. Put to good use. Just finished my junior year. On my way home actually, for the summer."

"Where do you go?"

"Down south. Partial baseball scholarship. Big Jack's gun money pays the rest."

"That's something."

"Yup."

"And Big Jack? He survived his wound?"

"Oh yeah."

"You see him?"

"He shows up. On occasion."

"And your mom?"

"Remarried. To a decent guy."

"That's good. And Homer? Did he back off? Stay away from her?"

Josh hesitated, then shrugged. "He saw her a few times."

"So what's he doing now?"

"Not too much. He's dead."

"Dead?"

"Fell off a ladder up at his place. Broke his neck. No one found him for a couple days."

"Jesus."

"I won't say he deserved it, but he did."

Before I could get all that straight in my head the train whistle blew. And seconds later, that train, after the long delay and all the rumors, pulled out of the station into the bright morning sunlight.

Made in the USA
Charleston, SC
10 October 2014